River

Bottom

Blues

Ricky Bush

Barking Rain Press

River Bottom Blues

Edited by Ti Locke

Cover artwork by Cassie Larish (www.twisted-pixie.com)

Title page inset by Virginia Bush

Barking Rain Press
PO Box 822674
Vancouver, WA 98682 USA

www.BarkingRainPress.org

ISBN print: 1-935460-28-5
ISBN eBook: 1-935460-29-3

Library of Congress Control Number: 2011946122

First Edition: January 2012

Printed in the United States of America

9 7 8 1 9 3 5 4 6 0 2 8 2

Dedication

To my wife, Virginia, who's been riding this
rollercoaster with me for some time now.

❧

Coming Soon From Ricky Bush
Soldiers of Satan

❧

WWW.RICHARDBUSHBOOKS.COM

❧

CONTENTS

CHAPTER 1

CHICAGO 1964

The last words J.P. Dillon heard before the ice pick slammed into his chest and pierced his heart were, "You'll be playing with the Devil now, blues boy."

Twenty minutes earlier, he held a mesmerized crowd of blues fans and harmonica aficionados in his grasp as he coaxed solid, soulful tones from his instrument for an encore at Rhoda's Roadhouse. "His People," as he called his fans, packed Chicago's best known blues club to standing room only and yelled for more.

He blew the final notes of his signature tune, "Baby Get Your Head Straight" and stepped from the small stage and ran the gauntlet of back slaps and handshakes. A strong arm hooked his elbow and yanked him towards a table surrounded by music industry types. A French documentary producer, who had filmed the night's performance, wore a smile as he towed J.P. along and yapped at him in broken English. J.P. understood every third word. He wriggled free of the foreigner and headed to the back door, followed by his drummer, Fat Frank, who was also yapping at him.

"Hey, J.P., don't you think you should go over and talk with Frenchie and his friends? He's gonna make you a star, man."

Peter Stiml had been in Chicago for a month, documenting the city's blues scene. European blues fans couldn't get enough of Muddy Waters, Howling Wolf, Lightnin' Hopkins, Willie Dixon, Sonny Boy Williamson, John Lee Hooker and other blues musicians. They had been touring overseas presenting a totally different style of music to sold-out auditoriums crammed with enthusiastic fans.

A couple of English chaps named Mick Jagger and Keith Richards formed a group called The Rolling Stones, named after Muddy Waters' "Rollin' Stone Blues," recorded back in 1950. The band's songs became major hits in the UK and their manager had them booked for their first U.S. tour. Columbia records signed Eric Burdon and his group, The Animals, who had built up a solid following in London by singing such blues standards like "House of the Rising Sun". They also had their sights set on a summer tour of the States.

Stiml had his hand on a strong pulse and he wanted to chase the potential before it weakened. He rounded up a film crew to seek out the music on its own turf and bring the results back to his people. Nothing prepared him for the lack of appreciation the musicians suffered on home ground in the U.S. Musicians who were idolized in Europe were relegated to small clubs in America and few white people ventured into such places to hear *le blues*. He discovered a society of racial segregation, where Negroes could not share dining counters, drinking fountains or restrooms with white patrons. In Europe, these musicians stayed in the swishest hotels and ate in the finest restaurants. Venues like London's Fairfield Hall were usually home to classical concerts, not music from Chicago and the Mississippi Delta, but the blues men were enthusiastically welcomed even there. They were featured on television and radio shows in London, Paris, Brussels, Hamburg, Stockholm and other cities throughout Europe.

This epiphany did little to dampen his enthusiasm and he found tonight's show exhilarating. He had high hopes that his project would shine a light on the Chicago blues musicians and perhaps raise their status even in their own, largely indifferent country. He was sure his efforts would be handsomely rewarded back in Europe.

J.P. Dillon had been tapped to accompany the next group of Chicago musicians to tour Europe. J.P.'s first studio sessions last year had two songs that reached the top ten on the rhythm and blues charts in the UK, and Peter had bought a box full of the records and distributed them to friends in Paris and London, and the bluesman was beginning to gain a favorable reputation even before his arrival. Peter fell instantly in love with the sound of the blues harmonica—or blues harp, as they called it here—because it was the perfect, wailing vehicle to express the deep, often sorrowful, feeling of the music.

He was in the midst of authenticity at Rhoda's Roadhouse on South Michigan Avenue, which had a reputation as the club that tolerated nothing but the blues. Proprietor Rhoda Williams had unplugged many an amplifier that dared to blast out anything but the real stuff. Her club could accommodate a little more than a hundred customers, or on a night like tonight, a hundred and fifty with standing room only. She kept it clean, because she wanted the ladies of the neighborhood to feel welcome.

"I've had enough of that stuff," J.P. said as holy hell broke loose close to the stage. Someone was screaming "the devil did this," "the devil did that" and raising a general ruckus. Both he and Fat Frank turned in time to see the club's bouncer, Big Bo Bo, drag a slender, wiry black man across the top of a table, scattering long-neck beer bottles, mixed drinks, and alarmed patrons across the room. The bouncer had both arms of the instigator pulled back, but the man kicked over another table and yanked loose long enough to grab a beer bottle and smash it over Bo Bo's head. The big man shook the broken glass from his hair, grabbed the trouble-maker around the neck and swiftly heaved him through the front door. When Big Bo Bo re-entered, tables were uprighted, and replacement beverages were issued.

"Guess the devil made him do it," J.P. shrugged as he swung open the back door to a cool breeze that whipped the sweat from his brow. He carefully settled a Fedora on his head.

"You know, I do remember that cat sitting at that front table staring a hole into you," said Fat Frank. Fat Frank had hopes of his own. He knew that if J.P. hit the big time that he would too and might get a chance to record some of his own songs for these funny French talking guys who loved the blues.

The wind whipped at the Fedora and J.P. grabbed his hat. "Those fellows are all nice and everything, but they drive me nuts with all the questions about how I play the harp and do this with it and that with it. I just blow, damn it! They want to know if Little Walter influenced me. Hell, no, he didn't. We came up blowing at about the same time. I've got my own style. And who my mama and papa was is none of their cotton pickin' business."

"By the way," Fat Frank said, "why'd you go and tell them how you picked cotton down in Mississippi? Hell, J.P., you were born in the 9th Ward of New Orleans just down the block from me. You ain't never picked no cotton in your life."

They had both moved up to Chicago together for one reason, and that was to play music. They were tired of playing on New Orleans' street corners, with Fat Frank beating on cardboard boxes and trash cans to keep time and J.P. blowing his soul. A guitar player sometimes joined them and they'd really make a racket and draw a pretty good crowd, who would pitch nickels, dimes and quarters into their tip jar.

J.P.'s laugh boomed down the alley, "That's the kind of crap they want to hear, so why should I disappoint them? Those guys that went over there in '62 had to fight promoters to keep from having to suit up in farm overalls and straw hats. Have you ever seen me in a pair of overalls? Man, my suits are Brooks Brothers. You can see your face in the shine on my shoes. This Fedora on my head sure the hell ain't made of no damned straw. But they think if you ain't no share-cropping farmer from Mississippi, then you ain't no bluesman."

Fat Frank watched his, tall, skinny, life-long friend walk down the dark alley and asked, "Where are you heading?"

"I'm calling it a night. I'm walking over to cousin Leroy's," he said. Leroy's place was only three blocks from Rhoda's on 14th Street.

A half of block down the dark alley, J.P. heard the tap, tap, tap of shoes behind him and he turned, but he could see no one in the darkness. He walked on and the tapping resumed.

He stopped, feeling spooked, and said, "Who the hell is back there? Fat Frank?"

The voice that answered said, "We are here to help rid the world of the friends of Satan, who corrupt the innocent by playing *his* music on *his* instrument."

J.P. could barely make out the man's figure as he stepped in close enough for him to smell the whiskey on his breath. *Another drunk idiot*, he thought.

Fat Frank walked back into the club and forgot just how smoky it could get. He snatched one more beer from the bar and headed over to Peter Stiml's table to offer apologies for J.P.—and a white lie that his buddy felt ill and had gone home to bed. The Frenchman smiled and said something, and Fat Frank had a harder time understanding him than J.P. did. But Stiml's smile and a hardy handshake indicated that the excuse was accepted.

They filed out onto the sidewalk, and Frank was flattered to have the film camera in his face. Everyone turned when they heard a woman shriek. Fat Frank saw his childhood friend stagger towards him with bloody hands clutching his chest. The film crew captured the final moments of J.P. Dillon's life as he collapsed into his drummer's outstretched arms, with Fat Frank yelling, "Cut that damn camera off, Frenchie, or I'll give you a reason to have the blues."

Wild eyes, searching for an answer, looked into Fat Frank's. J.P. opened his mouth and tried to say something. Frank whispered, "Shhhh. It'll be alright, J.P. It'll be alright." He turned and shouted, "Has someone called an ambulance! Damn it! Someone call an ambulance."

He pressed hard on J.P.'s chest, which was seeping blood and had soaked the white shirt. Rhoda gazed at them both in a state of shock. J.P. had played her club every Tuesday night for three years and she thought of the two men as brothers.

She tried not to look at the spreading crimson pool of blood around the two men as she put a hand on Fat Frank's shoulder. "An ambulance is on the way."

She looked into the wide eyes staring back at her, and J.P. said softly, "I see angels coming for me."

J.P. Dillon joined the ranks of Sonny Boy Williamson I and Henry "Pot" Strong on a list of unsolved murders on the streets of Chicago—a list of blues harmonica musicians.

CHAPTER 2

HOUSTON 2009

B ombs could have exploded. The roof could have caved in. I wouldn't have noticed. I was in the *zone*; that rare state of mind when an inner force takes over, the music flows, every note lands effortlessly, exactly where it should, and the musical tones wash down through the body and... well, musicians know what I'm talking about. We were cooking with gas and the audience was eating it up.

Deep into nailing a solo that Little Walter made famous, I spotted Pete Bolden walking through the front door of Little Queenie's, all one hundred and thirty five pounds of him. The man was still as skinny as a stack of dimes. Suddenly, the zone crapped out and I couldn't coax the right tones or hit the right notes to save my soul.

Pete Bolden hadn't shown himself in a club in at least fifteen years, since he got married, got religion and got off booze and drugs; not in that particular order. Seeing him threw me off my feed and shocked the zone out of me. It took the rest of the set to get my groove back.

Pete was a prodigy—a fellow blues folks called the "Real Deal". He was black, he could sing and he blew the blues harp as if his life depended on it. Back in the day his life did depend on his skills.

He had a natural talent and he taught me how to play tongue-blocked notes, how to create phrases and just how to suck the thing to get the fattest tone from the instrument. He was not successful teaching me to sing. Pete could sing like an angel or a devil, depending on the tune, but all I managed were froggy croaks.

He knew no limits, and that applied not only to musical boundaries, but to his indiscriminate taste for anything that altered his state of mind. All it took was, "Hey Pete, this'll get you high" and it didn't matter what manner of high he was being offered. He was in.

Most of his fans didn't notice his decline. They would claim that he was stellar up until he dropped out of sight.

We blues harp nuts knew, though. We could tell when that *something* that separated him from the rest of us began to dissipate. Oh, he could still blow and sing. Man, could he sing, but there was something missing from his harp playing and it saddened us to see it leave him.

Anyway, he'd caught himself in time, assisted by a wonderful wife and soul mate and Jesus Christ. He was alive and well and walking through the doors of Little Queenie's.

Little Queenie's received accolades year after year as one of Houston's Best Blues Clubs. Most of us considered Queenie's, The Big Easy over on Kirby, and Shakespeare's Pub as the only blues clubs in town; the ones that booked the most blues, anyway. There used to be more venues, but most were booking an eclectic roster of bands. Few of them were blues bands, even if they had blues in their name. The new House of Blues followed their corporate policy of going the rock route with popular flavor-of-the-month bands. Few national blues stars made Houston a destination any longer, and Little Queenie's just wasn't big enough for the big boys to play. But occasionally a few blues veterans cut their fees to play the club and support Franklin.

Franklin Pierce bought the club back in the early '80s when Stevie Ray Vaughan and his brother's Fabulous Thunderbirds were leading a mini-resurgence in the interest in blues music. Little Queenie's successfully rode the crest of the wave.

Nowadays, we heard the same complaint coming from his lips, "All I'm doing is subsidizing y'all's habit. I'm going broke here just so y'all can listen to the blues and play the blues. Y'all are just having a good time on my dime."

He repeated the last part of his mantra often. I told him that I was going to write a blues song based on that theme.

"You'll have to split the royalties with me," he said.

Truth was that Franklin—you didn't dare call him Frank and you'd get punched calling him Frankie—was a baby boomer who fell under the spell of the blues just like the rest of us. English cats like the Rolling Stones, Led Zeppelin, and Eric Clapton brought juiced up versions of Chicago blues back to our shores and slapped us around with it until we went out and bought Muddy Waters, Little Walter, Howlin' Wolf and Elmore James; and the blues gate opened.

Franklin never did drink much. In fact, he had once been into competitive body building and still kept in good enough shape to serve as his own bouncer. Few challenged him. He turned me into a gym rat for a while, but I never tried to keep pace with him. I do just enough nowadays to keep the ol' body from turning to milk toast.

The club had always been a neighborhood bar, but was just short of a dive when Franklin bought it and set to renovating it himself.

"I don't want to pretty it up too much," he'd tell us when we'd drop by to lend a hand and get a few free cold ones for our effort. He always kept a drum kit and a couple of amps set up and we would all jam at quitting time.

He prettied it up enough that our girlfriends or wives didn't mind spending an evening there, if they could handle listening to stone, solid blues, because that is all Franklin allowed anyone to play in his club.

Little Queenie's was juke joint chic without being pretentious. The club could accommodate 250 patrons comfortably and was laid out with a square floor plan. Along two walls he built booths made of oak and layered with enough coats of varnish to make a sailor envious.

He designed a modular stage. When all the modules were used, a band like Calvin Owens' could fit an entire orchestra on it with room to spare. When he wanted more seating for his patrons, he would break down, fold up and store the modules against the wall. He stuck the dance floor in the back. Some bands complained, but no one's big, tail-shaking butt blocked anyone's view of the action on the stage.

He brought in chrome-trimmed, Formica-topped tables, and padded chairs that he picked up from a '50s era downtown diner that had given way to urban renewal. Progress. Urban renewal was squeezing him too. Little Queenie's was close to the downtown renovation and he had what was now prime real estate.

His pride and joy was a highly-polished mahogany bar with shiny brass rails that had come from the officers' club at a military base in San Antonio. He never did tell us what he bid at the auction, but we know he paid way more than he planned.

Franklin had to have that bar. It came from the base where his dad spent the latter part of his career, and Franklin often pointed to the spot where he figured his dad's elbows had been propped many a night.

Franklin's father had risen to the rank of Lieutenant Colonel and was a casualty of the Vietnam War before most of the country knew any U.S. troops were even over there. Franklin had followed his dad into the same war and had gotten back stateside about the time the rest of us were draft age. He didn't come back a bitter vet, but a devoted patriot and he proudly flew the Stars and Stripes outside of Little Queenie's. Run down the U.S.A. in front of Franklin and you'd find out what kind of damage his twenty-inch biceps would do to your face.

The bar is where I found Pete Bolden resting his elbows at the end of our set.

"Hey, Peter, what in the blue blazes brings you out?" I said. We didn't grab and hug because we saw each other often and when the urge struck, I would venture into the Third Ward and listen to one of his Sunday sermons.

"Y'all sound pretty solid, Mitty. How'd you talk Rolf into playing lead guitar for you?" His curt little smile appeared to some as smart-assed. I always called his smile mischievous; he curled his lips slightly without exposing his teeth. No one came any friendlier than Pete Bolden.

"Billy couldn't make it and Rolf owed him one, so I got blessed with a bit of blues royalty tonight," I said. "It'll be business as usual next Tuesday. That's not what brought you out, though, is it?"

"I knew you wouldn't or couldn't answer a cell phone in here, but this isn't something that I would have phoned in anyway," Pete said slowly. "Listen Mitty, Bobby T is dead."

I was shocked, stunned speechless as Pete filled me in on the details. Pete's eyes always had a sad-looking slope to them, but they bogged heavily and filled with moisture as he told me about our good friend.

"Jean called about an hour ago and told me about it. His band was playing up in Kansas City and they were waiting for Bobby to get back to the stage for the second set and went looking for him after fifteen minutes. You know Bobby T; he's never late after a break. He's usually hassling and fining his band mates for that crap. He'd never leave the band hanging."

"Alright, already... heart attack? What?"

"Bobby T died from a heroin overdose."

"Bullshit! With a capital B," I said as Pete cringed. My quick temper was about to get the better of me. "Bobby never touched that stuff. He wasn't even smoking pot any more. Come on, Pete. What the hell are you talking about?"

"His drummer, Jake—you know Jake don't you?—he found him on the stairs of the hotel they were staying at next door to the club. He still had a needle in his arm.

"I know, I know," he said when he saw my eyes widen. "Bobby T would faint at the sight of a needle. But, you know Mitty, we haven't seen him for some time and take it from an old junkie, it can change people. Doesn't take much for the Big H to jump on your back and grab the driver's seat."

"Not Bobby T," I said, mad that Pete would even suggest it. "He had the strongest constitution of anyone I've ever known."

"Don't shoot the messenger," Pete said. "I'm just giving you the facts of what happened up there in KC."

"I'm not shooting anyone, and Bobby T was not shooting dope, and I know that you know better, too, Pete Bolden." I glared in Pete's direction and waved off a waitress taking drink orders.

Franklin came over to tell me how well he thought the band and I did.

"Mighty fine blowing, there, Mitty boy. You keep that up and I just might have to give you guys a regular weekend slot."

I rounded up musicians during the week and we hosted a jam once a month. Once in a blue moon, Franklin would toss us a weekend bone.

"Well, I'll be damned," Franklin said when he spotted Pete Bolden on the Captain's Chair next to me. "Sweet Pete Bolden. I haven't seen your ass in what? Ten years or so? Great to see you, dude. You're not off the wagon or anything like that are you?"

Franklin swept him off his chair, squeezed him and had Pete's eyes bulging. This time his smile showed teeth.

"Hell, no, I haven't fell off my wagon," Pete said when Franklin relaxed his bear hug. "If I ever do, though, I'll have Little Queenie's host the event. I'm sorry to show up here after all this time and be the bearer of bad news."

Franklin stared at Pete in much the same way I had when he heard the news about Bobby Tarleton. Bobby had blown more than a few blues harp notes at Little Queenie's over the years and had helped Franklin get the club off the ground.

"What the hell, Pete," Franklin said. "He wasn't no junkie. How the hell could something like that happen?"

"I only know what Jean told me on the phone." Pete said. "And I didn't want to piss Franklin off. I don't know what happened or what to think about it."

Franklin looked at me, with watery eyes, searching for an answer, and I could tell that he was choking up over the death of our good friend.

I looked at both of them and said, "I damn well know this; no overdose of drugs took him out. Something evil came Bobby T's way."

CHAPTER 3

I was easing into my third year of self-unemployment from *The Gulf Coast Gazette*, which was an alternative to the big boy *Houston Chronicle*. I was amazed how enjoyable life had become. *The Gazette* had reached a level of respectability over the years after being considered sort of hippy-dippy when I began my tenure with them. I worked twenty-three years of my life for the newspaper that promoted *"Truth, Justice, and Jitterbugging"*. The jitterbugging part is what convinced me to write for the rag a few years after graduating Southwest Texas State University (now known as Texas State) with a degree in journalism. The newspaper's focus was twofold: to report on the music scene; not just local, but statewide, and to advocate for our readers. We went where Marvin Zindler would not venture and did quite well at muckraking.

I wanted to write only about music; blues music. I convinced them to send me off to Austin and Antone's at least once a month to see the likes of Muddy Waters, Jimmy Rogers, James Cotton, or Eddie Taylor. Houston's blues music scene was also thriving at clubs like Rockefellers, Club Hey Hey, the Bon Ton Room, the Ready Room and numerous, wonderful hole-in-the-walls. Of course, Little Queenie's was my home base.

It didn't take long for me to get sucked into the consumer advocate role, which sounded better than being called a "muckraker," and "investigative reporter" sounded too haughty for what I did.

At first everybody had a hand in all facets of publishing the *Gazette*: editing, layout, paste-up, and selling advertising. We even had to throw the paper in our neighborhoods and enforce payment. As the business became more successful, they hired others to handle the donkey work and we could work at being real journalists.

I always used my given name for the watchdog pieces because "James Phillip Andersen" seemed more authoritative than my nickname—Mitty. Kids called me Mitts, then Mitty, back when I was a Little League catcher and I didn't mind it then. I tried to ditch the moniker at high school, but couldn't shake it. It just didn't seem mature for a professional, but that's what got stuck on my first blues story byline and that's why I'm still Mitty today.

However, when I went after politicians or school board members who needed a little exposure for misuse of public trust, "Mitty" ducked into a his phone booth to change his persona to "James Phillip Andersen," which pleased my parents.

I became skilled at getting to the truth, had many doors slammed in my face, and a few lawsuits filed against me. And we filed a few of our own; for information that we felt belonged to the public. I made enemies, but gained many more friends.

We never cared whose toes we stepped on as long as they deserved to be scrunched. We went after county commissioners, police chiefs, mayoral aides, real estate developers, the KKK, and the NAACP. We were an equal opportunity pain in the ass, but we laid it all out there for the public's assessment.

We got firebombed a couple of times for our efforts and I was cussed out, swung on, shot at, and run off the highway. I never did know who ran me off the road and into a tree. It cost me four weeks in the hospital with two broken legs. I held my own during most face to face confrontations and I was one of the first to apply for a concealed weapons permit when state law allowed.

The Gazette allowed itself to be bought out by a conglomerate out of North Carolina, which promptly fired the entire editorial staff and brought in their own people. I had the opportunity to stay, but they stuck it to so many of my friends that I told them where they could stick it.

A buddy of mine had guided me wisely through the maze of the investment world, and my nest egg was in place. I kept an income flowing from freelance writing for the blues publications, though sadly too many of those had closed up shop in recent years. I didn't like to think about the life insurance my wife carried and its pay out when she died from breast cancer. She bought that policy years before and never mentioned it until her final days with me. I haven't needed it and don't know if I could bring myself to use it, so it sits drawing interest. I think.

At fifty-two, I wasn't ready to call myself retired. It was time to open chapter two of my life.

I was up for anything, but now I was free to pursue my first love, which was blowing a blues harp with a band of individuals who shared my passion. I had jammed around town for years, but I rarely had the time to hone my skills. Franklin had given me a shot at filling the slow Tuesday night slot.

Mitty's Gritty Blues Band was a revolving door of musicians: there were always great musicians around who wanted something going during the week. We hosted the Wednesday night jams at Little Queenie's once a month and the rare weekend gig when something went awry with Franklin's bookings, like the night Pete showed his face. Franklin never admitted it, but I know he slipped a couple of extra twenties or more into our tip bucket each night.

I'd tell him, "Hey *'Boom Boom'* (he hated that nickname, but his mashed face did look like the prize fighter, Boom Boom Mancini), we ain't no charity case."

And he'd yell back, "What the hell you talking about *Pretty Boy* (he knew that I hated that name, but he thought that I looked like Robert Redford and he'd rub that in to get back at me), I saw some good looking blonde eyeballing you and that's her money in your bucket."

It didn't matter that there hadn't been a blonde, good looking or not, in the club for the entire evening. So, yeah, Franklin and I were tight buddies.

It was the same with Bobby Tarleton, whom I had always envied. He went for the dream that we both shared, but he refused to back off. He was renowned worldwide for the uncompromising blues music he brought to the stage and he had become a legend for his harp skills. They rewarded him with a Grammy for his exquisite *Get Your Spurs On* album. We shared lots of history.

Bobby and I met as freshmen in college at jams around San Marcos. He was the first person I ever heard in person blow amplified harmonica and the first person to turn me onto Little Walter. He practiced constantly and had the same passion for his music as an Olympic athlete had for his sport. I never could summon that kind of passion and always wished I could.

He had his stuff down pat already and he high jacked every jam when he took the stage and began blowing Little Walter's signature tune, "Juke," and oh, could Bobby sing the blues. Some snickered when Bobby walked into a jam in a suit, tie, and sunglasses, but when he plugged into his Fender Concert amp and started blowing; they quickly jumped on his bandwagon.

Bobby and I spent hours running up to Austin to catch the blues bands that cranked out their music every night of the week. We'd hit low down clubs like the One Night and the Vulcan Gas Company and catch Stevie Ray Vaughn and his brother Jimmy tearing it up. Bobby always insisted that we track down where Jimmy's band, the Fabulous Thunderbirds, was playing. His opinion was that no one could touch the skills of the band's harmonica player, Kim Wilson, and we'd sit and soak up every note at the Rome Inn and the La Cucaracha. Bobby could hang with this master, even back then, but he never would ask to sit in and prove it. Bobby strutted once he hit a stage, but shyness pinned him to his seat when he found himself in the same room as one of his heroes.

Bobby honed his craft once he got his own band cranking. College was out the window and Bobby hit the highway. I always wished that I'd had the guts to follow that path, but my resolve and talent lagged behind.

So when Bobby T's wife, Jean, called me, sobbing and asked if I would look into what happened to Bobby T, what else could I say but, "You bet I will."

CHAPTER 4

CHICAGO 1968

As the front tires of his Cadillac eased up on the sidewalk in front of Jimmy Miller's apartment building, Eddie Earl said, "If Muddy ever hears you blow, man, you'll be the next harmonica player in his band, and then big time's gonna happen."

"Yeah, *if* he ever hears me play," Jimmy said as he crawled out of Eddie's passenger side window. Someone had smashed up the door while they played a gig at Bobo's Lounge a month earlier and it wouldn't open and Eddie couldn't afford to get it fixed.

"I know Big Goose has talked you up to him and you never know when he'll be on the prowl for a new harp man," Eddie said. "All I'm saying is that you're just about the best that I've heard outside of Little Walter. I'd hate to lose you, but there are bigger and better things waiting for you out there."

Jimmy stuck his long arm through the window, shook Eddie's bear paw of a hand and said, "Sure, sure, Eddie. Listen, thanks for the ride. I'll see you the same time tomorrow night."

Jimmy Miller wished he'd get a chance to play for the greatest bluesman in Chicago, hell, the world for all he was concerned. All he wanted to do was blow a blues harp; ever since his Uncle Mo gave him one as an eleven-year-old growing up back in Monroe, Louisiana. He drove his parents and five sisters crazy playing, especially when his old hound dog Blue would howl along with him. They would send him off into the woods with his harps and out there he would wail away with abandon. By the time Jimmy turned fourteen, Uncle Mo had him jamming on stage with his band. Jimmy loved the way people took notice and clapped and hollered out his name when he played. The blues seeped deep into him and grabbed his soul.

Jimmy hit the streets of Chicago when he was eighteen. His Uncle Mo had steered him to Eddie Earl, and Eddie hired him immediately, telling him, "Boy, you got the real stuff going on. The folks here are gonna love what you're puttin' down."

Eddie played blues guitar superbly and garnered a long list of credits in the recording studio, playing for just about everyone in town. His band backed up many blues stars that came through without their own musicians. Eddie's mediocre singing kept Eddie Earl and the Dukes at the second tier level as far as gigs went, but between the backup gigs and recording sessions, Eddie made a good living. He did have two records out, recorded before Jimmy joined him. They sold better now than when they were released, thanks to the interest shown by young white people. It amazed Eddie to find his gigs inhabited by increasing numbers of college students.

Jimmy relied on his day job as a cobbler's apprentice to get by and was looking forward to the opportunity to play blues for a living someday. Eddie kept on at him about singing a little, maybe just a song or two. But he preferred to have his harmonica in his mouth and let it do more than words ever could. Eddie told him that he'd have to develop some vocal chops if he ever wanted to lead his own band. He told Eddie that being a sideman suited him just fine.

Eddie had chided him, "Don't be no fool. You need to develop all the talents you got. You're one good looking son-of-a-gun. Hell boy, women are throwing their panties at you on stage. You've got them swaying with that Mississippi Saxophone, and I'm telling you that you'd be killer if you'd add some singing in there. You would be dynamite, buddy."

Jimmy looked abashed at the mention of the panties. A very drunk lady had pulled off her panties one night at Domino's Parlor and threw them on stage during one of Jimmy's harmonica solos, and then she promptly passed out cold. The band wouldn't let Jimmy live it down, even though he was quite sure that her aim wasn't at him in particular. Earl's drummer, Bill Bender, started to call him 'Poon Tang Man', and it irritated him no end.

Jimmy had heard his singing voice at a studio session. Even with everything the sound engineer had to offer, his voice didn't impress him. He wasn't about to shove that on anyone else.

"Man, I think you have the perfect blues voice, Jimmy," Eddie said. "You don't have to worry about great vocal range, just put the song across with some emotion. You've got that happening. I felt the heartbreak in there when you opened your mouth. Start singing on the bandstand, dude."

Jimmy didn't think so. Maybe one day, when he felt that his vocals matched his talent on the harmonica. A representative from a small record company echoed the same sentiment at one of Eddie's gigs. The cat said he worked for the record company, but Jimmy thought he was just another long haired hippy, hanging out at the bar.

He gave Jimmy a card, though, and told him, "If you get your own band together and sing anywhere close as good as you blow, I promise you that we can sell your stuff big time."

Jimmy's mind still had big time on it when he open the door to his foyer and turned to go up the stairs. Eddie had found the apartment for him and had said that he wanted Jimmy to live in a safer neighborhood than he did. On the first landing, a kid of ten or twelve years old blocked his way. Jimmy was thinking how strange it was that the youngster had one blue eye and one brown eye, when suddenly he felt a thin rope sling around his neck and tighten.

Jimmy grabbed at the rope and managed to get three fingers under it. He pulled enough to keep his windpipe from being crushed. He threw one leg up on the stairway wall and shoved backwards as hard as he could. Both he and his assailant took a hard tumble down the stairs and onto the foyer floor. Jimmy ended up on his back on top of his attacker. The man gasped and loosened his grip enough for Jimmy to slide his entire left hand between the rope and his throat. He could breathe and gained the upper hand as he twisted around to his side, pulling his mugger with him. He had both hands in the noose now, and just as he thought that he had the strength to pull free, a hard-toed boot caught him across his right cheek bone.

He fell back and the rope re-tightened.

Just before the darkness crept in, Jimmy saw the kid with the strange eyes staring at him and smiling from the stairs. He heard him say, "You're gonna get exactly what you deserve, evil one."

ROBERT JOSEPH
1937-1968

"Hey TC, you coming back in? We're late kicking off the last set," said John Boy Raymond.

Robert Joseph was deep in concentration, muttering, "Come on baby, seven come eleven," as he tossed dice against the alley wall.

"Craps!" hollered one of his gambling buddies.

"Damn! Hey, man, I've just got to win my money back. Get Little Willie to fill in until I get back in there," he yelled back at his guitarist. "Half those people won't know the difference anyway." He looked up at his gambling partners. The alley light showed a face full of scars.

T.C. had been called Top Cat since his high school days on the basketball court, though most people thought it related to his proficiency playing blues harmonica. He'd had just come back from a successful European tour. Since Little Walter's murder two months earlier, and Jimmy Miller's before that, the

European Blues Coalition had been searching for a musician as talented on the blues harp. T.C. just happened to top everyone's list. Even though they stuck him with guitarist Jukin' Jake, who couldn't rock with his type of blues worth a darn, he thought that he fared pretty well and felt that the Europeans appreciated what he could do.

When T.C. climbed on the blues bandwagon, guitar-oriented blues bands were starting to incorporate rock and roll into their music. T.C. followed the trend, playing in a high-energy style, spitting out rapid-fire licks that no one could touch.

He owned the blues world during the late 60s, but drug and alcohol abuse began to take its toll. The Europeans loved him, but he had worn out his welcome on his home turf. The fact that he enjoyed his habits a bit too much led him to where he was now—in an alley outside a dive club, playing with whatever pickup players were willing to put up with him and his temper. Musicians still jumped at the chance to play with him and on a good night, flashes of genius on the harp, that only T.C. could create, would mesmerize an audience.

"Come on, T.C., let's go back in," said the other gambler. "We can shoot dice until daybreak and you ain't gonna break even."

"You two give me just a few more shots at getting some of my money back."

T.C. was still shaking the dice when they walked back into the club. He was squatting down and glanced up just in time to duck a pipe being swung at his head. T.C. could scrap with the best of them. He sprang at his assailant and connected with a strong right hook. The attacker stumbled back, and he smashed a hard left fist and then another right into the man's face. Then strong hands pinned his arms behind his back. His muggers pummeled him around his head. He struggled and slung his handler to the ground. They tumbled around until he was kicked in the head. He reached for his pistol, but it had fallen from his pocket.

"Hey, what the hell's going on?" yelled one of his recent gaming partners, who had stepped out of the back door. "Get back to the bandstand NOW. The club owner is hopping mad. Everybody wants their money back if you're not playing."

The two assailants fled down the alley and T.C. got to his feet.

"You okay, man? Let me help you inside." His unwitting savior gazed at the bloodied, battered face. "Want me to call an ambulance?"

"No. I'll be okay. Help me back in the door. We'll just go blow some blues away."

T.C made it up the back steps and into the club. Little Willie was blowing the blues in his absence and the bartender brought him a towel and ice for his face. He signaled to John Boy that he'd take the next song, but he collapsed before making it to the stage.

Robert "Top Cat" Joseph lingered in a coma at Provident Hospital for two weeks before dying from his injuries.

The *Chicago Defender*, the city's Negro newspaper, issued a call for action from authorities to investigate what they termed the serial murders of black musicians. The official response: the murders were being investigated the same as other incidents that took place late at night and outside a bar. After Martin Luther King's assassination, the Chicago police department made sure that statistics were released showing that more white people than black had been murdered in Chicago and they assured the public that all murders were being thoroughly investigated, regardless of the victim's race.

The officer in charge of the Robert Joseph investigation asked his partner, "Didn't some cop from down in Louisiana call up here last year looking for information about harmonica players being killed?"

"Hell, I don't remember. Seems like it. Who gives a rat's ass, anyway?"

"Well, hell, I do. That Negro newspaper is turning up the heat on this case. Didn't he say that harmonica players had turned up murdered down there and he was looking for a connection? What was his name?"

"Damn if I remember. And let me repeat: who gives a rat's ass?"

CHAPTER 5

Robert Cooley Tarleton flat out did not look natural surrounded by the white-padded sides of his polished mahogany casket with brass-and ivory handles. They had dressed him in one of his pinstriped gig suits, one with a Marine Band harmonica embroidered on the top pocket and a red kerchief sticking from it. I had overheard a couple of elderly ladies commenting how natural he looked, but he didn't—he looked waxy and fake, and they should have restored the smile to his face. His six-four, 240- pound frame didn't belong in this fancy box. I was wishing that it was *all* a fake and that this was a dream; that any minute Bobby T would climb out of the casket, step to the podium, and kick off a blues shuffle in E.

Wilder things have happened where Bobby T was concerned.

But this was for real. I stood with Pete and watched Jean Tarleton hug and greet the throng of people lined up along the outside aisle of the Boecker Brothers Funeral Home chapel. The line of Bobby's friends and fans extended out the door, down the hallway, and into the parking lot. Some folks already had taken seats in the red, cushioned pews with glossy oak backs. Visitation had begun an hour earlier and looked as if would go way beyond the posted hours. Bobby came back to Houston too seldom, staying out on the road at least 250 days of the year. He recently played a bunch of dates overseas, where audiences couldn't get enough of him and where the gigs were more plentiful. No one wanted to see him come home this way.

Jean's two grown daughters and their husbands flanked her and they all looked weary. Tess was a lawyer now and worked for a big outfit in Dallas. I'd helped Tammy start her journalism career at a San Antonio newspaper by putting in a good word with the managing editor, who was an old college buddy. I always felt very close to both the girls. They were the closest thing I had to children. My wife Suzie and I were still planning our brood when she died from breast cancer twenty years ago.

Even though Bobby ran the roads, when he got home he got involved in all aspects of his family's life. I went with him to high school football games to watch Tammy cheerlead, and to many of Tess' soccer games.

Bobby tried to make it back into Houston at least one week out of each month and often took a month off during the summer. He might be coaxed into an appearance at Little Queenie's when he came home, but for the most part, it was family time.

After a couple of hours of standing and greeting the well-wishers all three looked emotionally drained. I was feeling raw myself as Pete said, "Are you listening to me, or not?"

"Sorry, Pete. I was off somewhere else. What did you say?"

"I said, 'Exactly how are you going to do what you told Jean that you'd do?'"

"I don't know, yet, Pete. I'm just going to look into things. I spent a lifetime doing that for a living. Things just don't add up—you know what I mean? When you don't like the facts at hand, you've got to uncloak those yet to be found. I'll poke around and see what happens. I've always been good at poking around."

"Look, Mitty, I've seen plenty of people act different and do different out on the road. Maybe things got to Bobby and he needed to try a taste of something different."

"Pete Bolden! I can't believe you're even talking about my daddy like this!" Tammy was staring at Pete with eyes that were flashing fire.

She had a good six inches on Pete and a few pounds, and he visibly winced at her words as she lowered her curly, blonde head closer to his, so that she could keep her voice down and to make her point perfectly clear.

"Daddy did not do drugs; *at all*. You know that," Tammy said through clenched teeth. "He drank, but within limits. He hated not being in control when he played. Where do you get off suggesting what you just said? You owe him better than that, Pete."

"Tammy, I'm sorry you heard that. I was around that mess so long and saw so many people; people you'd never suspect, jump off into those waters. Maybe they try the junk just once, but I've seen that one time take plenty of people down."

"That is not the case here, Pete. Not with my daddy."

"I'm not saying it is. I'm just saying ..."

Tammy's husband, Earl, approached before Pete could finish his sentence, said his hellos, shook our hands and told Tammy that her mom needed her. I never had much use for Earl. No one was ever good enough for Bobby's girls as far as I was concerned. Fact is; Earl thought that he was too good for us common people. He had trouble holding down a job because he always thought that he knew how to run things better than his bosses. I figured that Tammy would have left him by now, but she saw something in him that I didn't. So I tolerated the pompous butthead.

"Whew!" said Pete, as Tammy walked off. "I guess I stepped deep off into it with Tammy."

"Well, hell, with me too." I shot him a look at least as mean as Tammy's.

I reddened as Pete said, "Now, Mitty, you know I'm not aiming to run down Bobby T's reputation. I'm just stating the obvious. I hope the hell that there is a better answer. That's what began this conversation, remember? Just what is it that you're planning on doing to get to the bottom of what went down?"

I said, "How about this? What are *we* planning on doing to get to the bottom of this? I know you and you are not convinced that Bobby T was shooting heroin during a break at a gig. I know you don't believe that at all, and that means somebody stuck that needle in his arm and murdered him."

After a pause, Pete said, "Okay, ya got me. Where do *we* start?"

"I don't know, Pete. I'm tired and clueless right now."

My attention was drawn to a tall, thin black man passing by Bobby T's casket. He wore a finely tailored grey suit with a red Bolo tie like the ones Gatemouth Brown sported. I might even have mistaken him for Gatemouth, had I not known that Brown had died after Hurricane Rita slammed the upper Texas Coast and drove him from home.

He definitely had the appearance of a musician. Takes one to know one, but I wasn't sure who this cat could be. His face was obscured behind dark Ray Bans, but I knew him from somewhere. What really stood out about him was a purple and black striped do-rag with a tail hanging a third the way down his back.

Pete chattered at me, but I fixed my eyes on the stranger and didn't hear him. I never was worth a damn at guessing the ages of African American males. I put this guy at somewhere between fifty and seventy. Something about him had my antennae crackling.

Pete said, "There you go again. Not listening to a thing I'm saying, are you Mitty? Mitty?"

"Pete, do you know the tall fellow with the purple do-rag paying his respects?"

"Who?"

"He was at Bobby T's casket just a moment ago." I looked around the chapel, trying to spot him again.

"Yeah, him and half the city."

"You *had* to have noticed this guy."

"Well, you and Tammy had me more than a little distracted." He followed me towards the door after I caught a glimpse of the purple do-rag bobbing above the heads of a mournful crowd that was getting thicker by the minute.

We threaded our way through the mob and headed into the heat-scorched parking lot. Sunlight ricocheted off car windows and blinded me. The stranger had vanished.

Then it dawned on me. "That was The Wizard. I knew he looked familiar. It had to be him."

Pete froze in mid-step.

"That's who it was, I know it," I said. "How could I have not recognized him?"

"He hasn't exactly been a public figure for, like, the past fifteen years or so," Pete said.

"Yeah, what's it been? A couple of years since his release?"

"Something like that." Pete said. "But why would he show up at Bobby T's funeral? Wasn't he sent up for murdering a harp player from Dallas? Big Joey, wasn't it?"

Damn. Had Bobby T's murderer just walked in and out of the door?

CHAPTER 6

I'd met The Wizard once, briefly, at his sister Sallie Ray's house, but most of what I knew about the man came from the numerous articles in various blues magazines and his sister. His talents had always impressed me.

The Wizard helped put Houston blues on the map, even though he had moved far away from the Bayou City for fame and fortune. Born Michael Ray Melton outside of Navasota, Texas, he hung around the legendary Mance Lipscomb long enough to master considerable guitar picking skills by the time he was a teenager. By his early twenties he had moved to Houston's Third Ward and played with Lightnin' Hopkins, one of the most recorded bluesmen of the time. He quickly fell in with fellow guitarists, Albert Collins, Johnny Clyde Copeland and Joe 'Guitar' Hughes. They were all honing their chops, learning from each other and stealing licks from each other in a thriving blues scene, undiscovered by most Anglo Houstonians.

Sallie Ray had told me, "Michael was a natural. He was full-blown good on that guitar by the time he moved to Houston. My auntie and me used to go up there and see him play. Michael packed those little clubs. People loved him."

While the Eldorado Ballroom booked the slick blues of BB King, Bobby Blue Bland and T-Bone Walker for the uptown crowd, Michael and his *compadres* were slinging it and stinging it at neighborhood working men's joints like Shady's Playhouse.

When Albert and Johnny Clyde bailed out to find the key to the highway and headed off to the west and east coasts, Michael Ray headed to Chicago. He said in interviews that he'd always loved the Westside guitar sounds of Otis Rush, Buddy Guy, Magic Sam, and Freddy King. They were playing his kind of blues.

His friends tagged him "The Wizard" way before he left Texas. Most in the blues world thought that the nickname referred to his guitar skills, which were considerable, and he never corrected them. His Third Ward partners knew better, though.

Michael always had a trick up his sleeve—literally. Seldom could he be found without a deck of cards in his pocket. He had spent as much time developing his sleight-of-hand skills as he had picking guitar notes. By the time he moved to Houston, he could amaze bar patrons with his magic. Michael supplemented his income handsomely with his cunning tricks and he quickly gained a reputation and the moniker to go with it.

"Michael learned them card tricks from an old tractor driver down on the farm we worked. He never would show me how he did 'em. All of us kids was his audience and our eyes would bug out when made cards disappear into thin air," Sallie Ray had said.

His card skills served him well in the Windy City too, while he worked at establishing himself as a musician. Established stars still dominated the club scene at Silvio's, the Alex Club, the Zanzibar and Theresa's, but he was always a persistent presence, soaking it all in and hoping for a chance to show what he had.

"He sent us tickets one time to take the Amtrak to Chicago," she said. "My brother brought the Texas swagger to the stage and he towered over most of his band. He was quite imposing. And he could play any style of blues guitar. All those King boys; B.B., Albert and Freddie. He could do T-Bone Walker or Albert Collins or Gatemouth Brown. He had 'em all down pat. But he pulled his own style together to record that first record *The Wizard's Magic*. That one became Windy City Blues Records biggest seller. All those music writers loved it and they started writing about him."

As the '80s rolled around, The Wizard soon headlined blues festivals from coast to coast and even grabbed a spot on David Letterman's show. His appearance on Saturday Night Live etched his name in fame.

As his popularity increased, so did his ego. His big mouth often got him in hot water with promoters and he began to rub other musicians the wrong way. Band members constantly had to challenge him for their share of gig money and he would claim that the promoters were swindling them, and him, too. He bad-mouthed whoever his record company executives were at the moment, and he became known—politely—as "difficult".

Then he inflamed every blues harmonica player in the world with statements in a national blues music magazine interview.

"Harmonica blowers have to be the most obnoxious musicians in the universe—if you want to call them musicians. Some of them think that they are the second coming of Little Walter and want to play just like him. Hell, the man's been dead for about forty years. They need to get their own style and move on with it. Some of them can ruin a gig fast and maybe mass extermination would remedy that."

Angry musicians wrote back, setting a record for the number of letters to the editor, but he remained wildly popular with the general blues-loving public even though he had not changed his set list in five years. Show after show, he played the same showy guitar gimmicks and employed the same stage routine. There were always fans that had never seen the show, fans who never wanted the show to change and plenty of others who idolized him and forgave him. He was still at the top of the blues heap in the early 90s. He loved his fans, showed it, and they loved him back.

"That's all that matters to me," The Wizard said. "The only reason I play this axe is for them."

He never planned on an audience of cellmates at the Eastham Unit of the Texas Department of Corrections.

That would be his only fan base for fifteen years.

CHAPTER 7

DALLAS 1994

Andy Rodriquez sat wide eyed after his buddy, Big Joey, put his fist into the sheet rocked living room wall. He knew he shouldn't have shown Joey the magazine article.

"Just who the hell does he think he is? He got some of his licks from cats that have been dead for forty years. Hell, I don't like trombone players, but I sure the heck wouldn't be bad-mouthing them in public. Harmonica players get dissed enough without someone like The Wizard bad mouthing us."

Andy had seen his friend angry plenty of times, but he'd never seen this much rage. Sometimes the permanent scowl creased into Joey's forehead made it hard to determine whether or not Joey was mad or not. There was no doubt that furious fit the bill at the moment. Big Joey was a generally mellow fellow and soft spoken—unless someone pissed him off. And when it came to music he could get really riled up. As Joey's voice rose, Andy once again realized that he should have just thrown the magazine away.

Andy and Big Joey had been pals since their school days at Dallas High. They were a Mutt and Jeff duo: Big Joey was just shy of six-three and 290 pounds and Andy barely stretched to five-eight at 165 pounds. They became buddies on the football field, where Joey's blocking skill made Andy a better running back than he really was. Joey would pancake anyone who risked stepping into his path. Andy merely had to sprint past Joey's victims and rack up enough yards to garner All-District honors by the end of the season.

Joey could have had his pick of any college in the nation. Football recruiters hit on him hot and heavy to sign to a scholarship, but he quit school after his junior year and became a full-time professional bluesman. Andy had seen it coming and knew that Joey's mind would not be changed, but it left the pundits scratching their heads over what could have been.

"Ain't too many young black guys doing this anymore, but as athletes, we're a dime a dozen," Joey told him. "I'm going to do it and keep the blues going. I told my daddy I would."

Rumor had it that Joey's dad had made a dying request that Joey carry on the blues tradition. Andy knew it wasn't true. Joey was across town at a blues jam when his dad suffered a heart attack on the stage at the Mojo Rising club and died before the ambulance arrived. If anything, Kenny would have been proud that his son may be able to continue his education on a football scholarship. Andy had heard Joey's dad say many times, "Son, you'll be the first in the Brooks family to make it into college."

Andy had half-heartedly argued with Joey that his daddy didn't want him to follow in his footsteps, which were big ones to fill in the DFW area. Kenny Brooks had won regional success on the circuit that swung from Dallas to Houston, along the Gulf Coast of Louisiana, Mississippi, Alabama and into Florida. He slowed down his road running to raise Joey and his five sisters. While the kids were growing up he led a local band that backed up or opened up for every famous blues musician touring the area. Many traveled to Dallas without their bands, knowing that Kenny Brooks had them covered.

Big Joey had been a part of those early bandstand days. At twelve he was already known as Little Joey Brooks and he grew from a kiddie curiosity into a respected musician. He began paying his dues to play the blues and often played with his dad's band four or five nights a week. On school nights he was sent home by eleven o' clock, but he would often head to someone else's gig and sit in with them—as long as he could beat his old man home. Blues veterans around the city no longer looked at Joey as a novelty, but as someone serious about the music and at sixteen, he could play with the best of them.

Joey had worked long and hard to gain respect for himself and his instrument. Too many felt that the harmonica was a toy, even though Little Walter had disproved that in the 50s, and in the hands of Big Joey and others like him its status was solidified by the 80s. It bugged Joey that harp guys still had to prove to others that they were *real* musicians.

Andy had read The Wizard's interview a few months earlier and figured that Joey had also seen it. He should have known better. Big Joey didn't read about the blues, he just played the hell out of it. Since The Wizard was booked to play the Piñata Theatre on Friday night, Andy thought he would ask what his buddy thought of the article. Joey's reaction reminded Andy of the time his hot-tempered friend had busted a guitarist's nose because he was sticking some Albert King licks into a Big Walter tune.

"That bozo ain't getting away with this crap," he said. "I'm just going to check out Mr. Wizard in person."

The Piñata Theatre was one of the upscale clubs that opened during the grand plan to restore Dallas' historic Deep Ellum district as the entertainment Mecca that it had once been. Deep Ellum had been a blues haven as far back as the 20s, when Blind Lemon Jefferson shouted his blues in the neighborhood and had more records on the market than any other blues singer.

Big Joey's dad had told them how the construction of the Central Freeway project in the 60s ripped through the heart of Deep Ellum and businesses closed or moved out.

"Yeah, boys, the powers that be killed the best damn entertainment district in the U.S. of A. But it was entertainment for our kind, so it didn't matter. They didn't give a skunk's ass about what it was destroying. Back in the day, every big name star played clubs in Deep Ellum. Count Basie, Cab Calloway, Louis Jordan, T-Bone, B.B., Bobby Bland. You name 'em and they came down to Dallas and played down there," Kenny Brooks had said. "Then those power that be, that shouldn't be, wanted to resurrect what had been for us, but would be for them."

Andy and Big Joey watched the new and improved Deep Ellum develop and it was obvious that it catered to an entirely different crowd—mainly middle-aged, affluent, white blues fans. A few restaurants opened, along with clubs aimed at the twenty-something crowd. Deep Ellum was far from being the center of an African-American community and the *real* historical preservationists put a stop to what they felt was the destruction of a piece of Dallas' heritage by modern day carpetbaggers. Lawsuits slowed the renewal efforts, clubs closed, restaurants moved out and businesses failed to draw customers. Deep Ellum began to revert to its recent identity as a warehouse district. One of the few remaining venues was the Piñata Theatre, which was part of a national chain like the House of Blues. They had deep pockets and booked nationally known acts. They seldom featured local bands.

The Piñata Theatre inhabited a renovated movie theatre and it was as far removed from the low down juke joints where Big Joey spent most of his early professional life. The club had a red carpet sidewalk and velvet ropes channeling the uptown chic patrons through the ornate, gold inlaid trimmed doors—with a doorman, no less.

Even though some of Dallas' finest blues veterans made up his band, the club snubbed Big Joey and the Jokers and they could never find their way onto the bill, even as an opening act. They had two strikes against them: they played gritty low-down blues and they were local. Big Joey and most of the musicians he knew returned the snub and vowed never to set foot in the Piñata.

"The hell with 'em," Joey said. "They don't need me and I don't need them. I'll be here, though, still doing it, when they are long gone."

Big Joey never stepped foot in the place, but Andy saw that he was hell bent on doing it now, "Just to have a word with The Wizard," he said.

"Hey, I respect the man. His dedication to the blues and his guitar playing has always impressed the devil out of me," Big Joey said, "but he darned sure should show a little more respect for harmonica players. He could have kept that to himself and not blabbed it to some stupid writer."

Joey and Andy's good friend, Paul was the chief cook and bottle-washer at the Piñata and had told them to call him anytime that they wanted him to slip them in free to see a show. Andy had gone a couple of times, but Joey always refused, until now, and since The Wizard's show had sold out long ago, they needed a way in. Andy called and Paul agreed to meet them in the back alley.

As Joey and Andy walked up the back steps leading into the kitchen, Joey almost tumbled off as a loose board flipped up.

"Look at this. The back part of this place is falling apart," he said.

"Yeah, I guess they figure that no one's going to venture back here but us peons," Paul said as he walked up the alley decked out in a shirt that resembled the Texas flag. Paul considered himself a true Texan and let people know that he was born and bred in Dallas. Andy didn't think that the pleated Dockers slacks and the rubber clogs that Paul wore advanced that claim very well.

"I've got a few boxes of produce in back of my truck around the corner," he said. "If you guys go and grab a box, that'll be your way into this gig. Shift change is about now, so there's a lot of milling around. Just follow me in like you're making a delivery and then slip down the hall and head towards the men's room and then out into the venue. You won't have any seats, so just hang out at the bar and no one will hassle you."

Everything proceeded as Paul had planned and Joey said the place looked pretty much the way he figured it would with the faux weathered wood siding, and neon Jax, Falstaff and other vintage beer signs glowing on the walls, evoking a bygone era.

Scattered strategically around the club were reproduction gig posters from the 50s and 60s, touting appearances by Muddy Waters, Howlin' Wolf, Elmore James, Guitar Slim and other blues stars.

Joey wasn't impressed and said so, "Anyone who would book Metallica, just for the bucks, should feel real shame for sticking those posters of blues royalty up on their walls. Give me a break."

Red and white vinyl checkerboard table cloths covered the fifty or so tables in the eating area. A sloped floor—hinting at the building's theatre history—led to the large stage. There were two bars. One was along a wall close to the dining area; another, shorter bar was along the opposite wall, closer to the stage. Joey and Andy headed for the latter, where the vintage vibe ended with the international beers listed behind the barkeep. Andy ordered a dark Bavarian and Joey shook his head and said, "Bud long neck."

Joey placed the leather pouch of his favorite keyed harmonicas on the bar, and Andy knew that this meant trouble.

"Okay, Joey, I have never heard you Gus anyone, ever," said Andy. "Tell me you don't plan on doing it tonight? You despise guys who play along in the audience. Don't know why y'all call 'Gus', but please don't be one tonight, please."

Andy had seen Joey stomp a Gus's harmonica flat when it happened at one of his shows. He silenced another by threatening to shove his microphone stand up his butt. Gussing made Big Joey lose his mellow.

"The difference will be that I can play and a Gus can't," Joey said. "I'm going to give him a good reason to hate us harmonica players."

"That won't matter, it'll still piss him off," Andy said. "They'll toss both of us out. If I had known that you planned to do this crap, I wouldn't have come and if you follow through with it, I'm out of here."

Joey did and Andy left. It was the last time that he saw his friend Big Joey Brooks alive.

Paul found Joey in the alley behind the dumpster, several hours after closing, with a two-by-four nailed to his forehead.

CHAPTER 8

As we watched a group of church kids kick a soccer ball around the spiffy new Discovery Green Park in downtown Houston, I thought that Mayor Bill White must have been a Joni Mitchell fan, because he saw to it that they built paradise after they tore up the parking lots. Plenty of citizen input resulted in the creation of a splendid oasis for the urban dweller's enjoyment, replete with a lake and fancy water fountains for kids to frolic, event centers, and entertainment stages. The planners even had century-old oak trees hauled in to line sidewalks. After all that they still needed parking space, so they constructed parking garages underground.

"The Wizard always claimed that he didn't kill Big Joey Brooks," Pete said.

"Well, a jury of his peers sure the hell didn't believe him," I said. "They had pretty overwhelming evidence. *The Gazette* covered the trial. It wasn't my assignment because I always hated sitting in a courtroom, listening to lawyers.

"I still can't believe that I didn't recognize him at the funeral. I met him at his sister's house a few years before he went to jail. He wrote me a letter thanking me for promoting his sister's talent in *The Gazette* and said that any friend of hers was a friend of his.

"The transcripts said he and Joey had been seen yelling at each other as they stepped out the back door of the Piñata Theatre and only The Wizard returned. Then they found Joey, nailed with a two by four. It had The Wizard's prints all over it. He disappeared after that night and claimed he had no idea Big Joey had been murdered or that he was wanted for questioning. He claimed he returned home and isolated himself from the rest of the world by watching no news, answering no phones, and working on no computers, except to work on his music. That, he had said, was his normal routine between gigs. They grabbed him on his way to buy groceries."

I thought at the time that The Wizard was lucky that he wasn't assigned a due date for lethal injection. His lawyer had a heck of a time getting him to plea to manslaughter, when Michael kept insisting his complete innocence. Given the evidence, the lawyer finally convinced him to accept a seven- to twenty-five-year sentence. Too many people in the club had witnessed the verbal assaults slung back and forth and watched the two leave together, screaming threats at each other.

"Okay, so what *was* he doing at Bobby T's funeral if he hates harp players so much?" I said.

"You know, there are rumors that The Wizard was seen at Big Joey's funeral, but in disguise, so nobody was sure," said Pete, peering at me over the top of his gold-rimmed glasses. I still wasn't accustomed to seeing him in glasses. They gave him a wise, maybe professorial appearance. "Others said that they doubted that he was there because he would have used it in his defense if he had been mourning Big Joey. Then again you hear about murderers doing weird stuff all the time. Maybe he knows something that we don't about Bobby T's death."

"Maybe. I do know that he couldn't have held Bobby T down and shot him full of heroin. Bobby T could twist The Wizard into a pretzel," I said.

"No, but maybe he talked him into a getting little high and it was more than he could handle. I'm telling you, Mitty, this is experience talking. You'd be surprised at the faces that turn up in the old neighborhood, looking for a taste."

"Bobby T did not shoot heroin, period!" I flushed with anger, stood up and walked around in a circle, glaring down at Pete. "Why do you keep bringing that back up?"

"Okay, okay. Relax, don't have a stroke," Pete said, flinching. "I'm just saying that maybe Michael Ray knows something that we don't about Bobby T and maybe he would be a good starting point for your—our—investigation."

"You may be onto something as far as The Wizard goes," I said. "I'm not going to accept any of your theories about Bobby T and dope, and never will."

"All I'm saying," Pete said, "is that Bobby T is dead of an overdose and we have no idea how it happened. I hope that I am way off base."

"You are, but I do think I need to find out just how often Bobby T and Michael Ray Melton's paths crossed and how recently," I said.

I pulled into an internet café in Jersey Village on the way to my country kingdom. I worked my Silverado pickup around the tiny parking lot and squeezed into a spot that absolutely was not designed for my vehicle. That sure seemed to be the trend. Tiny parking spaces, even though a couple of million Houstonians drove pickups or large SUVs.

A few college age students occupied tables at The Javanet. The place felt home-like with large, overstuffed chairs that enticed a nap more than a session on the computer. They provided cooler trays that perfectly poised a laptop at the right angle. And a cup of good coffee cost just seventy-five cents.

My laptop showed me that Bobby T still had a website up and running. His webmaster, or webmistress, was his longtime drummer, Jake Peters' wife, Karen. She had already put up a memorial page which allowed fans to post comments, and there were a bunch of those. I clicked on the gig button and discovered that the page listed just one date and mentioned that he was now swapping licks with Gabriel. The only contact information was an e-mail address.

I needed phone numbers and it dawned on me that I didn't have Jean Tarleton's number and I knew that Bobby T kept his home phone unlisted. I ran through the contact list in my cell phone and found an old one of Bobby T's and decided to try it, hoping that Jean had his phone. I hadn't called him in a long time, but I knew that he was adverse to change and probably kept the same number all these years.

My body tingled when Bobby T's blues harp notes greeted me and then Bobby T's voice mail said, "Hey, podner, you are my most favorite fan, leave me a message and I'll be back at you, directly, for sure." An overwhelming sense of sadness washed through me. My thoughts unfocused for a few moments after hearing the voice of my old friend. I don't know how long I sat there, staring at my cell phone as if it were alive, but a waitress, asking if I wanted a coffee refill, snapped me out of it.

"Jeesh," I said out loud to myself and remembered that I had Tammy's cell number. We had stayed in touch after she began her professional journalism career. She was always calling for advice and I would tell her, "Hell, don't even think about doing anything close to the way I've done it. It might just get you fired."

"Hey, Uncle Mitty," she said, before I had a chance to say anything. I never did like that caller-ID phone feature. "What's up?"

I never kept anything from Tammy and told her about my conversations with Pete and what my next move was, but that I needed her mom's phone number to see if she knew what her father's final itinerary might have been.

"I know a club up in Kansas City was the last venue he played, but I don't know which club," I said.

"You know Mom knew where Dad was at every minute of every hour of every day when he was on the road," Tammy said. "He would call her to make darned sure that she knew exactly where he was laying his head for the night.

Good thing that Mom searched out the best phone plan for them or they'd have gone broke paying for all those calls."

Tammy thanked me for checking into things, gave me Jean's cell phone number, and began to cry. I apologized for ruining her day and she said, "Nah... it's my weepy hour. If I don't let it out now, I'll just have to cry later.

"Let me know if there is any way I can help," she said. "I'm getting pretty good at rooting out trouble makers here in San Antonio. I can damn sure help you find out what the hell happened with my dad."

I smiled into the phone because I knew she would jump on it like a buzzard on road kill. "Well, whenever I figure out what the hell I need to figure out, then we'll go from there, Tammy. Don't worry; I'll keep you up to snuff. Love ya."

Jean answered the phone and apologized for not giving me her number. She started crying when I began asking questions.. *Second time that I've made someone's day for them* and now I felt like crying myself.

"Mitty, you don't have to do this," she said. "I wasn't in my right mind when I asked and it isn't fair for me to even think of asking."

"Hush, Jean. You know and I know that something ain't right here," I said, thinking about how much time Bobby, Jean and I had spent together over the years. "You also know that I've never shied away from getting to the bottom of something that just ain't right. Now that it involves someone I loved, do you really believe that I'm not going into the deep water with both feet?"

"I know. We both can see how Bobby's death is going to be written off," she said. "I know you well enough to know that you aren't going to let that happen."

Truth is that I just might have needed Jean's phone call more than she thought. I had gotten pretty complacent since my retirement, with no pressing 'must dos'. I was starting to drift along in a self-centered fog: live and let live; leave me alone and I'll leave you alone.

I'd always thought that retired life out in the country would include my wife Suzie, and since that wasn't happening, I was adrift. Hitting a small stage weekly, with a blues harp helped add a little color, but I got jazzed about little else. I would have pursued the truth about my buddy without a push from Jean.

"Okay, here it is. You want to write it down," Jean said, as she began to read off the list of Bobby T's last gigs.

I thanked her and told her we'd swap calls frequently. Just to talk, if nothing else. She thanked me and began crying again. This time huge sobs.

I pulled up the website of the Flim Flam Club in Kansas City and saw Bobby T's name booked for the Friday night of his murder. OK, it *was* murder as far as I was concerned and it was a murder that I was going to investigate.

His band was also booked the following Saturday night. From there it looked like a gig in Salinas, and then a prestigious blues festival in central Kansas. I pulled up both those pages, and something caught my eye on the Flim Flam Club site:

Sunday Brunch:
Jumpin' Joseph and His Flyin' Fingers
Special guests expected

I called the club and got a space cadet on the other end of the line, saying, "Hey, dude, that was like last weekend. You can't see that anymore."

I patiently explained to him that I knew that, but was just curious as to who showed up as the special guest. I knew that Joseph Williams had been the piano player that lured Michael Ray out of Chicago and over to Milwaukee. Space Cadet went away from the phone and then came back and said, "Some guitarist they called The Wizard."

CHAPTER 9

As I cut through the rolling countryside from my house, heading for the Brazos River bottom, I created a fantasy of Michael Ray Melton, a.k.a. "The Wizard," killing another harmonica player. Or maybe Pete was right. Maybe Bobby T had been using heroin

I argued myself out of that ugly thought as James Cotton wailed "One More Mile" from my pickup truck speakers. Bobby T had the strongest will power of anyone I had ever known. I was heading down that dark road by myself to see if The Wizard had some answers to my questions. It was just too strange that he was at the same club during the same weekend that Bobby T blew his final notes.

I was still arguing with myself when I noticed the road sign pointing the way to Navasota. I recalled pleasant memories of the blues festival founded there a decade earlier. The city had a statue commemorating the French explorer LaSalle that sat in the middle of the main street. It took a migrant Yankee blues fan moving to town to point out that Mance Lipscomb deserved a statue more than a Frenchman killed by Indians somewhere in the area 'way back in history. Enough like-minded natives felt the same and the Navasota Blues Festival, honoring the highly talented Lipscomb, took root.

The festival stayed small over the years. The organizers went after area talent, whether they played blues or not. As long as their music was close in spirit and they understood that proceeds went to a high school scholarship fund in Mance's name, then they found a spot on the program. Purists would holler about a country and western band being booked, but Mance wasn't strictly a bluesman. He was a songster and pulled tunes from many genres. His purported 300 plus song repertoire pleased a wide range of audiences.

They always had someone on the bill who could pull in folks from outside the area. Houston blues harp master Sonny Boy Terry had been on board from the beginning and he would bring in legendary talents like Joe "Guitar" Hughes or Ashton Savoy to give the crowd some authentic Gulf Coast blues. I'd covered the festival for *The Gazette*, become fast friends with Sonny Boy and got to know some of the Houston cats a lot better.

As the festival grew, blues talent from around Texas, Louisiana, and even California found their way to the stage. They always booked someone on the bill that had played with Mance personally or had recorded his songs, and who could replicate his music note for note. It was always a treat to interview them and hear their Mance tales.

Michael Ray Melton could pick up an acoustic guitar and play Mance as good as Mance. He would have been one of the biggest supporters of the festival and a bill with his name could have gotten the festival off to a roaring start. Except that when the festival was getting its start, Michael was already in prison. The Wizard's sister, Sallie Ray Robertson, could also have been their star. She had become a blues diva by the time the festival began. I always told her that if it hadn't been for me that she would still be playing coffee shops in Bryan, Texas and she would agree with me. That was far, far from the truth.

I did interview her and got the story published in a national blues magazine after listening to her, in one of those Bryan coffee houses. She took the licks that her brother had taught her and sang out the blues in a three octave voice that needed no microphone.

Sallie Ray became a real student in all styles of country blues. She stomped out a set, the night I saw her, covering the sweet melodies of Mississippi John Hurt, the Delta intensity of Son House and Charley Patton, and the exquisite Piedmont picking of Blind Blake and Willie McTell on quite an expensive Martin acoustic.

"Michael gave me this guitar," she had told me. "I refused to take it from him, telling him that my string banging didn't deserve the torture that my fingers would inflict on its fret board. He didn't take 'no' for an answer. Had to improve my playing just to justify picking it up. Oh, it does sound sweet, don't it?"

Her vocals really set her apart from anyone on the local scene. She'd growl out a Charley Patton song and then take it uptown with some Etta James. I really couldn't think of one female blues singer any better at belting out the deep stuff than Sallie Ray. She was going to be a star regardless of what I wrote.

Sallie Ray also had the looks to make her a star. She was long and lean, like her brother, but had shapely athletic curves, high cheekbones, and elegance reserved for models.

We talked a long time after her last set that night, about our music, her dreams, and her brother and created as tight a bond as one could in an evening's time. It didn't surprise her that a white boy knew as much about the music she played as she did.

"I've never had a black audience listening to my stuff," she had said. "Hell they had no clue who Son House or Robert Johnson was and didn't care for that 'plantation music'. Mance Lipscomb farmed with 'em and played fish fries, so they knew him. Even when I was learning to pick down on the farm, kids my age were listening to what was on the radio. Joe Tex was from Navasota, so he was the 'King' down in the bottom with his soul jive music. Wilson Pickett, Sam and Dave, Marvin Gaye and all that Motown sound is what grabbed them. You white folks dug up the past."

She would call me whenever she wrangled a more lucrative gig in Houston and I would always make sure that *The Gazette* ran a nice blurb touting the venue. She always expressed her appreciation for the little things that I did to help her professionally.

Actually, by the time my national article found its way into print, Sallie Ray had moved to Austin and quickly became the darling of the Antone's set. Everybody wanted to work with her, and she had no problem getting a full-blown blues band cranking. She did claim that my article boosted the band's ability to book gigs out of the area, which led to a recording contract, which led to a national tour. I told her that I refused to take any of that credit, but that I would accept her willingness to be my friend.

Sallie Ray moved out to the West Coast as the Austin blues scene began to wane and about the time that the Navasota festival took flight. Stevie Ray was gone, Clifford Antone was in prison and his club was booking bands that could turn a dollar, whether they could play a blues note or not. It fact the entire genre was suffering a slump, but West Coast retro blues was still popular and Sallie Ray found a fresh audience in California. The new scene offered her new recording opportunities and even a few small acting parts. Slowly, she moved away from the hard blues and drifted off into the more radio friendly R&B pop, dominated by songstresses like Whitney Houston, Mariah Carey, and Beyoncé. I had heard that she was peeved when Beyoncé played Etta James in *Cadillac Records*. Even though Beyoncé was the executive producer for the movie, Sallie Ray thought that other singer/actresses should have had a shot at least auditioning for the part.

We had lost touch with each other, so as I turned off the highway and headed out across the flat bottom lands of the Brazos River, I was hoping that she would return the voicemail message I'd left. I wanted to feel her out a bit about her brother, find out where his place was in the river bottom, and see if she knew what he was about since his release from prison. I needed a little insight as to what to expect when I tracked him down for a little "chit-chat".

"Boom, boom, boom, boom..." John Lee Hooker was singing as my cell rang and I had to turn him down to hear, "Well I'll be damned! James Philip Andersen called me on my phone," Sallie Ray said in her snappy way. "To what do I owe this rare pleasure? Did you forget that I existed, or what?"

"I rang you up last year," I said in defense, "and besides, that cuts both ways, you know? My phone accepts calls from celebrities too busy to stay in touch with old friends."

"Okay, Mitty, you've got me there," she said. "That call was two years ago, though. It's a shame when we do that to those that we care about. I think about you a lot, though. That's the truth."

"With all the modern gizmos I have for keeping in contact with people, it seems I do it less than ever. No excuses here, though." I replied.

"Last time we talked, you had gotten fired," she said. "Who are you working for now?"

"What...."

"I know, you *said* you quit," she said lightly and I knew that she was teasing me. "I know your temper though, remember? I figured that you got pissed off and then pissed someone off and got yourself fired."

"No, what I said was that we came to a mutual understanding that I would never walk through their doors again. There's big difference between that and getting fired." I said. "You could say that I fired myself and I'm still unemployed, basically doing what I damn well please and a lot of that has to do with the blues."

"Damn, you ain't had a job in two years?"

"Starting on three," I told her.

"Well, just what the hell do you do all day?" she asked.

I gave her my pat response, "I don't know, but it takes all day and I still don't finish. The pretty part is that there's always tomorrow."

She laughed at that.

"Let me ask you what you do all day," I said.

"To begin with, I don't put up with all that California crap any longer," she said. "They pissed me off for the last time. Kinda sounds like you, huh, Mitty? Too many people wanting to run Sallie Ray Robertson and you know me, hon, ain't nobody doing that but me. So I bailed out of there and hit the highway home. They can come to me now."

"You're back in Navasota?"

"No, lord, no. Navasota was never really home, we were river bottom folks, and I've been a city girl for too long now. I'm back in Austin. I've only been here a month. You have no excuse to not look me up and offer a visit."

"That a for-sure deal," I said.

"I can run my career from here as well as anywhere and at least they'll have to travel to Texas to lie to me in my face. There are just too many hucksters in this business, Mitty, and don't even get me started talking about those movie types. Lordy."

"They're in every business, Sallie," I said. "Anywhere there's a profit to be made, someone has their hand out."

"Now... did guilt prompt this call or do you have something on your always inquisitive mind?"

I cut to the chase and said, "I need to talk to your brother. I know he bought some property back down in the bottom, but I'm not sure where his place is located. I just turned off on Monnigan Road and figured that if I didn't hear back from you, that I would stop by Snowball's Place and Mary or Bo could give me directions."

I could almost see Sallie Ray's glare through the phone. "You mean to tell me that after not hearing from you for over two years, that you want to talk about my brother. Well, that's a fine howdy do!" she said irritably.

I knew Sallie Ray well enough to know that she wouldn't take any bullshitting right now. I came out straight shooting, but I just didn't have enough finesse.

"I apologize, Sallie Ray," I said, "but I wasn't going to pretend that I was calling you for old time's sake. Eventually, I was going to have to get to the point, so it was 'piss you off now, or wait until later'."

"Okay, well, I'm pissed off now and probably will still be later," she said. "You could have at least asked a little bit more about me and how I'm getting along and how much you liked my last record before you jumped in about Michael."

"You're right and your last record was really good, but it needed a little more nasty ol' blues..."

She cut me off with, "Alright. That's enough. I don't want to hear you spouting your blues propaganda at me. You know the blues is my only love. When I catch these new fans and reel them in, they won't know what hit 'em when I put out a pure blues album. Those record people are going to scream and pitch a fit, but I'm going to do it."

"Wow, that'll be great, Sallie Ray," I said consolingly.

"Shut up! It's too late to suck up! I'll tell you this. Bitter can't even come close to describing my brother since he's been on the outside. Now, just what do you want with Michael Ray?"

It's a good thing that she gave me directions to Michael's house before she demanded to know why I was looking for him. Her temper blew through the phone and I had to pull it from my ear to keep my hearing.

"So, you think that my brother had something to do with Bobby Tarleton's death? How dare you even think such a thing? He just got out of a hellhole of a prison for a murder that he did not commit and he ain't ever getting over that shit! He won't ever be the same. Now you want to pin another one on him. What the hell kind of friend are you?" she hollered.

"No, no, that's not what I'm saying at all, Sallie," I said.

"Well it damned well sounds like it to me," she said.

I was in the middle of trying to tell her that since he was at the same club on the same weekend, that he just might know something that could help find out what went down the night that Bobby T died, but I lost my cell signal.

"Damn! No bars at all," I said to myself and thought, *this river valley must be a hellhole for Ma Bell.*

I really didn't want to leave it there with Sallie Ray. I'd try to call her back and convince her that I truly didn't think of her brother as a killer and I was hoping that I could make it come true. The Wizard held the key and that was a for-sure deal.

CHAPTER 10

The fields of cotton made it look like it'd sprinkled snow on the flat bottom lands in the middle of summer. Fields of soy beans alternated with the cotton, the one-time king of cash crops. For years farmers simply plowed the soybeans back under as a "green" fertilizer, but once they found that folks in Asia ate soybeans for their chief source of protein, a new cash crop was born. Then someone convinced us just how healthy the soybean could be for the body, and soy burgers, soy cakes, soy milk, soy ice cream, and any other soy products anyone could think up increased the demand.

I occupied myself with some ecological thinking as I drove down into the river valley. The Brazos flooded frequently and left ample fertile silt behind, but the flooding also destroyed crops, and rivers had to be tamed with dams. The dams created a supply of reservoir water for irrigation during a drought, and a drought is what we had been in the middle of since May. Less fertile soil meant applying more commercial fertilizer which had a tendency to wash away into the river, developing pollution problems. I'd been an ecology freak in my college days, but I hadn't thought about such things until now, as I looked across the fields to the tree line that marked the edge of the Brazos.

I had traveled this route a few times over the years. I always made sure that I had some country blues playing and at the moment it was Charley Patton belting out "Boll Weevil Blues," which I was thinking was real appropriate. These were old plantation lands. These were the same kind of farms that Mance Lipscomb wrote about in "Tom Moore's Farm," a song he would never sing around his hometown. He drove a tractor for a living and wasn't about to bite the hand that fed him. Lightnin' Hopkins had no trouble with it and made its message a hit record, singing about a farm boss with a streak so mean that he wouldn't even allow the narrator time off to attend a wife's funeral. These were corporate lands now, owned by huge conglomerates and the shacks that dotted the landscape were inhabited by migrants from Mexico. Some were legal citizens, some not so much.

The flat fields gave way to wooded terrain of post oak trees and the two-lane blacktop began to wind into snaky curves away from the flat stretch of the previous fifteen miles. I flew right past Snowball's Place engrossed in listening to Blind Lemon Jefferson singing "Matchbox Blues". I slowed and made a U-turn. Sallie Ray had said that Michael's turn was five miles past the club, but I certainly needed to drop in on old friends first. Plus, they might just be able to provide me with a little more insight as to what The Wizard had been up to since gaining his freedom.

Snowball's Place might have been miles from nowhere, but it served as a community center for the small collection of families who had once share-cropped the land. It was just an old fashioned juke joint and where Michael Ray Melton first played his guitar in front of people and got paid for it.

Jim "Snowball" Washington's premature crop of white hair earned him his nickname. Snowball hosted weekend fish fries at his house. His large front room served as his dance floor and a front porch that wrapped around one side allowed folks to spill outside and into his yard. Several musicians from the area, including Snowball himself, kept the customers well entertained. Traveling blues minstrels made an occasional appearance. Snowball claimed that Blind Lemon Jefferson came through more than once in the '20s. He eventually remodeled his old barn, constructing a large stage and a planked oak dance floor. In the '50s, he bartered for an attic fan, which he sat up at the barn's front door to suck the Texas heat out of the building. Snowball's became the Brazos River bottom's entertainment enclave and began attracting customers from the surrounding cities.

Back in the '70s and early '80s, word had it that the likes of Johnny Clyde Copeland or Little Milton would drop by Snowball's and play.

I had heard that Copeland had relatives in the area and he would stop off on his way to lucrative gigs in Austin, Dallas or Houston.

"I never saw him at Snowball's," Sallie Ray had told me. "Word was that he'd show up out of nowhere, rock the joint and disappear. Nobody could belt the blues like Johnny Clyde Copeland. He should have been as big as James Brown."

Even after he lit out for New York City to advance his career as a premier blues singer and guitarist, he never seemed to forget his roots. I hoped his daughter felt the same. Since his death, Shamekia had successfully picked up his blues torch and was taking the music to a younger generation, and keeping the tradition alive.

I always wanted to check out Snowball's Place back then, but I didn't know how receptive a white face in a black crowd would be. *Would I be intruding on something sacred?* The same reservations kept me out of Houston's Third Ward during the same era. I learned later that I was being foolish. I missed the opportunity of seeing some great blues played on its own turf, where the artists let it all hang out for the native population—much more so than they would for an Anglo crowd.

Most folks said that it was a good thing that Snowball had passed away before his club caught fire and burned down or it would have killed him.

Mary Johnson, Snowball's great-granddaughter, was running things in the '80s when the place burned and was resigned to the loss. Snowball's Place never carried any insurance and her main source of income was being the postmistress for the community. The federal government had even built her a nice new post office. She got to see most everyone at least once a day, and if they wanted to know who was playing Snowball's Place, she needed no printed advertisement. She just told them when they picked up their mail.

Plenty of theories flew around as to how the fire started, from a pissed off drunk arsonist to a match eating goat. The burning of Snowball's Place actually afforded me a reason to check it out, even though it no longer existed. The Bryan newspaper ran an article about the historical aspect of the club and the suspicious nature of the fire, and *The Gazette* loved to pick up these stories. Of course, it was my idea to send myself, the investigative reporter, who also covered the blues scene, to interview Mary Johnson. Mary and I hit it off pretty quickly, once we started talking blues. Mary's own crop of white hair perched atop her short, squatty body gave her the appearance of being older than forty. Or maybe she was nearer to fifty. She never divulged her age and I knew better than to ask. People said that she was an exact replica of Snowball, but I knew better than to breach that subject, also.

She had said, "Hell, no, there wasn't any funny business about the fire. I could have told them other reporters that, but I didn't like them. They were pretty uppity and acted like it was beneath them to be out here checking out the story. The fire had been out for two weeks before any of them showed up and then only when they thought they had some kind of story. The customers milling around told them more than I would.

"See, I've still got customers sitting out under the shade trees. They bring their own bottles, but they're happy to be drinking at Snowball's Place. There ain't no other place to go."

She told me that a county policeman, who lived in College Station and played pretty good guitar, brought out a fireman friend of his who investigated fires.

"He found the rat's nest of old cloth-style wiring that Granddaddy had strung together," she had said. "He said that everything was outdated and overloaded and that he didn't know why it hadn't caught fire before. Bottom line is that Snowball's Place ceased to exist. I loved the place, but without insurance, I'm not about to spend the money to rebuild it."

Mary had said that The Wizard actually got to ball rolling as far as resurrecting the landmark.

"Don't you worry none, Miss Mary," he had told her. "I ain't about to let ol' Jim's dream die on the vine."

He insisted and Mary said she resisted, until he started passing the hat at his gigs, and even donated entire proceeds from performances, and brought the donations around to Mary. He began throwing impromptu jams together whenever he was home and made sure that the word had gotten out.

"There was no building and no stage, but that mattered to no one," Mary had said. "Everybody kept coming out for the jams. People spilled out of the parking lot and into the pasture across the road. Soon, folks from all over were jumping and jiving on the ashes of Grandpa Jim's place and giving me money."

Back in those days Mary would give me a call to let me know when Michael was headed in her direction and I would see that an ad and an article ran in *The Gazette* promoting the parties. Blues fans from Houston chartered a bus one weekend to be a part of the festivities. By the time I got around to making it over to the jams, Mary's bartender/bouncer/handyman, Bo, had built a sturdy stage with a blue tarp for a roof. The jams began to run whether or not The Wizard was around. I never did see him there, but got to sit in on some kind of great jamming with great musicians.

Snowball's Place soon rose again. The community pitched in for an old-fashioned barn raising and soon a large metallic barn housed the grand reopening, attended not only by blues fans, but also politicians looking for a hand to shake. There were county judges, commissioners, and even an incumbent state representative. He even had a resolution passed in Austin declaring Snowball's Place the Official Juke Joint of Texas. It was quite an event and it put the club on the map. Mary thoroughly enjoyed being the toast of the town. Conspicuously missing, and it dampened Mary's spirit considerably, was an appearance by Michael Ray Melton. He couldn't leave his new home at the Texas Department of Corrections.

She sent him photos of the grand opening and subsequent shows and told him how busloads of tourists came through from as far away as Japan wanting to see a "real" juke joint. "He never answered any of those letters," she told me. "I always got 'em back 'Return to Sender'. It broke my heart, because then I knew that prison was breaking more than Michael Ray's heart."

Mary never knew when a tour bus would stop in for a visit. She had taken to cooking meals for a lunch crowd on the weekends and always had something on the stove or the barbeque pit to feed supper to the regulars. Some called it "Soul Food," but she knew it as just country food that she and everybody she knew ate growing up around there. Smells of collard greens, pinto beans with ham hock, pork chops, sausage, and cornbread permeated the building throughout the day.

Mary lived next door to the club in a double wide mobile home and Bo had moved into a room built for him in back of the building. If the club was closed and a tour buses came through unannounced, Bo would hit one of many buzzers installed around the building, all of which buzzed Mary's house. She would come over and begin meeting and greeting blues fans from Germany, Belgium, Japan, the Netherlands, and all points in between. A great deal of the time, the buses would stop by during a weekday and she would open the large front and back doors and crank up the only thing remaining from her granddad's original club—the huge attic fan.

If it was close to a meal time, Mary would heat up leftovers or offer sandwiches with chips. She said that she was always glad that it wasn't her climbing back on a bus full of people after eating a mess of her collard greens and a bowl of her beans.

She bounced around like a ball of energy and she knew how to put on the dog and offer entertaining information to her visitors. Mary gave them what they wanted: tales about Granddaddy Snowball and his stories about the old time blues legends. The truth being stretched a tad never mattered.

She would have the juke box cranking out the blues and then Bo would bring out his old Sears Silvertone flattop sunburst guitar, put a glass slide on his finger, and sing blues songs well enough to satisfy the tourists. She never let them talk with Bo, claiming that he was just way too shy and if they persisted, she would send him out on an errand. Bo could sing the blues convincingly, but he spoke English very poorly. He was a very dark Mexican, but as long as no one knew enough to ask, Mary wasn't telling. She sure wasn't going to allow Bo to let the cat out of the bag that he wasn't a black bluesman.

But Bo Vega could have been related to the early blues masters. Bo was from a little Mexican Gulf Coast fishing village inhabited by descendants of African slaves who had fled from Caribbean plantations.

He had found his way into the Brazos River Valley with a wave of migrant farmers in the '80s and stayed. He hung around Snowball's Place and soaked in the music that he had grown to love. Farm work and Bo were not a good fit and the longer he hung around, the more chores Mary would find for him to do and soon he helped her run the place. Some people thought that he was Mary's brother. It was a toss-up as to who was physically stockier or squattier.

They never charged a tourist to hang out, unless they were there for a weekend gig. She sat out plenty of tip and donation jars around and they overflowed by the time a bus rolled out. She let Bo keep any tips that his fans threw his way and his wide smile and genial demeanor had him emptying his jar for refills.

They had tacked up posters and flyers advertising past gigs and future gigs onto the oak veneer paneling covering all the walls. She had wished that she still had some of the ones from her great granddaddy's day, but the fire had consumed those too. I had offered to have replicas printed for free, but she declined the offer because she just didn't think that they would look right and she felt that it would be messing with Snowball's spirit.

Little shops sprang up around the community run by people who could care less about Snowball Washington's spirit. They offered replica gig posters promoting more artists than ever really played the place. They also offered all kinds of blues paraphernalia and pieces of boards that they claimed came from Snowball's Place.

Mary contemplated hiring a lawyer to end all that, but often said, "What the heck. Let 'em make a buck. They've got to put up with all this traffic coming through." She refused to compete with any of it and let her neighbors hawk the t-shirts, tank tops, caps, and packaged beans; all claiming to be "Brazos River Bottom Blues Approved".

Each time a bus rolled out and the blues fans were deposited back into their own environment, the reputation of Snowball's Place grew and soon approached legendary status for being an authentic "Real Deal," juke joint. Mary was a purist and didn't want her river bottom to end up being a vanguard of the Second Coming of the Commercialization of Mississippi Delta music. But she knew that it was out of her hands.

I looked forward to seeing Mary and Bo again. The smell of barbecue smoke oozed its way through my air vents and had my mouth watering before I could turn into the parking lot.

CHAPTER 11

P ete Bolden read the story in the paper slowly, shaking his head. He peered at the wall over the top of his gold-rimmed glasses. *First Bobby T and now Damon Stokely. Maybe Mitty was right, there is some sort of evil going around.*

Bluesman Damon Stokely Dead
by Don Deal, exclusive to *The Chronicle*

Talented blues harpist Damon Stokely was found dead in his van outside the Texas Blues club in New Orleans yesterday evening, according to News Orleans Police.

Stokely, a known drug user, was first thought to have died from an accidental overdose. However, police are treating this as a murder investigation and are exploring several leads, though no person or persons of interest has been identified.

Damon Stokely was the son of acclaimed blues harpist Glenwood Stokely. The elder Stokely disappeared under suspicious circumstances in 1977. Damon claimed that his father had been murdered, but no body was found and the case remains unsolved.

Stokely spent many years touring in Europe and recently returned to the U.S. He played harmonica for the Clarksdale Five, a popular blues band and a feature at Jerral and Gene Deloney's Texas Blues club, one of the few musical venues in New Orleans to survive Hurricane Katrina.

He'd be sure to tell Mitty about it, if he could get him to answer his cell phone.

CHAPTER 12

When Snowball's Place came back into view, good-time memories from the Grand Opening flooded through me. I knew many of the musicians playing that day, and I was invited to sit in numerous times on harmonica. I blasted out all the harp licks that had been caged up inside me with some kind of wonderful musicians.

The Grand Opening of Snowball's Place jammed until the wee hours of the morning. Mary's re-application for a liquor license had not been approved yet, so she didn't have to obey liquor laws and close by 2 a.m. She got around the rules by hosting a "private party" with locals donating the keg beer. Cash donations overflowed their buckets.

Bo had his chair propped back against the front wall of the building when I pulled into the gravel parking lot. A hot, hair-drying breeze took my breath away as I stepped from the cool confines of my Silverado. The large front and back garage type doors of the club stood wide open and the old attic fan pumped hot, humid air out. I could see several customers inside the building enjoying a cool one. Bo's head pointed down and he looked to be working on something.

"Hey, Bo," I said and when he looked up, I could see that he had a harmonica in his hands with the cover plates off.

"Hey, Mitty, it's about time you come back," Bo said, in his best English. He flashed a huge grin that made his eyes smile and revealed a chipped front tooth which he didn't have the last time I saw him. He told me later that he was showing off for tourists by opening a longneck Lone Star beer bottle with his teeth, even though they all twist off now.

"How you fix this?" he said, holding up what looked to be a Hohner Marine Band harmonica.

"I didn't know that you'd taken up the blues harp, Bo," I said. "Let's get out of this sun and I'll take a look at it."

Bo hit the red button right inside the door as we entered and I knew that it would summon Mary over to the club.

Bo started to draw me up a beer and I waved him off as I sat down at the bar with his harmonica. The barbeque pits out back billowed smoke up through the post oak trees. Four men, playing dominoes at one of the tables, never looked up from their game; nor did two younger fellows, with caps turned backwards, at the pool table. Between the big attic fan and ceiling fans, Snowball's felt fairly comfortable. Mary had installed air conditioning, but rarely ran it unless she had a band booked to help pay for running it.

"If you have some of Mary's sweet tea back there somewhere, I'll sure take a jar of it," I said. Mary served all of her liquids, that weren't bottled or canned, in pint sized jelly jars from the days when she preserved most everything that grew in her garden.

I was picking at the reeds of Bo's harmonica with a toothpick when Mary scooted in through the side door, squealing, "Well, Howdy Doody, witty Mitty." She always called me that, even though my wit was far from being one of my strong points. Her long, blousy Mexican peasant dress hid a few pounds. She had taken to wearing them after migrants moved into the river bottom. She had befriended most of the women and sold their tamales for them, so the dresses had been given to her as gifts. Bright yellow flowers covered the red material of the one she wore today. A red and blue bandana tied do-rag style hid most of her white hair.

I handed Bo back his harmonica and told him to try it now as I got up off the bar stool and met Mary with a halfway hug, which she pulled into a tighter one. I never knew how close to hug women because their breasts always got in the way and Mary's were particularly problematic, but we squeezed them tightly between us.

"Where the hell have you been, boy? You forget how to get here? Aren't we your friends anymore? You still playing in a band and writing them stories? They still send me that paper of yours and I haven't seen your name in it in awhile. Nobody's shot you yet? What brings you out in my neck of the woods?" she rapid-fired at me.

"Whoa, whoa, wow," I said. "Let me think about where I need to begin answering. You know Mary, you haven't changed a bit. I always told you that you would make a much better reporter than me."

Bo turned my head with a few nicely played blues harp notes and I said, "Nice, Bo. Are you adding harmonica to your tourist repertoire?"

"Hey, Mitty boy, I'm not through talking here," Mary said impatiently. "Naw, Bo's just doing it all for fun. He's gotten to be a pretty decent musician, but the tourist buses just aren't coming through the way they used to do. Maybe once or twice a month during the summer and a couple of times during the fall or spring. You know how blues music goes, up and down. It never stays down long, though."

"So, are you making it okay, Mary?"

"Wait a minute," she said, "I thought that I was asking the questions here. We're okay. I still have my post office job and we've become a pretty popular place to eat and we still have live music on the weekends and get pretty good crowds and the Thursday night jams are really good. The rest of the week, we run the juke box and sell beer and food. Now, back at you."

"I quit the paper because I didn't like the new people who ran it. I have a weekend warrior band and I'm allowed to run a jam or two and hold down a week night slot and open up occasionally for some star attraction," I said.

"Can't be much money in that honey," Mary said. "So, are you making it okay?"

"Oh, yeah, I spin out a few freelance articles when I feel like it and dumb investments from quite a few years back have turned out to be smart investments. What I really need to do is write the story of Mary Johnson and her faithful sidekick, Bo. Now, that could make me a rich man," I said.

"You've always been full of it, Mitty. Right. Me and Bo would make about a one page story. You know I would book you and your guys to play Snowball's," she said, "but, no, no one's called *me*."

I smiled as Bo hit the opening harp lick to "I'm A Hoochie Coochie Man" and said, "Well, my band is actually not my band. I've kind of got a rotating cast of characters that I call a band and I call it mine, but not one that would follow me out on the road to anywhere."

"Well, that still doesn't excuse your absence from Snowball's over the last few years," she said.

"No excuse," I said. "Sometimes I just need a swift kick in the pants to get me jump started in the right direction, especially when it comes to staying in touch with old friends."

"So, who supplied the swift kick to get you over to my place today?" she said.

I decided it best to get to the point and said, "Michael Ray Melton. I need to sit down with him for a chat about some matters. I figured that since he was a free man, that Snowball's would be his second home."

I wasn't about to bring up Bobby T, unless she asked. I had already learned better with my phone call to Sallie Ray.

"Oh, I see," she said. "This wasn't about dropping by to see us old friends. This was all about The Wizard."

Here we go again, I thought, and opened my mouth to explain my way out of the hot water that I had just stepped off into, but Mary just told me to hush my mouth.

"I'll tell you about The Wizard. He is just not the same Michael Ray since he's been out of prison. It changed him bad, Mitty. He used to be outgoing and gregarious and he never met a stranger he didn't like, and now, you can barely get a look or a word from him.

"He dropped by a couple of times on Tuesday nights, when we cooked up pork chops and collards. I quit trying to get him to talk and he would sit off by himself and eat and have a couple of beers and leave. When he did have something to say, it was always about how he was innocent and not a murderer and such. I know a few of his old friends from around here tried to go by his place to cheer him up and he ran them off with a shotgun. He just isn't right in the head, Mitty."

As she poured me another glass of her sweet tea, I said, "Prison does awful things to people. I think they come out like someone returning from combat. Some handle it and others get shell-shocked, PTSD. Maybe he'll talk to me."

"I really hope he does, and doesn't pull a gun out on you," Mary said. "I love Michael Ray. The marvelous things that he always did for me means that he has the right kind of heart and he can't keep that hidden by the darkness that is bothering him. Now, how about a plate of beans and brisket?"

I couldn't resist that invitation and Mary heaped up a plate with sliced barbeque beef brisket slobbered in homemade sauce, and filled a bowl with her famous pinto beans and ham hocks. It made for a five napkin meal.

After I had stuffed myself, I thanked Mary and shook hands with Bo. Mary said, "You tell Michael Ray that we love him."

"You know I will," I said.

"If he doesn't shoot me first," I thought as I headed out the front door of Snowball's Place, listening to Bo's harp licks accompanying the jukebox blues.

CHAPTER 13

T he road to Michael's place cut off to the left from the main two lane blacktop, some seven miles past Snowball's. I had to look hard to find the gravel road without passing by. I missed it, but not by much and I backed up and swung onto it. It was a well-kept road maintained by the county and wide enough for two automobiles. I was to look for a narrower private gravel road off to the left after four more miles. That road would lead to Michael's and eventually would wind down to the Brazos River.

Potholes dotted the road as it twisted and turned through the dense post oak woodlands, and they made travel a slow go. The heavy oak limbs, hanging over the road in some places, gave the road the appearance of a magical, darkened tunnel. I expected that elves or some other fairy tale creature would appear at any minute.

The thick yaupon undergrowth provided an impenetrable jungle wall on either side. The gravel had worn off the surface in many places, leaving hard-pack sand, which I was sure that a good rain would turn to mud. There were hardened, rutted trails on each side of the road that indicated that negotiating the road in foul weather would be a challenge.

Not a problem today. The hot July sun had been cooking and steaming whatever water vapor existed and provided a natural summer sauna. Daylight was just easing off and the light blocking canopy made it seem later than it was when I rounded a sharp turn in the road and it opened up into a large pecan orchard with the nut trees planted in precise rows diagonally to the road. The orchard looked a bit neglected.

Nestled in the middle of these trees was a large old farm house. Its unpainted clapboard siding had weathered gray and a long porch extended along the front and down the left side of the house. What might have been a later addition jutted out from the back right side. The tin roof looked more modern and it was reflecting the last bit of sun before it disappeared in the forest.

I pulled in next to what I assumed to be Michael's late model 4 x 4 Toyota Tacoma. I imagine he found it valuable getting him home when the road got sloppy. I debated about honking my horn and decided no. I would rather be a little closer to Michael if he did pull a gun and maybe I could reason with him, so I eased up onto his front porch.

Two front doors, equally spaced from the ends of the porch and from each other, stopped me momentarily. Before I could decide on which door to knock, a single, loud, deep bass of a dog bark sounded and around the right side of the house loped a dog the size of a small pony. I grabbed a door handle nearest to me and thanked God that it twisted open. I leapt into Michael's house as the dog skidded by on the porch.

I found myself in a room that belied the shabby outer shell of the house. The walls were decked out in knotty pine paneling with the high gloss sheen of many coats of vanish. Gold Record awards were mounted along one wall with photos of Michael taken with various other blues stars and politicians. This was a studio. Amplifiers of numerous brands and vintages, p.a. equipment, an expensive sound board, and various recording paraphernalia lined one wall. Guitars, electric and acoustic, hung and covered most of the paneling along another wall.

There was a tan couch that appeared to be real leather, a rolltop desk with a chair that didn't match, and what looked like a bar stool with the legs shortened. A Grammy statue resting on the desk caught my eye, and I was moving to get a closer look when...TUNK!

The last time I heard that sound I had stepped in a little too close to the plate from my catcher's position. Then the lights went out. The song remained the same, just with a different verse this time around.

When I was able to focus my eyes, they were looking at Michael Ray Melton's and he stared hard at me. An aluminum bat leaned against his desk chair. I tried to sit up and remembered the problems associated with doing that after a whack on the head. The room spun and I lay back down on the leather sofa, which felt like cement against my swollen skull.

"What the hell are you doing, Mitty?" Michael said, still glaring at me. His frowning, dark, bushy eyebrows gave him a menacing appearance.

"How the hell was I supposed to know that was you standing in my living room, uninvited?" he added, sounding pissed off. "You scared me half to death and I might have killed you. I heard the door slam, grabbed a bat and swung at the first thing I saw and that was your head. What the hell, man?"

Still trying to focus my eyes, I struggled to sit up and I had trouble producing much of anything outside of a croak for a voice.

Michael got up and left the room. He returned, threw me a baggie of ice, and sat back down. He waited as I put the ice on back of my head. I had trouble collecting my thoughts enough to begin a sentence.

"Okay, let's try this again," Michael said. "To what do I owe the pleasure of this visit?"

"That behemoth of an attack dog gave me the choice of being eaten alive or jumping through the nearest door," I said. "I chose the latter and here I sit. Thanks for not shooting me."

"You're welcome and you're lucky that the bat was handier than my gun. People just don't pop in like that, way out here in the country, and Wolf wouldn't bite a hot biscuit. He's just a loveable galloot of a Great Dane and was just looking for a hug," Michael said. "Now, keep talking to me. What brings you way out here in the country? I know that you weren't out for no Sunday drive."

I tried explaining the reason for my trip and worked hard on avoiding making it sound like I had suspicions about him. Seeing those dark brows furrow again assured me that my attempt failed.

"Let me tell you something, Mister," he said fiercely, "if you're insinuating that I had anything to do with Bobby T's death, then I should have hit you harder and then shot you."

Michael stood up and towered over the sofa. I tried to look up, but lost focus and felt dizzy, so I just bowed my head and hoped for the best.

"Bobby was closer to me than any of my kin, other than my sister," he said. "Bet you didn't know that me and Bobby's dad drove tractors together on the Monnigan Brothers' farm before I split for Houston. Bobby hung around me like a little brother or nephew. He always called me Uncle Mikey."

I began to understand why Sallie Ray got so pissed off at me for suggesting that Michael had any involvement in Bobby T dying.

"He'd sit and watch me try to pick out a blues tune every evening and once he got himself a harmonica, he tried his best to make it fit what I was playing. He figured it out on his own and was getting pretty good at it by the time I left the farm. We lost touch for quite some time.

"Bobby's dad moved them to Houston to take a job in one of those chemical plants around Deer Park. I think Bobby was thirteen or fourteen when I found out that he was in the city. I began dropping by to visit his family and pick a few tunes with Bobby. He had his blues harp chops down and could do some kind of wailing."

The ice pack began to numb the knot on my head and I tried easing up into a better sitting position, as Michael continued. At least I had him talking.

"Bobby wanted really bad to come and sit in with my band, but we're talking the late '60s here. Lots of civil rights bullshit and we played mainly in the Third Ward clubs. Lyons Avenue and Dowling Street were no place for a paleface. After I headed up to Chicago, I heard that he began to do that anyway and the old blues cats respected his playing so much that he was accepted as a member of the community and they looked out for him."

"Yeah, it was obvious that he had done some serious woodshedding by the time I met him in college," I said in a weak voice.

"He honed his skills with some of the best bluesmen to ever pick a note and in some of the roughest clubs. He got to know Billy Bizor and Juke Boy Bonner. Those cats could blow a mean harmonica," he said. "They didn't let just anybody share their stage. You had to be a player and not the kind they talk about today."

The Wizard was pacing the room now, as he said, "Once Bobby got things going for himself, I rarely made it back to Houston, but we met up on the road every chance that we got. He lined up a sit-in gig for me in Kansas City. That was the first time we saw each other after I got out and my first gig. He wanted me to play with his band the night before, but I really didn't want to taint his show, so I sat back in the shadows and watched a hell of a bluesman put on one hell of a show. Some of my old fans recognized me during the first set, so I slipped off over to my hotel next door. Bobby even booked me a room next to his. So, hell, yes, I was at his funeral. Now, look at me!"

Michael was glaring down at me as I did my best to look at his piercing eyes.

"I'll tell you one damn thing is for certain. I'm going to find out who killed Bobby and I'm going to make damned sure that they pay for taking him away from here," he said sternly.

I lowered my head to keep vertigo at bay and said, "That means that you don't think that Bobby died from an overdose, either?"

"Hell, no!" he boomed and I thought that he would swing at me again. "I don't know what happened, but I know that Bobby never, ever did any hard stuff, ever! Period!"

"Michael, I promised Jean that I would find out everything I could and you just happened to be first on my list of people to talk to."

"You know, I met Bobby's wife only once and he raved about her," Michael said.

He looked at me for a long time and said, "I know why I was first on your list. Everyone has been saying for years, *The Wizard kills harmonica players*."

I just sat with my mouth open and looked at Michael. My brain had trouble working up any kind of response.

"Do you know what I've been doing since I've been out of the pen? I've been trying to track down who killed Big Joey Brooks. I know that you and the rest of the free world thinks that I killed that boy." Michael was seated at the desk chair again and his face was mellower.

I wanted to say something about the overwhelming evidence against him, but I needed his help. I kept my mouth shut. It hurt to think enough to talk and he still had a bat at his side.

"Let me tell you a story that no one believed, but it's the truth," he said.

He retold the same tale that I had read in his trial transcripts and had been printed in the *Dallas Morning News*. He said that, yes, he was extremely mad at Big Joey for ruining his set and that, yes, that they screamed at each other as he came off the stage and were still yelling when they took it outside.

"Once we got outside, I could see that Big Joey could most likely break me in half, so I calmed down and got him to relax a little, also," Michael said. "I told him that I got why he was mad, but that the magazine article that he was so angry about took my quotes out of context and made it sound as if I hated harmonica players. I explained to him that I my comments were aimed at amateur harmonica players doing what he just did—being a "Gus" by playing from the audience and poorly at that. I even gave him a brief outline of my friendship with Bobby T and he finally got where I was coming from."

Michael said that Big Joey told him that he hated those guys, too and that they gave all harmonica players a bad reputation and that Big Joey apologized for "Gussing" the gig.

"Mitty, we shook hands and I returned to the club," he said. "I had no idea what had happened that night. My prints were on that two by four because it had come loose from the steps and I almost took a tumble while we were loading in our gear. I picked it up and set it back in place and stomped on it a bit to re-set the nails, not knowing that it would be the murder weapon."

The story had always sounded plausible to me, but a jury of Michael's peers thought otherwise. Then again, who would have come along, picked up a board with Michael's prints on it, and have chosen it as a murder weapon?

"Hey, and you know what, the hell with all of them," Michael said with a little fire returning to his face. "I'm going to find out who murdered Big Joey, because they probably murdered Bobby, too. I will hunt them down and they'll have to die."

"Wait a minute," I thought. Michael Ray was tying Big Joey's murder in with Bobby T's death. He just suggested a relationship between two deaths that were something like fifteen years apart from each other. Now, I was doing the hard staring and was way more focused than I had been, because I wanted to make sure that I heard right.

"Come on, Michael," I said. "You're saying that there is a connection to be had here?"

"Exactly," he said. "You hear things when you're locked away with other criminals. Lots of claims of innocence, a few proud claims of guilty, and plenty of nonsense swirl all around the cells. After awhile, though, you begin to realize who just might be worth a listen."

"You're saying that someone in the pen gave you the idea that the same person is responsible for both killings?" My eyes began to focus and I tried to get my mind to do the same.

"Oh, I'm not saying just these two murders. We can go all the way back to Sonny Boy I and keep it up going all the way up through Bobby," he said in a voice that was rising with excitement. "I'm talking about unmitigated, unchained evil at work."

"Wait a minute, Michael," I said. "This sounds like a load of voodoo hoodoo crap that you're trying to lay on me. Come on, Bobby T's killer also killed Sonny Boy Williamson some sixty years ago? One guy? You're talking about a serial killer?"

"I'm talking serial killers killing harmonica players as far back as the 1940s and they are still at it because they got Bobby and I'm going to get them," Michael said all in a rush and with a dead serious glare.

"Man, I heard that prison time really worked on you and that you weren't in your right mind," I said and regretted it as I did. Stupid.

Michael stood up abruptly and he had the bat in his hand again. He slung the door open and it banged against the wall.

"Get your butt out of my house before I hurt you again," he said.

I stood to walk out, my head spun, I fell straight back, and felt the black night again.

CHAPTER 14

As Yogi Berra said, "*This is like déjà vu all over again...*" I opened my eyes to see Michael staring at me again.

"We might have to get you to a hospital, Mitty," he said, and I was happy to hear that he was showing concern for my well-being.

"Oh, I've had a concussion before. I just need to remember to move my head very slowly, stand up carefully and not to smash it anymore," I said as nonchalantly as I could. The story was getting good and I didn't want to go to the emergency room. "How long was I out this time?"

"Listen, Mitty, I know what I said sounds crazy," he said without answering my question, "and believe me, I have had trouble believing it myself. I believe it now, and if you'll listen to what I've got to say, then maybe you'll understand that this evil stuff has been going on for a long, long time."

What I thought was that he was beginning to believe in his "wizard" nickname and had wandered into la-la land. Prison just might have whacked him out like Mary had said. But I needed to know a lot more about Michael Ray Melton and what made him tick, so I apologized and tried to focus on his fairy tale.

"An old black inmate sat down across the meal table from me every day. I always acknowledged him with a 'hello' and he never responded. He would just look at me as if he were sizing me up. I figured that he had gone a little bit daffy from his years in the slammer and just left it there. Then one day, out of nowhere, he spoke to me in a very articulate voice, and in a very serious tone. And from that very day, that I never doubted a word that Silas Guyton said.

"The old man told me, "I know that you are an innocent man and I know who should be serving your time."

Michael said he quit chewing his food so that he could hear the soft-spoken voice better.

"Here was this old man who had never said a word to me for the past month," Michael said, "telling me he knew who set me up for murder. I was more skeptical then than you are now, Mitty, believe me. I had to know more, though, and the more he told his story, the more I believed him."

Michael told me that the old man told him that he had listened to plenty of inmates declaring their innocence and that he knew plenty who had convinced themselves that they were when they weren't. The old man said that they would tell anyone and everyone who would listen that they had been set up, framed, or that the law was just out to get them off the streets.

Silas said to me, "I know that you are innocent, because the same people that killed your boy killed my daddy."

Michael said the man must have been in his sixties and couldn't understand how Big Joey's killer could have possibly been the same as the one who killed the man's father. Michael said he figured that it was something that the elderly inmate had dreamed up in order to have something to talk to him about. Something he knew he would find irresistible. Silas Guyton had him and he let the dreamweaver draw him into the family's tragedy.

He said that Silas told him, "Yeah, I see how you're looking at me as if I'm some old coot without all his senses, but I've been an honest man all my life and I lie to no one. I've got nothing to gain here. Just lend an ear to this crazy old convict is all I'm asking."

"Mitty, once Silas got started, it was like the flood gates opened to his life," Michael said. "Our meals were very short affairs, so he had to pick up where he left off over several days. I could barely wait for meal times to roll around, just to hear the next episode of Silas Guyton's tale."

I was a fairly good blues musicologist and I was trying to recall whether I had ever read or heard about Eddie Guyton. My head was still too foggy to do that and listen to the Silas Guyton story at the same time:

I was raised up in the country outside of Alexandria, Louisiana, which was the same area where Little Walter spent a good part of his youth. Lots of folks don't know that Little Walter came out of there. They think he came from Mississippi like Muddy Waters and all of them. They think that bluesmen had to come out of the Delta, but they didn't. My daddy was one of the best blues harp players around and he told me that he even taught Little Walter a lick or two. You know what? You can hear some of those Eddie Guyton licks on some of Muddy's records via Little Walter. Daddy didn't go about bragging about it to people, though, so nobody knows that, but us family.

Daddy was a tenant farmer, but we owned our own patch of land. He was more interested in making an honest liv-

ing, *being a good father to us kids, and a good husband than running off to be a traveling musician. But I'll tell you what: everybody who was anybody coming through Alexandria playing the blues, wanted Daddy to blow harp with them. They'd try to get him to leave town with them to go over to Baton Rouge or Shreveport and he'd always decline. If he had ever cut a record, he would have made a name for himself.*

That explains why his name didn't ring a bell, I thought. Lots of excellent musicians and local legends never saw a recorder, but influenced those who migrated on to fame and fortune. Many a blues star gave credit to their back home mentors, who often died in obscurity.

Michael was apparently thinking the same thing, and said, "Eddie Guyton must have been the local Jimmy Reed or Slim Harpo."

Daddy sometimes played guitar with his harmonica in a rack and was first call for parties and fish fries. He played in a bunch of different bands and had several of his own through the years. He could play anything on the harmonica. Everyone loved him.

The great piano player Rooster Sylers came into town in the early sixties and asked dad to play a gig at The Big Club off of Broadway Avenue.

"Mitty, that club was still around when I was backing up Big Rocky's band in the early seventies. And it was big and still catering to the black folks who could afford the high class entertainment on the 'Chitlin Circuit'. Silas said that every top name in the blues business always stopped in Alexandria. He said that whenever Little Walter came back into town, that even The Big Club wasn't big enough."

I'd never seen my Daddy so excited. He had played with some pretty heavy hitters, but Rooster Sylers had been recording since way back in the '30s. Daddy said that everybody

had his records and that he expected a huge crowd. He was nervous about it. He laid out several ties to wear with his best pinstripe suit. Daddy always dressed to the nines for a gig. It didn't matter if it was for a fish fry or in a place like The Big Club. He said that you always dress better than your audience. That would have been hard to do at The Big Club, because folks always dressed in their finest. Well, anyway, he ended up driving into town to buy a brand new red tie. But that red tie topped off the gray pinstripe jacket and white shirt perfectly.

Daddy pulled out each of his harmonicas and give them a blow making sure that no reeds were stuck and that none of the notes were flat. When he got up to leave, I jumped up and grabbed his old Gibson amplifier and followed him out to the Oldsmobile. I asked one more time if I could go, but being only sixteen, I knew the answer. "Even if I could get you in, I don't want you around people drinking."

The last time I saw my daddy alive, he was driving off to the best gig of his life.

"I had to wait until breakfast the next morning to hear how Silas lost his dad," Michael said thoughtfully. "Silas' story had to be spilled out during those thirty minute meals—and sometimes both of us forgot to eat."

When I walked into the kitchen early the next morning and saw my mother drinking a cup of coffee with a worried look I knew that something was bad wrong. She didn't like coffee—and then she said, "Your father hasn't come home."

Daddy never, ever laid out all night, even if he played a juke joint, he would be home before sunup. I climbed up on our old Farmall tractor and headed off towards town. We lived way back off of Highway 107 on a packed oyster shell road and were about ten miles from town and I knew that it would take me at least thirty minutes to get there, but I had the tractor wound up as fast as it would go.

I spotted my daddy's Oldsmobile before I got to the highway. It looked as if it had slammed to a stop off in a deep ditch just past the creek bridge. My brain felt like it was swelling or something, because suddenly I couldn't think right and I felt all jangly inside. The driver's side car door stood wide open and I could see that no one was in the front seat. I slowly peered into the back seat and saw that my daddy wasn't in our car.

I didn't know what to think. I was relieved that he wasn't dead in a car accident, but then I began thinking that he might be in a hospital. I thought that they would have called us, everybody knowing my daddy and all, but maybe not. I walked up and down the ditch, just in case the car had thrown him out. I then climbed up on the tractor and slowly crept down the ditch back towards the house. He might be injured and tried to walk home and didn't make it—all kinds of thoughts were racing through my mind. When our house came into view, I turned the tractor around. I wasn't ready to face my mother without having found my dad.

I got back to the car, and decided to walk the ditch back to the creek bed and soon found myself in waist-high weeds. I could see a trail where maybe my dad had walked, and then I found one of his spit shined, wing tipped Florsheim shoes. I thought that he walked off in the direction of home, but got turned around and that he was injured out there somewhere. I followed that trail that led off to the wooded creek bed and my heart stopped when I realized that blood smears were streaking the path.

I found my dad. Someone had stabbed him, hung him from a tree in that creek bed, and set him on fire. They had stuffed that new red tie in his mouth.

Good God, I thought. I forgot about my own aching head for a moment. "KKK?" I asked Michael.

"Nope," he said. "Those people harassed the uppity black folks who didn't 'know their place'. Hell, they would have hung my smart assed, black butt back then, but the Klan usually didn't hassle musicians like Eddie Guyton. Like Silas said, his daddy could play anything, you know, like Mance Lipscomb playing "Shine On Harvest Moon". White folks booked him for parties as many times as our own people did. Of course, he had to know his place and all that."

"I'll assume the authorities investigated," I said, "and that they caught up with the murderers eventually."

"Are you kidding? This was in the early sixties and federal hate crimes laws weren't in effect. The civil rights movement hadn't exploded onto everyone's TV sets yet. A national spotlight certainly wasn't shining down on Alexandria."

"OK, will you let me finish Silas' story?" Michael asked as he handed me a cup of black coffee.

I cut daddy down. The only piece of clothing that had not burned from his body was that new red tie stuffed in his mouth. I had to stop several times carrying the body out of the woods. I found the car keys on the floorboard and drove daddy back home. I parked the car far enough away from the house to keep mom from seeing Daddy and I went back to get the tractor. She heard the tractor coming, saw the car and I had to hold her down to keep her from trying to get a look at daddy's body.

"Silas cried softly over his food tray the day that he told me about finding his father," Michael said. "Lunch time ended and I was glad, because I felt like crying, too. I didn't care a whole lot for my dad, but if I had found him like that, I think I would have been scarred for life. Well, I was anyway, but the damage might have been worse."

"So, you know what the cops told him when they got to his house don't you, Mitty?" Michael asked.

"He shouldn't have touched the body and messed with the crime scene?" I said.

"Yeah, and Silas said he wasn't about to leave his daddy swinging on a tree limb and that he knew who did it anyway and that they should just go arrest them."

"Wait a minute. Silas knew who the killer was?"

"Killers," Michael said. "Silas said he told them that Joe Badou killed his daddy and probably had help, because no one man could have done that to his daddy. But they laughed it off and said, 'Crazy Joe's been claiming that he's been killing harmonica players since his wife ran off with one. He even claimed that he went up to Chicago to kill them. Nobody believes half the crap that Crazy Joe says—and don't you believe those tales either, son'. Silas said he screamed at them to get after his daddy's murderers."

"Now we're getting to the serial killer theory," I said. "It doesn't sound like the cops thought much of that scenario."

Michael gave me a look that told me to shut up and listen to what Silas told him:

Crazy Joe Badou. I told the cops that if they didn't arrest Joe, that I would go after him. They didn't take me seriously and my mama told me to mind my manners and quit talking nonsense. The cops acted all sympathetic and told mama that they would find out who murdered her husband.

I knew that Crazy Joe and most likely his crazy boys killed my daddy. Daddy always believed that Joe was pure evil and told us to keep our distance from his boys. I only really knew the oldest, Leonard. He was several years below me in school, and after some kind of accident that severed his vocal chords he wasn't in school any longer. Joe Junior and Davey were a lot younger and they were always in trouble.

Daddy did have a face-to-face with Crazy Joe one time and me and my brother Patrick were both with him when it happened. It scared the hell out of us.

Daddy ran hounds every weekend when he didn't have a gig. We had eight hounds that could chase a fox or a wolf plum out of the county, so farmers always allowed him to let his hounds loose on their land. He would always take us boys with him, and there'd be a couple of other kids with their dads. We felt like grownups, sitting around a campfire with Daddy's friends.

They would sip on coffee with a little whiskey added. They would try to be sneaky about the liquor, not wanting us to see. We knew, though.

Those hounds would run all night long, and the men could tell whether the dogs had jumped a fox or were just baying at a deer. They could pick their own dogs' barks out. "Now, that's Old Red's bark," one would say and another would add, "Yeah, sounds like he's lost." They'd rib each other and then brag about their own dogs.

When all the hunters decided to call it a night or early morning, each would pull out a special horn made out of a cow's horn and blow their secret signals to their dogs. Most of the time they would all come dragging back in and we would load them all up and head home. If a straggler didn't make it back, we would stop off at farm houses to see if they had tied or penned up the stray. They all had collars with tags, and sometimes a farmer would call us and tell us that they had one of our dogs. But lots of folks didn't have phones back then, so we would make the rounds, and Daddy would blow his cow horn out the car window. That's how we met up with Joe Badou.

We lost a dog over by Hinson Bayou one night, and the next morning we began looking for her. We passed by one house that was set back off the road a ways, and I told Daddy that he missed a house and he said, "That's Crazy Joe's place. If we don't find Sadie, we'll come back. I'd just rather not talk to that evil man."

Nobody had our dog and we were driving slowly, with Daddy sounding out his secret signal. Sadie could have caught up with us easily if she was wandering around and heard us. As we got close to Joe's, Daddy stopped and turned the engine off, saying that he had heard Sadie. He blew his horn and we all heard Sadie's bark and then a yelp. Daddy took a deep breath and turned off onto Crazy Joe's drive, which was littered on each side with tractor pieces, car fenders, tires, and plenty of other junk.

Joe stepped out from around a pile of junk and appeared in the drive with a shotgun pointed at Daddy. As he walked up to Daddy's window, he said "Lookee here, someone done sent me a harmonica player to shoot. What a day this'll turn out to be."

He looked at Patrick and me with bloodshot, yellow eyes, and his crooked smile looked more like a devilish smirk. Both of his top front teeth were jagged—they looked broken in half. He was a light-skinned black man, what we called "redbone."

Daddy told him that he wasn't looking for trouble, just looking for our dog and thought that he recognized her bark. Joe stuck the gun in the window and said, "There ain't no dog of yours around here. I've got dogs you might have heard."

He poked Daddy hard in the cheek with the tip of the barrel and said, "Why don't I just pull the trigger right now, and rid the world of another scumbag harmonica sucker?"

My Daddy didn't break a sweat. He just stared at Crazy Joe, and I thought that he was about to swing the door open at him when Joe said, "Eddie Boy, you're just damned lucky that you've got your boys with you. I ever catch you by yourself, though, you ain't gonna be so lucky. Now, get the hell off my property.'"

"Not until you give me my dog back," my Daddy said.

"Like I said, I got a few dogs of my own," Crazy Joe replied.

Just then Sadie came running down the drive, dragging Davey behind her. Her nose was bloody and she had a rope so tight around her neck that she could hardly breathe. We opened the door and she jumped in. Davey tried to yank her out of the car, but I grabbed the rope and pulled it out of his hands. Her collar was gone, but it was Sadie, all right.

Crazy Joe kicked at his son, who ducked away. "I told you to hang on to her, you idiot!" He leaned back into the car, "I'll get you one of these days, harmonica boy..."

Patrick had been gripping my arm so tightly the whole time that it had gone numb, and his eyes were opened big and I'm sure mine were too. Daddy sat there, glaring at Joe and we were pleading with him to back up and get off this scary man's land.

From that day on, I believed all those tales about Crazy Joe. I knew that he killed my Daddy, and I wasn't going to let him get away with it. I didn't give a damn what the police thought. Mama called up Ray Raton, down at the sheriff's office, to ask about Daddy's case. It had been two weeks and no one had called her.

"No, we have no suspects yet, but, yes, we are following up all leads and maybe there will be a break in the case soon," Ray said.

Blah-blah-blah. That made my mind up for me. I waited until ten o'clock that night and pulled Daddy's single-shot shotgun down from the hall closet.

Patrick woke up while I was searching in my dresser for dark clothing and said, "I'm going with you."

"Absolutely not!" I told him. "And you better keep shut about it!"

He started crying, and I held him for a long time and told him that I had to go. Pushing the big Oldsmobile down the drive exhausted me, but I wanted to get it far enough from the house so Mama wouldn't hear it start. I cut through the countryside towards Hinson Bayou on back roads because I didn't have my license yet and I didn't want to get pulled over.

I parked just past the Hinson Bayou Bridge, right before the Badou place. Since the bayou flowed just behind Crazy Joe's house, my plan was to creep along down inside the banks and keep peeking up until I could see the house. Noise jammed out of Joe's place, so I had no trouble determining where to raise my head above the bank. Someone was wailing slide notes on an electric guitar and making more racket than music.

The house was less than fifty yards from me, and there was Crazy Joe sitting in front of a fire in the back yard on what looked to be an old tractor seat planted in the dirt. Whatever was burning smelled really bad.

My heart pounded. I slipped a couple of times trying to get up the bank of the bayou, but the guitar screams covered the noise. I crept slowly through the dark, getting closer to vengeance. Joe occasionally tilted a liquor bottle up and took long swigs.

Then the music stopped and I froze.

Joe said, "What you looking for, boy?" I didn't think that he could see me in the dark, but I guess he could.

"You looking for your dog? Ain't left much of her in this here fire, but you could sift through the ashes." Then he laughed at me.

Well, now I knew he was crazy because Sadie was safe at home. Then Joe said to me, *"Hey, come a little closer. Are you chickenshit or what?"* When I stepped into the firelight he said, *"Yeah, you're a chickenshit. Just like your old man."*

I pulled the trigger and blew Crazy Joe Badou off his tractor seat. He went all glassy eyed and that evil grin was still on his face. Then I felt something around my neck, choking me and the darkness closed around me.

Leonard Badou looked me straight in the eyes when I came to. I was strapped down to a chair on the back porch. I could still see Joe, through the screened porch walls, on his back, the fire flickering dim, and it looked as if day was about to break. Leonard's wide nostrils flared as he stared, and I could see the thick, rope-like scar across his neck.

A mouth right up next to my ear began whispering, *"Your old man could fight, but it didn't do him no good. It took all of us to drag him out of his car after we ran him off into the ditch. I think our papa just planned to whip up on him a little, but your daddy came out swinging and broke Davey's nose. That was that. We went wild on his ass, and then Davey started stabbing him, and we dragged him, kicking and screaming, to the creek bed. Papa sent me after a rope we brought to hog tie ol' Eddie Guyton. People didn't believe Papa killed harmonica players, but I'll bet your daddy did just about then."*

Joe Junior wouldn't shut up, and just kept talking. *"We thought that your daddy was dead by the time we threw a rope over the limb and pulled him from the ground, but he wiggled around enough so that we knew that HE knew that we were hanging him. Davey shoved dry weeds up his britches legs and set them on fire. He's always been a little firebug."*

Then Joe Junior and Davey dragged my brother Patrick before me, wrapped in rope with a rag in his mouth, and his eyes wide with fright.

"Davey wants to burn your brother in front of you, so you can watch. Papa should have killed your daddy back when y'all was looking for that bitch dog. He didn't want to kill a man in front of his own kids. That makes him a better man than you, Silas Guyton. You little bastard! You killed our daddy in front of us kids. Now, watch the show!"

Davey picked up a can of lighter fluid and began spritzing Patrick all over his clothes. Davey looked at me and I'll always remember those devil eyes—one was brown and the other was blue. They pulled Patrick out the door and into the backyard. I bounced my chair and all four legs were off the floor, and the chair flipped me over on my side, and my head banged the porch, and I looked out the door at Patrick—both of us helpless.

Suddenly, all heads turned to what sounded like hounds howling in the wind. Davey was still trying to light a match, but the wind kept blowing them out. Meanwhile, his brothers bolted towards the bayou when they realized that it wasn't hounds barking—it was sirens!

The police had arrived, and I yelled at Davey, who was in a trance, lighting match after match, "The police are here, you asshole! You'd better run!"

It worked. Davey took off before torching my brother. They caught him before he could make it to the woods and escape with his brothers.

Ray Raton just shook his head as he untied me and Patrick, scolding us like wayward children. "You boys are damned lucky that your mother is a vigilant woman, and that there's a telephone in your house. What the hell happened out here?'"

Two sheriff's deputies pulled Davey back into the house. He was screaming about me shooting his papa dead, and my evil family, and how he hoped that I rotted in hell. I haven't yet, but I sure as hell have been rotting in prison since that happened."

72 — RICKY BUSH

CHAPTER 15

The knot on back of my head began to complain to the rest of my body. "I'm guessing murder charges for Silas," I said.

"Murder in the first degree," Michael told me. "Silas admitted that he had planned to go to Crazy Joe's for one reason; to shoot him for hanging his daddy. That's what they call premeditated, so even though the jury might have been sympathetic, they really had no choice but to send him away. Of course, most of them were probably damn glad someone got rid of Joe Badou. Most likely he got life instead of the electric chair because of that."

"What'd they do to Davey?"

"Davey went to the juvenile reformatory. They never found enough evidence to prove the Badous killed Eddie Guyton, and Leonard and Joe Junior vanished from the area."

Michael got up and brought back a fresh baggie of ice and two Tylenol tablets. He asked me to lean over so he could look at the bat's damage. He said he saw no blood, just a nice goose egg sized lump.

If circumstances had been different, we would be talking music and playing through some of the vintage amplifiers in the room. My eyes fell on a pristine Fender Princeton amplifier, and I knew that blowing my blues harp into it would result in some sweet tones.

Then reality settled back in. There were too many loose threads weaving around in my head.

"Wait a minute, wait a minute. The state of Louisiana convicted Silas of murder, so what was he doing in the same Texas prison as you?"

Michael smiled and said, "Well, I questioned him about that. He escaped, ended up in Texas, and was charged with murdering a harmonica player. That's the short version."

I know the look on my face told Michael that I needed the long version.

"You ever hear about Angola Penitentiary, Mitty?"

"Sure," I told him. "Robert Pete Williams and Leadbelly were both there and wrote prison songs. Story goes that Leadbelly sang his way out of Angola."

I sorted through my aching head for more details. I knew that the prison is surrounded by the Mississippi River on three sides, making escaping a difficult activity.

I recalled my research for an article I had written about bluesmen who had served time in prison and the songs they had written about their experiences. Angola Prison held the largest population of maximum security inmates in the United States and at one time was the most brutal prison farm in history. Ten thousand or more floggings reportedly took place between 1920 and 1940, and inmates sometimes spent as long as thirty years in solitary confinement. In 1952 thirty-one inmates—the "Heel String Gang"—sliced their own Achilles tendons to protest the brutal working conditions.

The 1970s brought lawsuits and prison reform. The current Warden, Burl Cain allowed "Dead Man Walking" and "The Green Mile" to be filmed on prison grounds. I can remember listening to 91.7FM while traveling through Louisiana. The inmates ran the radio station and called it "Incarceration Station" and "The Station That Kicks Behind the Bricks".

I shared what I knew with Michael.

Michael pulled the desk chair closer and leveled his eyes with mine. "Mitty, people squawk and holler now about how suspected terrorists are treated. You ain't telling me nothing that I don't know about that hellhole. They tortured Americans in Angola for decades and nobody cared. Angola was built on an old slave plantation, and they farm it the same way today. The only difference is that the convicts do the slave labor in the fields. I thought the Texas system was bad, but Silas told me that we were in heaven."

Michael told me that Silas had reluctantly taken part in what became an infamous escape attempt from Angola. Twenty-five inmates launched the attempt at freedom, and they killed a guard. News reports stated that the attempt failed, that no one escaped, and that two convicts were held accountable for the murder.

"Silas refused to detail the escape, but said that he and five other inmates got away from the prison. He said that three of them swam the river bordering Mississippi, but that he and the other inmate swam to cross into Louisiana. He told me, 'I guess they caught those guys in Mississippi, but I made it into the countryside of West Feliana Parish. The boy with me got caught up in a whirling river current, and I never saw him again.' He had heard later that no one escaped, and he damned sure didn't want anyone thinking different. He had also heard that they beat the holy hell out of the inmates, whether they were involved in the escape or not. Even as he told me about it, beads of sweat popped up and ran down his face. He wanted no one sending him back to Angola."

"Bottom line," Michael said, "Silas ended up in the Piney Woods of East Texas working in the saw mills and lumber camps and doing a pretty good job of lying low. He said that he kept a keen sense of awareness to everyone around him and stayed nervous, and it helped him steer clear of trouble. Then, he said that trouble found him anyway.

"*I was drinking beer and listening to a duo play and sing the blues at a lumber camp juke joint outside of Woodville. The harmonica player brought tears to my eyes, not because he was much good, but because it made me think of my daddy even though my daddy could have played circles around this guy. I noticed a man standing close by the musicians who looked real familiar, but I couldn't place him. He had a bushy hairdo about the size of a basketball. You couldn't hardly miss him.*

"*It was Leonard Badou.*

"*I watched him walk out the door with the two musicians. One turned to Leonard and asked him a question and he replied in sign language. Then he looked straight at me. I bolted for the door. When I got to the front porch, the guitar player had a cigarette lit and offered me one, and I told him no, just tell me where his buddy went. I knew that Leonard meant him harm.*

"*He told me around the corner to take a piss, and I took off and didn't see him.*

"*I looked around the back of the shack and there he was on his back. I went over to see if he was alive and went to feel a pulse and his throat had been cut. The guitar player rounded the corner and started yelling bloody murder, and I was all bloody and people grabbed me.*"

"Mitty, they hauled Silas off and convicted him of manslaughter, so that's how he ended up at my lunch table in an East Texas prison. It didn't matter that they had no murder weapon. He expected to be hauled off back to Angola any day.

"Mitty, Silas said that Leonard Badou knew that he was sitting in that juke joint. He didn't know how, but he was sure of it and he told me, 'I think Leonard showed up there to take me out, but the harmonica player offered too much temptation, so he got him first and he probably would have gotten me, but then all hell broke loose and I ended up here.' Plenty of prison time thinking about it convinced Silas that the Badou boys are still out there removing blues harp players from the world. He said that the death of every harmonica player since John Lee Williamson's damn well could have been orchestrated by Crazy Joe or his sons."

I focused on the much mellower face of The Wizard. Everything Michael had said seemed plausible up until now. "Let me get this all straight. Silas can pretty much nail down the murders of his dad and the lumber camp murder; but does this really have anything to do with Big Joey or Bobby T? Do we really have a serial killing scenario?"

"Mitty, stop and think about all the harp players that you know about that died way too young. Think about it."

I did. Little Walter, Alan Wilson, Bob Hite, Paul Butterfield, William Clarke, Robert Lucas, Gary Primich, Paul DeLay, Big Joey, and now Bobby T. None of them made it to fifty, some never saw forty, and hell, some were gone before they were thirty.

"Well, hard living claimed some, heart attack and other natural causes took others, but I don't think murder applies except to John Lee Williamson, Henry Strong, or Little Walter. I'm pretty sure that they arrested Strong's wife or girlfriend for accidentally stabbing him.

"Besides, those guys were killed back in the early 1950s, except for Little Walter," I said. "Crazy Joe's wife hadn't left him yet, according to your story.

"All I see is that Crazy Joe murdered Eddie Guyton, and his boy, Leonard, committed the murder that framed Silas," I continued saying. "Silas fed you some kind of wild conspiracy theory. Hell, let's just throw in all the guitar players who died too young and go looking for some shadowy killer."

Michael Ray Melton's eyes narrowed. He was angry again. "Yeah and I killed Joey Brooks and Bobby Tarleton died a junkie. Is that how you want to leave it, Mitty? Maybe he didn't kill those cats back in the fifties and maybe he was crazy before his wife left, but I know of at least three Chicago harp players that were murdered in the sixties, including Little Walter.

"Silas said that Crazy Joe taught his boys the meaning of evil, and they are way smarter than anybody gives them credit for. I don't know who has done what to whom, I just know that when I sat down and listened to Silas Guyton that the old man convinced me that some serious bad is going on out there."

"Alright, he convinced you with a great story. Maybe he can convince me, also. How can I get in for a visit? If nothing else, I want to hear more about Eddie Guyton. He seems like my kind of harmonica player," I said, if for no other reason than to ease Michael out of his fierce laser-beam stare.

"Here's the clincher. It was for me anyway," Michael said in a softer voice. "Silas convinced me that I could track these guys down whenever I got out of the joint. He had a contact inside feeding him information on the Badou boys. They seem to be moving targets, Mitty, and they don't stay put in any one spot for too long. Silas felt sure that he knew where to find them, but he thought the best plan would be to draw them out."

"How so?" I asked when Michael paused, swallowed hard, and seemed to have difficulty continuing.

Michael's eyes appeared to be watering up as he said, "Lunch ended before we discussed details, but basically Silas said if I rounded up a band and booked gigs around their known habitats, that they would show themselves—especially if I had a blues harp player on board. We were going to discuss details at supper and go over his list of just where the Badous might be hanging their hats."

"Oh, I see, bait the hook with some poor schmuck who had no idea that sharks just might eat him," I said, rather intrigued with the idea, actually.

"You damn sure don't know me very well, you jackass," Michael said. "I'd make sure that everyone in the band knew the agenda, agreed to pack a piece, and could watch each other's back. We'd take those bad boys out, without a doubt."

"Okay, sorry, Michael. What details did Silas lay on you at the evening meal?"

"Silas didn't show at the evening meal," Michael said slowly. "He didn't show at breakfast, lunch, or supper the next day. I really thought that maybe they dragged him in and shipped him back to Angola. Two days later, I found out that someone slit his throat in the laundry room where he worked. They buried him in a pile of dirty prison garb, and it took a while to find him."

I looked at Michael without comment. Silas Guyton's murder was pulling heavily at The Wizard's heart. He stood up and walked away through the door leading into his hall. I sat quietly. I had a lot to absorb. His boot steps tapped on hardwood floors as he moved through his house and shut a door. I leaned back on the couch and felt the tender knot at the back of my head. I'd gotten way more answers than I expected. More questions flooded through my mind as my eyes lost focus and exhaustion swept me away.

Freddy King's "San Ho Say" ripped through the air as I opened my eyes to see Michael Ray Melton picking the tune on a Gibson ES355 guitar plugged into a Fender Deluxe amplifier. With eyes shut, he reeled off lick after lick from the vocabulary of one of the best damn blues guitarists to ever bend a string.

"Gotta play this upbeat shit when you're down, Mitty Boy," Michael said smiling large. "Nobody picks me up like Freddy."

My toes began to tap out the beat as Michael's fingers segued into "Hideaway" and then he stopped abruptly and looked my way.

"They got to him in prison, Mitty. I don't know how, but they reached out and grabbed him. That freaked me out, and I knew that maybe they would come after me and kill me next. Murders inside just don't get investigated the same way as on the streets."

Michael said that he slugged a guard hoping to get solitary confinement. He said he had to get away from the general population. His good time earned went out the window, until the warden called him in and questioned him. He spun Silas' tale. The warden found it ridiculous, but agreed to remove him from other inmate contact.

"Silas was the only friend I had the entire time I was doing time and I knew that I couldn't trust anybody after that. I believed every word Silas Guyton told me and solitary confinement gave me a lot of time to reflect. The man knew who set me up and got me sent up," Michael said.

"I keep tryin' to tell Silas' story. No one believes me, and they damn sure don't want to be in a band with a crazy-ass convict."

Michael told me that he never had trouble hiring musicians, but now no one returned the call of an ex-convict, especially one with a crazy story. Michael had been locked up for years. Most people had cell phones now and he didn't have the new phone numbers. He left voice mail messages for those that he did contact and they seldom replied.

When they did call back, they bailed once he spun his plan based on what sounded like a fantasy.

"Hell, some people got offended that I'd asked them to risk their lives," he said. "I'm thinking about saving lives. I'm not even sure that you believe what Silas Guyton told me."

Michael looked at me and before I could answer him he said, "People don't want to be in my band, but, Mitty, you could put one together, then I could join your band. Yeah, that would work."

My mouth had to be wide open, along with my eyes, at Michael's suggestion. "Look Michael, I get a few small time gigs around Houston and very rarely on prime weekend nights. You're talking about booking clubs out on the road and convincing the owners that Mitty's Gritty Blues Band will bring 'em in and pack the place. Pretty much a real long-shot plan."

"You get a band up, I'll get the gigs," Michael fired back. "I've talk with my old booking agent. He's retired, but he still has plenty of contacts that would be willing to take a chance on the comeback of The Wizard. But, if you don't think Silas Guyton's story is for real, then forget it."

"His story sounds absolutely real, Michael," I said as sincerely as I could. "Sure, parts seem to be a bit implausible, but my skills as an investigative reporter involved playing the part of a skeptic until facts can be revealed. We do know that Joe Badou killed Eddie Guyton, and that Leonard probably framed Silas with the lumber camp murder. The old man's story convinces me that he just might have been onto something, plus he turns up dead after telling you his story. But I still don't know how to tie the Badou bunch into Big Joey and Bobby T's murder."

"In the beginning, Silas' story left me doubting the man's sanity," he said. "But he won me over with his kindness, his honesty, and just the fact that maybe he did know Big Joey's killers, who took twelve years of my freedom. He swayed me enough to believe in him.

"Let's go get 'em, Mitty, or get them to come after us."

CHAPTER 16

As Big Walter Horton played his boogie through my truck speakers, I was lost in thought about promises and how they always get me in trouble. Promises to Jean and now promises to Michael Ray Melton. When will I ever learn? How many promises did I make as a reporter? Promises to find answers, to expose corruption, to right some wrong. How many times did I disappoint people by making promises that I couldn't keep?

Damn too many.

I'm trying, Jean, I told myself. *I'm trying to get to the bottom of what happened to Bobby T.*

I didn't exactly promise Michael that I would join in his band of vigilantes. I didn't tell him that I wouldn't either, but wanted to do a little investigative research and then get back with him in a few days.

I'm pretty sure he felt that he had me.

I'm pretty sure that he did, too.

My cell phone had been off since losing signal, and it beeped at me after I pushed the on button. Eight missed calls and three voice messages. I'm a horrible multi-tasker and just can't drive and operate a cell phone simultaneously. The messages could wait until my butt was planted in my easy chair at home, which was just three more hilltops away. Then the phone rang in my hand with Pete's number showing, and I debated answering it, but knew that half those missed calls were probably his. "Hello, you've got Mitty."

"Well it sure the hell is about time you answered this damned thing," Pete said. "What the hell, Mitty?"

"Sorry, Pete," and I offered the dead zone excuse. Which was true.

Pete said, still obviously irritated, "I guess you heard about Damon Stokely."

"No," I answered, but anticipated bad news.

"He died of a heroin overdose in the alley outside of Texas Blues in New Orleans."

After the news sunk in, I said, "Well. He was a junkie."

"Here we go again. Let me tell you something about junkies, Mitty. They don't die of an overdose, unless they want to. A junkie knows how to handle heroin, and I'll bet my bottom dollar that Damon's death was no accident. I think somebody took him out."

"Damn!"

"That's what I say, damn."

"No, damn, I just ran a mile past my place," I explained. "Listen, Pete, can you come over to my house tomorrow? We can discuss all this business then, and you can hear what the Wizard pulled from his sleeve. What is today? Friday?"

Pete said, "It's Saturday, Mitty. What the hell is wrong with your funky butt? Yeah, I'll go to early church service and get out your way soon after."

Damon Stokely, I thought, after wheeling the pickup around and pointing it back towards home. The Clarkesdale Five had just kicked ass last month as the opening act at the Gulf Coast Blues festival. They set the bar high for all that followed them that day, and Damon absolutely smoked the harmonica, and no one came close to matching his singing. Matter of fact, my glowing review of that show should be published in next month's *Blues You Can Use* magazine. *Damon has risen to the top of his game and could certainly challenge the heavy hitters now,* I wrote then. Seems that all ended. Maybe Silas Guyton had it all right.

As I pulled up the long, gravel drive that split my forty acres of beautiful Washington County countryside, and my house came into view, my thoughts turned to Suzie. She insisted that we get the hell out of the city and found the old farmhouse, and then insisted that we could remodel the place and that the commute wouldn't be so bad.

Her insistence paid off.

We did remodel, even though our carpentry skills sucked. With "how to" books in one hand and a hammer in the other, we tackled the job. We added to the front porch and wrapped it around two additional sides to take advantage of the views from our hill and throw a little more shade than our four ancient oak trees provided.

During the spring, a gorgeous blue blanket of Bluebonnet flowers dazzled the eye on about twenty of those hilltop acres. Tour buses stopped on the blacktop so pictures could be snapped. Suzie also always insisted that I not shred the pasture with my old trusty John Deere tractor until all the wildflowers went to seed. The weeds sometimes reached two feet high in order to guarantee a repeat of nature's splendor for the next year. When I tackled that job, it made me wonder why in the hell I thought I needed forty acres, but the fact that I could crank up my biggest harp amp and not have any neighbor complaints helped justify the purchase.

Although most of the old farm sat in Washington County, the house itself split the county line with neighboring Austin County. The original builder either had no idea or a sense of humor and let the tax assessors to figure out what county the house belonged in. We found that the master bedroom determined residency. Wherever you laid your head at night was the deciding factor, so Washington County claimed the house and the taxes. We never admitted to building a new master bedroom in Austin County.

The commute turned out to be a pleasant one. Cutting down back roads to *The Gazette's* northwest Houston location could not have been easier, and Suzie's commute to her job as a school counselor took her even less time.

The things I missed most in life always slapped me whenever I pulled under the old shed where I parked my pickup. Chipper, our faithful Australian Sheppard, should have met me already, barking at the truck coming up the drive, but she had passed on and could never be replaced. YoYo Meow, named for his habit of leaving and returning, had the typical attitude of a farm cat and did as he pleased. He still chased mice, but rarely showed me affection. I missed listening to him purr, burrowed down in Suzie's lap.

Suzie I missed most. As I stood on the porch and looked over the hillside toward Brenham, Suzie's spirit surrounded me. She permeated every inch of the place. As I walked through the door, her essence thickened like the Texas humidity. No way to shake it off, and I had quit trying.

RIIIIBBBBBIIIITTRAAT! said my electronic greeter frog as I entered. The one thing that Suzie had insisted, and I had resisted, was installing an alarm system. I tried to reason with her: way out where we were, an alarm would not scare off a burglar. I gave into the plastic frogs at each entry and they still startled me with their loud croaks. I eventually named the front door frog "Bud" and the back door frog "Wieser". My plans were to ditch them, but like everything else associated with Suzie, I lacked the will to do so.

After Suzie passed on, my stabs at developing any type of romantic relationship failed miserably. I couldn't move from Suzie's house and therefore, I couldn't move on from Suzie. I admired people who could move on, but I couldn't and didn't want to. Getting on with my life had not been a problem. I just had no need to share it with anyone. Maybe someday, but not now.

I walked through our living room overflowing with antique furniture. For years Suzie insisted on hauling back purchases from the Round Top Antique shows. I lacked her enthusiasm for those road trips, but I always kept my eyes peeled for vintage microphones from the Little Walter era that could help me produce a sound close to his. I found a few, too.

In the kitchen, I opened the old pie safe that she loved so much and pulled out a bag of coffee and my favorite mug, and then retired to my music room while the pot brewed. I flipped off the timer to my stereo designed to blast out burglar retardant blues in my absence. I knew such a ploy would never stop a determined thief, but it made Suzie feel better.

Oddly, I lacked the desire to listen to blues and stuck Doug Sahm's first record on the turntable. As I stood from that task, my head spun a bit, and my concussion reminded me that all was not well right now, with me or the world around me. I settled into my chair, placed my feet on the fat ottoman, and drifted away.

CHAPTER 17

I heard the crunch of Pete's tires on the gravel outside while I was on the phone with Tammy. "B-a-d-o-u," I spelled out to her. "See what turns up with this bunch from Alexandria. I've got a feeling that they're the type that no one forgets. Okay, little one, get back with me on this. I love you."

I knew Tammy would bite into the Crazy Joe investigation and rip the facts from the rumors until the bare bones of the story emerged, especially since it might shine a light onto what happened to her father.

At some point during the night I stumbled from my chair and off to the bedroom in Washington County. The essence of Suzie remained way too strong for me to stay put in "our" bedroom. Sometimes I went in there to talk to myself, hoping that she'd be listening.

I had spent the better part of the morning returning calls logged onto my cell phone. The cellular service worked where it wanted: in the middle of the kitchen facing north or alongside the front window of the living room. Tammy, Jean, Mary, and Michael had all left messages, and I called them all back, except Michael.

I filled the others in on some of the details, but left out Michael's scheme. Tammy had begged me to let her help in any way that she could. She had a few press contacts now, and that's why I put her on gathering background on the Badou wild bunch. It wouldn't hurt to verify a few facts and had nothing to do with doubting Silas Guyton.

I waved Pete in when his face appeared in my front door window and watched him jump as my alarm frog croaked at him. He still wore his Sunday go-to-church clothes. "Can't you cut that damn thing off when you're home?" he complained.

"That's the whole point, Pete. It's supposed to alert me to intrusions," I said, grinning at him.

"Don't be smiling at me. I'm still more than a little bit pissed at you. Gone for two days visiting a murder suspect and nary a word. No returned phone calls, and then you want me to drive sixty-five miles to talk to you. What the hell kind of friend is that?"

"Forgive me, Pete. Really, forgive me. Things just got flat weird for me after entering The Wizard's Twilight Zone." Pete's look told me that I'd better get on with the explanations.

A couple of pots of coffee later, Pete surprised me with, "Okay, we can't let these bastards keep getting away with murder. We'll show them that you don't mess with Texas."

"Forget the *we* shit, Pete. I am not getting you involved in this crazy mess. Besides that, Michael's even having second thoughts. He called sometime last night and left a message. Listen to this," I said to Pete as I walked out to the front porch with my cell phone.

"Mitty. I want to apologize for even suggesting that you get involved in my plans. I was ready to give up on the idea myself, then you showed up and the idea sparked in my head again. So, forget about it all."

"Call him back. Tell him that we can do this. And, yeah, I said *we*, Mitty. Tell him that we'll slam them with a band featuring the return of The Wizard and Pete Bolden. How the hell can anyone resist that, and then when we throw two blues harp players into the mix, those badass Badou boys will crawl from beneath their rock and get exactly what they deserve. Boom!"

Never have I ever seen Pete Bolden so animated and excited. Pete's willingness to jump feet first at any adventure and ask questions later just seemed to be his nature.

"Come on, Pete. Just hold your water a minute," I said. "You've got a wife, and if you think for a second that I want her to think that I'm responsible for dragging your ass off into this kind of stuff, then you are wrong. Let's just drop the idea, Pete."

Pete would not let it go. "Then why did you bother to tell me the whole Badou story? I've kept my chops up, Mitty. I can still play circles around your ass. We could be a dynamic duo. There're guys in Houston that I know that could get us booked in every state that we could possibly want to play. Michael had a good idea. These guys need to be stopped."

I told Pete that he would have a giant bull's eye on his chest and that I still didn't think the risks would be worth it. And then he *told* me his tale.

Pete said that back in the day, when he played the part of the harp hero out on the road, that he always loved playing Corpus Christi's Bootlegger's Inn. A blues harp fanatic owned the club, he said, and booked harmonica players at least five nights a week, and the club drew aficionados of the instrument from all over the state.

"Many times they could be a bother, asking about how I hit this note or that, and whether I tongue blocked, u-blocked, or puckered my notes. Heroin had me by the balls pretty good by then, and as long as I fixed before they peppered me with questions I could be fairly tolerable. One eighteen year old kid reminded me so much of me that I always dished out pointers to him, and he attended every one of my gigs and had been sneaking into them since he was fifteen."

I knew the club. Plenty of times in college, especially during Spring Break, we would head to the coast for fun in the sun and catch touring bluesmen at the same time. I knew the type of kid, too. I could be quite the pest in my younger days.

Pete went on to tell me the familiar story of how he'd show him his techniques for getting deeper tones, hitting octaves precisely, and slapping the tongue for percussion. He'd show off his latest harp mic or amp and then dart off for his fix.

"The last time I played the club, I got him up on stage with me, handed him my mic, and told him to 'Get it on'. He did and he lit up that crowd. I started blowing through the vocal mic, and the kid matched me note for note. He had it and played like he knew it.

"At the set break, he came out back looking for me. He found me sitting in my van, nodding out with a needle still stuck in my arm. Even though I could barely focus, I'll never forget the look of horror on his face as he backed away. I just shot his Easter Bunny and Santa Claus with the one syringe.

"I looked around the club as we played the last set and saw him nowhere. My playing sucked during that set and I really didn't care."

Pete said that they returned to the Bootlegger's Inn a couple of months later, and the kid never showed; and after asking around found that he had never been back.

"I felt so ashamed, Mitty. It didn't dawn on me until that last gig there, that I never asked him his name, which was Jimbo. That's all anyone ever called him, and those that knew him said that he just disappeared. They said he always just talked about blues harp and nothing about his personal situation.

"That night laid the lowest of lows on me, and heroin couldn't touch it. I gave it up then and there, spent a couple of months in rehab and realized I had to grab hold of a different lifestyle. I still think about Jimbo. He could have been a contender, Mitty and that ain't just a cliché."

Pete had never told me this story, but I wasn't about to call him out on holding out. "I imagine that old Jimbo is blowing the blues somewhere out there," I said, trying to cheer him up.

"No, Mitty. Jimbo could blow the hell out of the harmonica. He kicked ass that night and if he kept that up, then his star would be shining today. We'd hear about him. Something happened, and I don't know what, but I've always blamed myself for him chucking his talent," he said.

Pete gave me a determined look and added, "You and I both know that it would take a lot more of a disappointment than me to sidetrack a harmonica addict like Jimbo. We both know the type—just like Bobby T. They ate, breathed, and slept harp notes to get to the ultimate level. I've thought long and hard about Bobby T's passing and have come to believe that someone definitely took him out, and I began to think along the same lines as far as Jimbo goes. Throw The Wizard's story into the mix, along with Damon Stokely, and you've clinched the deal for me.

"I'm in. I don't care if it leads to any answers about Jimbo or not or Bobby T or not, we've got to try and come up with something. So, hell yeah, tell Michael that *we* will be his bloodhounds."

I knew Pete well enough to know that once he set his mind that no one could change it. He said bloodhound, but bulldog best describes Pete Bolden's demeanor.

I still couldn't convince myself to drag one of my best friends into such a danger zone, but I told him, "Okay, Pete. Let's get back together in a couple of days. I'll meet you in Houston somewhere."

CHAPTER 18

H ot and humid. I felt the dew from the early morning evaporating and rising around the park bench, where I awaited Pete, in Discovery Green Park. Ninety degrees and it was just now ten o'clock. An earlier meeting might have been cooler, but the ferocious, relentless mosquitoes would have been worse than the humidity.

I gazed at the remarkable skyline, and remembered that not everyone found it remarkable. The old historic neighborhoods that I admired had been razed in the efforts to revitalize Houston's downtown. Minute Maid Park and the Toyota Center had driven real estate prices as high as the skyline. Places like the Third Ward, where Pete grew up and still lived, were on the endangered list. However, Pete liked the park, which he thought was a nice addition to the neighborhood, and suggested meeting there again.

It was darned hot, though.

While I waited I thought about ways to convince him *not* to get involved in any monkeyshines. I should have kept my mouth shut, but I had to clue him into what was what. I hadn't expected him to jump in so darn enthusiastically.

If Michael Ray was right, then there were serial killers targeting harp pros just like Pete. He had turned his life around, had a ministry, a wife, and his home life smacked of tranquility and bliss.

I was different. I had no one at home to guide me away from danger and far-fetched schemes. Suzie might have protested; she had gotten used to my rough-and-ready life as a reporter. I wanted to think that she would have wanted answers to Bobby T's death as badly as I did. I imagined talking things over with Suzie and a sagging, nagging sadness swept down my back.

My cell rang as I watched Pete, dressed in blue plaid shorts, a red t-shirt, and flip flops, stroll across the damp grass towards my bench. Beatrice Bolden's voice met my ear, and I expected to get an earful of expletives accusing me of sucking her husband into bullshit.

Shockingly she said, "You've got to let Pete help you and Michael, Mitty. No one can cover your back like Pete and you can trust him."

After this meeting, I had fully intended to call Beatrice to see if she could talk Pete out of joining me, but no, it seemed that she was going to insist otherwise. I attempted an answer, but was met with, "Shut up, Mitty. Pete's going to do this. He needs to excise a ghost that has been haunting him for too long. He never told you that he almost overdosed the night that young Jimbo caught him shooting up, did he? No, I know he didn't. That was his low point, that's when he decided to walk away from drugs and that life."

I looked at Pete as he got closer to the bench and wondered why my good friend had kept so much from me.

"He was so ashamed, Mitty. And he still is. He always hoped that the young man would turn up again, and never seeing him again made things worse. He needs to know if Jimbo is alive or not. If Jimbo is alive, then Pete wants him to know how he's turned his life around. If he's dead, then Pete wants to know if your bad guys got to him. Pete needs some kind of closure."

"Okay, Beatrice, just let me say this...," I began.

"Shut up Mitty. I've said my piece, and you have my blessing," Beatrice said and hung up.

"Hey, Mitty," Pete said as he sat down on the bench. "Ain't she something?"

"How do you know who I was talking to?" I said.

"Because you were just listening and I know my Beatrice wasn't about to let you get a word in edgewise," he said. "Besides that, I could hear her voice ten feet away."

I told him that she'd volunteered him for hazardous duty and he said, "Does she love me or what? Anyway, I've got us a drummer and he's all in."

"Oh, yeah?" I said.

"Yeah, you remember Buddy Kirkland? He's a bit like you. No wife, no kids, no one at home. I remember something he told me years ago. I called him and asked him to repeat the story."

"Yeah, I know Buddy well," I said. "You're saying that he wants a part of this, and he knows the risks? Okay, what's his story?"

Pete began spinning out Buddy Kirkland's tale and it rang familiar.

"Buddy had an aunt in Slidell, Louisiana that he visited as a young pup back in the late sixties. She always bragged about how Leon Buller always stopped by her place for a visit whenever he passed through. Buddy said that his family doubted his Aunt Tilley knew Leon, since he was the most popular blues harp player in Mississippi back then. Remember him being called "Neon Leon" for his flashy dress?"

I nodded, "Yeah, Leon could put on a show and he did hit it pretty big with some hit records—at least around Texas."

"Buddy said that he believed his Aunt Tilley and listened to her stories when no one else did. She told him that Leon was convinced that the Devil was after him," Pete continued.

"Oh, him and every bluesman since Robert Johnson," I said skeptically, playing the Devil's Advocate.

"Exactly," Pete said, ignoring the sarcasm in my voice. "Buddy said that according to his aunt, Leon figured that everyone would think that he was crazy. You might get away with claiming that hellhounds were trailing you in the thirties, but not the sixties. Remember the story of the bullet that Leon took in the leg back in the mid-seventies?"

"Some jealous husband nailed him is the way I heard it," I said.

"Leon said that a She-Devil tried to kill him. Leon picked her up after a gig at Silvio's in Chicago. He said that she had some kind of bad voodoo stuff in her hotel room and what's more—that *she* was a *he*.

"He bolted for the door after discovering that and he heard 'her' yell to someone in the hallway, then he heard a gunshot and felt the bullet slam the back of his leg. He yelled and screamed as he tumbled down the hallway, went limping down the sidewalk, passed out three blocks away, and awoke in a hospital bed. The police found no one in the hotel room when they went back to investigate."

I believed the story, but kept playing the Devil's Advocate, "He was quite the ladies' man and I'll bet Neon Leon's getting shot surprised no one back then. Heck, I've heard at least four different versions of that story."

Pete said, "I have too. This is the one I believe, though. Neon Leon convinced Buddy's Aunt Tilley that evil spirits meant to do him in.

"Did you hear about the second attack after he fled Chicago and moved back to Mississippi? This time Satan hit him at a crossroads. Literally. Leon said he saw the car headed right for his driver's door, and that he swerved just in time to keep from being t-boned. He got clipped on the back fender and his car spun out of control.

"He was thrown from the car and he crawled to his feet in time to see the attack car speed off with three people inside. Police found the car abandoned outside of town. It had been stolen in Louisiana."

"Hmm, could have been the Badous, huh? Maybe with a cross-dresser in the family. I guess that's one way to lure your victims in," I told Pete.

"That's what I'm thinking, and also what Buddy thought after we swapped tales, but it doesn't end there," Pete said. "Aunt Tilley told him that Leon really wanted to stay in Europe when he traveled over with a group of blues all-stars. He wrote her letters and Buddy's aunt kept those letters as proof that she and Leon were an item. His family accused her of mailing them to herself, even though they had European postmarks."

"Is Buddy's aunt still around? Sounds like someone we need to interview," I said. "Maybe we could stop off in Alexandria on the way to Slidell and poke around a little."

"No one has seen her since she showed off her letters from Leon. Buddy said that she just dropped off the face of the planet in 1977."

I must have looked dubious, because Pete said, "Yeah, I thought the same thing. People don't just disappear. Did your Badou boys do her in? What would they want with an old woman?"

CHAPTER 19

I had called Michael to respond to his voice mail. I left messages for him for six days straight. No response. I called Pete and told him that I was heading back to the Brazos River bottom.

"He called and apologized for getting me involved, but I want to tell him that I want to help," I explained. "I know the cell phone signal is hit or miss at his house, but I've been leaving messages for days. You'd think he would call back."

"Does he have a land line?"

"That's the number I called first, but all I get is the voice mail."

"Did you call Snowball's? Talk to Mary Johnson?"

"Sure did. She said that Michael dropped by a few days ago, happier than she had seen him since he got out of prison. He told her how much I believed in him and gave her an overview of his plans. She says that if I agreed to help him that I've lost my mind. He had told her that he had changed his mind about it all, but was thrilled just to get everything off his mind. She thought that Michael took off to the river for a little fishing, and if so, that I wouldn't be able to reach him on a cell phone. She says he sleeps in his Toyota pickup 'cause it has a camper shell."

Pete said, "Now, that sounds like a nice getaway."

"Yeah, I need to talk to him, though," I said. "He should have called me. I told him that I would think about his plan. Well, I've thought about it and talked to you about it and it's time to act. I'll let you know what's what as soon as I can."

"Right, the last time, I didn't hear from you for two days," Pete said. "Why don't I just tag along?"

I thought about that. It might be nice to have company, but I didn't want Pete to get into anything just yet.

Pete said, "I'll answer my own question. I've got some loose ends to tie up with the ministry before we can set sail as vigilantes. You take care of yourself. You got a piece?"

"I've got a couple of Rugers."

"Better take it along."

⚛

I turned down the volume on Kim Wilson, playing fat toned licks on his blues harp with the Fabulous Thunderbirds.

I wanted to try Michael's cell phone one more time and before the signal became hit or miss.

A tractor, pulling an extremely long disc harrow, took up both lanes and had slowed me to a crawl.

I dialed Michael's number. Nothing. This time I left no message as I turned to head across the flat expanse of the bottom lands.

I debated about stopping in at Snowball's Place, but the sky darkened off to the west enough for me to nix that idea and get to Michael's before the storms rolled into the valley and turned his driveway into mud. The one time I traveled his road clued me into just how bad it could get in nasty weather. It seemed like the Brazos River valley right up to Cleburne was a thunderstorm magnet. Maybe the storms were sucked along the path of the river.

The storm took me—uncharacteristically—by surprise. I've always taken pride in my ability to keep kept abreast of the weather: a habit I developed after taking meteorology in college. I was way out of sync, and I wondered to myself just how long that had been going on. I don't like being knocked off my routine.

The wind rocked the truck around, gently at first, but by the time I turned off the blacktop onto Michael's road through the woods it whipped at me pretty good. Heavy clouds rolled in and huge drops of rain pelted my Silverado. The canopy of tree limbs dipped and flipped up, down, and sideways. Daylight turned greenish-black, forewarning of tornado activity nearby.

I could feel my blood pressure going up.

Pea-size hailstones began falling, and leaves and twigs fell onto my pickup hood and windshield. My windshield wipers were doing a poor job keeping my view clear.

I closed in on Michael's house, as the winds whiplashed the trees and the rain started coming down in sheets.

Michael's front door was swung wide open. Most of his lights were lit and it gave the house an eerie, jack-o-lantern look. I pulled my Ruger Security Six.357 from beneath my seat and set it beside me. I took a couple of deep breaths. My chest vibrated and I thought that maybe this was what a panic attack felt like.

I honked my horn, but could barely hear it myself above the roar of the wind, rain, and booming thunder. I jumped from the truck and dashed and splashed through the rain and leapt onto the front porch. I almost landed on Michael's dog, and the dog didn't move.

He was dead.

My skin prickled. My breathing quickened and my knees wobbled. I thought my legs would collapse as fear raced through me. I called out from the front door as the rain slashed across the length of the porch.

"Michael! It's me, Mitty!" I didn't want another encounter with the baseball bat.

No answer.

I slowly entered the house and closed the front door to keep the driving rain from following me inside.

I heard a voice in Michael's studio and froze, then laughed nervously. It was Bill Wax on the satellite radio, introducing a Magic Sam tune. The guitar and vocals competed with the howl of the wind. I opened the studio door with trembling hands. No Michael. Everything appeared to be intact, which relieved me somewhat. I tried to keep my mind from racing away from me, took some more real deep breaths, and relaxed a little.

I flipped off the stereo and Magic Sam died out, but a clap of thunder rattled the window, shook the house, and re-ignited my adrenaline rush. The wind slammed the front door open and I whirled around.

"Man, I've never been this jumpy," I said out loud to myself.

I closed the door again, engaged the deadbolt, and stepped across the foyer into Michael's bedroom. The bed was made and the room looked neat. A picture of Michael and his sister, Sallie Ray, stared at me from the dresser, and seeing her brought a smile to my face. An open box overflowed with flat picks, finger picks, venue ticket stubs, a wrist watch, coins, and other items normally cleared from pants pockets. A pair of golden, wire rimmed glasses sat in front of a photograph of a woman who I guessed was his mother. No father pictures.

I stepped closer to one of several oil paintings hanging on the walls. They all seemed to depict life on a plantation, except for one that looked like Sallie Ray, and a closer look revealed Michael's signature at the bottom of them. Another louder thunder slap snapped me back to reality.

Fear sucked the air out of my lungs as I made my way to the kitchen. I spotted blood smears before I reached the entry. I stepped through the door, and the remnants of a mighty, violent battle greeted me. My body buzzed as if a Taser had hit me.

The table and chairs had been upended. Pots and pans had been thrown about the room. *Blood. Everything* covered in blood. It pooled in the middle of the room, it was splattered on the walls, counter tops, and on the refrigerator.

I couldn't get my breath, I couldn't think, I felt faint.

I retreated back to Michael's studio, reached for my phone and realized that I had left it in my truck. I sat down and tried to sort things out in my mind. The howling, booming, electrifying storm didn't help.

I sat until some semblance of rational thinking returned, and then I went searching for Michael's land line phone, which was not in the studio. Not in the foyer. Not in the bedroom, and I damn sure did not want to re-enter the kitchen.

I dashed outside and jumped into my pickup and watched a bolt of lightning smack at something close. It deafened me. More deep breaths. My cell phone beeped out the *No Service* signal. Damn. I was hoping that there would be a ray of a signal. One bar, at least.

Michael's house took on a ghastly, ghostly sheen each time lightning lit up the front. Blood pounded through my brain. I felt like a motor was whirring deep within my gut. I tried to relax, but couldn't. I had to leave. I had to flee.

I cranked the engine, put the truck in reverse, and went absolutely nowhere. The tires spun and sunk, and rocking the truck back and forth just buried me deeper. My spirits sank along with my tires.

I cut the engine and sat silently, staring at the house. If I wanted to find a phone I had to go back inside. I made a mad re-dash back to the house. My feet slipped and slid as I jumped back onto the porch, tried not to look at the dead dog, and dove through the front door.

My insides were bubbling as I moved slowly towards the kitchen in hopes of finding a phone. I surveyed the bloody scene a little closer, but still from the doorway. I did not want to step off into...into...into... and I giggled at myself as I thought *"mess hall,"* and then realized that my mind had just about had it. There was no phone on the bloody counter or the red smeared walls.

I noticed the blood trail leading out the back door. Michael had been dragged outside. What to do?

I eased back into the studio and sat down once more. I tried to think. My mind cleared a bit. The whirling, crashing weather seemed to have calmed down.

I walked out on the front porch, stepped into the mud, and headed for the back of the house. Rain had washed away much of the blood trail by the kitchen door. The dark clouds parted slightly and a welcome sliver of sunlight shot through the holes.

As I tried to keep my balance in the sloppy mud, I looked into the orchard and saw Michael Ray Melton's body swinging by a rope from the limb of a pecan tree.

CHAPTER 20

There was no doubt as to what evil had swooped through the trees out there—it had to be the same evil that killed Eddie Guyton.

"No need to go any closer," I told myself stupidly. I pulled out my cell phone. Two bars! I have two bars! If my feet had not been anchored in mud, I would have leapt for joy.

The body in the tree had been stabbed, burned, and hung. I knew it had. No need to examine it more closely. Don't think about it. Don't go out there. My mind raced as my fingers punched in the number at Snowball's Place. Mary answered, I told her to dial 911 and why. Told her that I didn't want to answer the dispatcher's inquisition. I sounded a little deranged, even to me. For once, Mary didn't pepper me with questions. She told me to hang the hell up so she could make the call.

I hung up, walked back to the front of the house and sat down on the front porch, far away from Michael's dead watch dog.

It seemed as if hours had passed before I heard the first squalls of a siren through the dense woods. Two county patrol cars splashed into sight, and I guided them away from my truck's muck.

Two uniformed Billet County Sheriff's Deputies stepped out of one car, and another deputy and a plainclothesman came from the other. The summer sun came out and the steamy air suddenly felt thick and heavy. The plainclothes officer was small and wiry and spoke in a casual manner, in a voice much deeper than I expected. He had the same East Texas twang as my own, "We got call from a Mary Johnson. Our dispatcher says she sounded pretty hysterical. We don't know what the hell she tried to tell us, except to get out here because someone murdered The Wizard."

He extended a surprisingly powerful hand to me and said, "Detective Perry Thompson. Did you call Ms. Johnson and then she called us?" He glanced at my Silverado, "Looks like you might need a tow truck. Hey Jerry, call into dispatch and get the Winch Brothers to send a truck."

"Yes, sir, I did call Mary," I said, perhaps over-politely. I've always believed in addressing officers of the law with respect. I was raised that way and my years working as a reporter stressed the importance of mutual respect. "I'm James Andersen." I thought about telling him to just call me Mitty, but I'd been around enough cops to know that they'd rather keep things formal when conducting the initial investigation. Detective Thompson would call me Mr. Andersen until he didn't want to.

"Mr. Andersen, tell me what's going on here. Just roll me a story, and I'll ask questions as I need answers. Is there a body in the house?"

He took his sunglasses off as I shook my head, and he turned to his officers, who still had their Ray-Bans on their noses and said, "You guys get out of the sun. When Mr. Andersen fills me in with what we should be looking at, then we'll go to work."

The three Billet County deputies—two white, one black—who stepped up on the porch were downright huge. They weren't fat either; just big. Their biceps bulged in the brown short sleeves of their uniforms.

"Someone hung Michael Ray Melton from one of his own pecan trees out back," I said. The black deputy stopped scraping mud off his boots, lifted his sunglasses, and stared at me, hard. "I suspect that he's been stabbed full of holes and set on fire, also."

"Did you examine the body?" asked the detective.

"No, I didn't have the stomach for it."

"So, you really don't know if the body hanging in the tree belongs to Mr. Melton, is that correct?"

"Yes... no... I wanted to remember my friend the way I last left him."

"Alright, guys, let's earn our pay," Detective Thompson barked. "Let's go have a look at the body. You guys meet me out back. Don't touch anything. Okay, Mr. Andersen, let's go inside."

I politely declined the invitation. "Go do what you have to do, but I'm not going back in the house. You might have a look at the mess in the kitchen first."

He nodded and walked into Michael's house. I could see him moving slowly into the studio and after a few minutes across the foyer to the bedroom. He headed toward the kitchen, and I heard him groan as he got close. He didn't enter, but stood in the doorway for quite some time.

The three deputies returned from their gruesome, grisly detail out back, and they were visibly shaken, especially the black deputy. He slipped his shades in his shirt pocket, wiped his brow with a handkerchief, and ran it around his neck. His eyes looked like they had been full of tears, though he had wiped them away with his sweat.

I looked at him, he returned my gaze, and I asked, "Is it Michael out there? I couldn't go closer to look. Did you know The Wizard?"

"It could be Michael. He's burned to the bone in places, but it could be him." The deputy stopped, rubbed at his eyes again. "Why? Who would do such evil to a generous and kind man like Michael?"

I held out my hand. He shook it and said, "Benny Williams, and yeah, I knew The Wizard very well. Everybody around here did. I live over in College Station, but I grew up over close to Snowball's Place." He moved in closer, so only I could hear what he said next. "I'll tell you something else; they railroaded an innocent man and sent him away to prison."

He leaned away from me and kept talking. "I'd finished my shift when the call came in, and had to get out here. I told the deputies that I knew the area real well and could get them here quickly."

Before Benny finished talking, Detective Thompson eased out of the house, and if the scene inside had affected him, it didn't show on his face. The deputies confirmed that yes, a body had been hung and burned in the pecan orchard. He asked a deputy to call into headquarters and report what they had observed.

"Okay, Mr. Andersen," the detective said, "Let's pull up a yard chair under that shade tree and have a little chat."

We sat. He said, "One hell of a struggle took place in that kitchen. If that is Michael Melton hanging out there, he did not go quickly or quietly, and it took more than one person to subdue him."

He paused, and then said slowly, "Lynchings draw serious attention, and the hate crime laws will bring out the wrath of law enforcement agencies everywhere. The Texas Rangers, the state police, the FBI, and who knows who else will come swooping in and will turn this little homestead inside out. They will thoroughly investigate and interrogate each and every person involved, including me. They'll jump my ass for taking a statement from you now, because this case will pass out of my jurisdiction very soon. But I'd really like to know why you were here? You know what I mean?"

We sat under that shade tree for a long time as I told my tale. I went all the way back to Silas Guyton's tale and the Badou boys and forward to my plans with Michael. It was therapeutic to pour my story out. My body relaxed. The sweat dried out of my shirt. The rumbling in my guts eased as I rambled on and on.

A few quizzical, doubtful looks crossed Detective Thompson's face, but he summed up what I had told him.

"A hoodlum family from Louisiana who killed a convict's daddy back in the 1960s is connected to this mess. And this lynching is the latest in their series of murders. Is that about the gist of it?"

He sounded doubtful, but I wasn't fazed, even though my mind felt mushy.

"Yeah, that's about the gist of it." I said. "I struggled to accept Silas Guyton's tale too. But I believe that somebody killed Bobby Tarleton. Somebody besides The Wizard killed Joey Brooks. Somebody has just killed Michael Ray Melton in a way that mirrors how Eddie Guyton died. I really don't know what to believe beyond that."

He looked at me for a few moments and said, "A hell of a lot of conspiracy theories get hatched out behind prison walls. With enough time, the imagination can conjure up plenty of wild scenarios. We've heard our share, believe me."

"I thought the same thing, but Michael made a believer out of me," I said, "and his efforts cost him his life."

"We don't know if the lynched body belongs to Melton. We won't know until we examine dental records or run the DNA samples," the detective said. "Here's another scenario for you. Maybe Mr. Melton recognized his attackers, killed one, hung and burned him, and then hit the road."

"Whoa! That's enough of that. OK, I guess I can imagine Michael killing someone in self-defense, but hanging? Burning? I think some kind of evil visited The Wizard, viciously attacked him, hung him in a tree, and torched him," I told him with plenty of anger in my voice. "I don't care if you believe me or not."

"It really doesn't matter what I believe," he said calmly. "Trust me on that. We'll see what the evidence says. This place will resemble a stirred fire ant mound before sundown. Like I said, a case like this—a modern-day lynching—will have every fact, every thread of evidence, and every motive investigated ten times over. I'll soon be taking orders and not giving them, and they damn sure will not care what I think or believe."

The rumble of a vehicle splashing up the road interrupted us. A large, mud-splattered, white tow truck with "Winch Brothers" stenciled on the side came into view. Two very skinny men jumped from their truck, hooked on to mine, yanked it up onto solid gravel, took my payment, and headed back down the road: all in the space of 20 minutes.

"Unless you'd like to spend the better part of your night re-answering questions, I'd advise you to head on out of here," Detective Thomson said. "I don't know how much of this investigation they'll allow me to retain, but I'll damn sure keep up with what happens. Here's my card. Give me your contact information. I'll tell whoever takes over the case all that you told me, and yeah, they'll get pissed off that I let you leave. You'll hear from them, and then the real interrogation begins."

We shook hands and looked each other in the eye. With mutual trust.

He had one last bit of advice. "Badou boys or not, the killers involved with this murder know their business. Do not even think about going after them, especially with your friend's harebrained vigilante-blues-band plot. You keep that to yourself. Your interrogators can make do without that information. You understand?"

I nodded.

Benny Williams approached me and gripped my hand tightly and said, "Mr. Andersen...."

"Please call me Mitty," I said.

"Okay, Mitty, and you call me Benny," he said. "Can you keep me up to date with anything you know about who did this to Michael? I'd really appreciate that. The man meant a lot to me."

"If it is Michael. Detective Thompson says we'll have to wait for a positive ID." I was hoping against all odds that maybe it wasn't Michael out there.

His eyes began watering as he slid his shades back on his nose. "I don't know about you, but I'm sure it's Michael," he said

I kept a firm grip on his hand and said, "I'll keep in touch, Benny."

Chapter 21

I headed straight to Snowball's Place and was slightly less depressed by the time I arrived. The air conditioned pickup blew maximum cool at my face as I pulled into the parking lot, scattered with a few cars and trucks.

Mary also had the air conditioning pumping. It was four in the afternoon and the heat and humidity were fierce. The cool, dark interior of the club beckoned. The sounds of pool balls knocking around and dominoes slapping down on table tops mixed well with Junior Parker's "Mother-in-Law Blues" cranking from the juke box. The Astros had the Mets down four to one in the fifth on the television above the bar. Ah, yes. It felt like home. I almost felt okay.

But not quite okay. Mary and Bo both looked up from back of the bar, surprised when I ordered a shot and a beer. They knew I usually drank lightly, rarely more than a couple of beers in an entire evening. Bo grinned his big grin at me and asked what brand, but Mary stopped him.

"Hold on a minute, there Witty Mitty," she said. "That ain't your style. You ain't no drinker. What happened out at Michael's?"

"Just set 'em up, Bo. Jack Black and a Bud," I said as blaring sirens, one set after another, screamed down the road. That drew everyone's attention, and patrons headed to the door to check out the racket, Bo and Mary included.

Bo came back, began pouring my liquor and said, "Man, I ain't ever seen that many cop cars going down a road like that in my life. Especially this road."

"Okay, Mitty. It takes a hell of an event to bring out that many lawmen. You hung up the damn phone before you explained just what the hell all happened. Get on with it," Mary said.

Bo placed my drinks on the bar, and before he had time to get to the other end of the bar, I said, "Hit me again, Bo."

"Damn, boy, you sucked that down," Bo said as he pulled another draft.

"Sorry, Mary," I explained, "but getting a cell phone signal is difficult down at Michael's place. Making the message short and sweet seemed to be the thing to do. I didn't want to lose the signal before telling you to get the authorities to Michael's and why."

Mary and Bo both deserved a full disclosure from me and I spent the next hour drinking and telling the story again. At some point Mary stopped Bo from serving me, but after hearing the story she understood my need for a sedative.

She and Bo had a couple of shots themselves while I talked, and Mary wailed loud enough that other patrons turned our way. She grabbed and held onto Bo's arm more than once before my story came to its gruesome end.

"OK, but listen. The detective said we'd have to wait for dental or DNA to know for sure. But I'm sure it was Michael," I said, slurring my words.

"I should call Sallie Ray," I said, my tongue thickening. I looked up at the television and saw two batters swing at a pitch.

"I'll call her, Mitty," Mary said. "You can barely get your words out."

"No, it needs to come from me," I said catatonically. Leaving my barstool gracefully proved to be impossible. Mary led me off to her office

My first words, "They hung your brother, Sallie Ray," represented a poor start on my part, and the conversation deteriorated into mournful screams, moans, and cries from her and me losing track and repeating myself. Mary grabbed the phone from me. She calmed Sallie Ray down, straightened out my story and told Sallie Ray that I would call her back when I wasn't plastered.

Mary looked at me sunk deep in the couch with my head wobbling and led me off to what she called her Gigger's Rooms, where she offered free room and board for bands booked at Snowball's Place. A queen sized bed and lamp table were in each of the five small, neatly kept rooms, and allowed Mary to book bands for less. Musicians always left well-rested, well fed, and it didn't take long for word to get out to definitely book Snowball's Place when traveling Texas.

I banged shoulders on each side of the doorway as she directed me into a room and said, "Michael went through hell in his life and now this. There's a shitload of stuff that we need to discuss, Witty Mitty. I don't believe you'd remember any of it tonight, though. So, good night."

She grabbed me and hugged her short heavy frame to mine, heaved a sob, turned and left. My bed spun out of control for a while, but the day had been temporarily washed away from memory.

CHAPTER 22

F oggy mind. Nauseous stomach. Pounding head. I remembered why
I got my drinking under control fifteen years before. I swear, only
humans possess the ability to go from feeling wondrously good to devastat-
ingly bad by choice.

Suzie tended to me and kept me level headed while she shared life with me,
and once she passed on I knew just what trouble I was headed towards if I kept
drinking. I quit drinking altogether for quite some time, and then resumed
with the very occasional beer. I sat on the edge of the bed, really regretting my
recent transgression, and I knew that Suzie was frowning somewhere.

My eyes twitched with every heartbeat, which provided a backbeat to my
hangover. I felt as if a layer of sand coated the insides of my eyelids. My pores
were sweating out alcohol even though Mary kept the temperature freezing in
the small room. I raked my cell phone, wallet, pocket knife, change, and St.
Francis medallion from the night stand. I guessed that Mary had kept the truck
keys. I feebly rose to my feet with both my head and stomach complaining.

I called Sallie Ray first thing from Mary's office phone. It did not surprise
her that I had no memory of last night's conversation. She told me that Mary
had called her back and filled in the gaps.

"Did she tell you that there isn't a positive ID yet? We're not absolutely
sure if it's Michael," I said.

"Yeah, but I guess I'm expecting the worst. And good god, will they
call me to identify the... the... body? I just can't make any sense out of all of
this," Sallie Ray said, her voice shaking. "Feels the same way as when they sent
Michael off to prison. That it wasn't really happening."

Silence weighed long and heavy when she said nothing else, and I couldn't
focus enough to say much of anything.

Finally I offered, "Why don't you let me help you with funeral arrange-
ments. That's tough business to go it alone."

She said, "I buried my sister and mother, and I can handle things just fine.
My cousins run the funeral home and that'll take most of the load off of me.
You just take care of yourself, Mitty. I've never known you to wallow around in
alcohol like you did last night. Another thing: the stupid plan that my brother

schemed up is exactly that—stupid. Don't even go there, Mitty. Let the cops do their thing and catch the bastards."

I hung up and dialed Pete's number. He had left a voice mail. When he answered, he said that he had called Snowball's Place last night after I had passed out and Mary pretty much brought him up to speed.

"Evil begets evil," Pete said. "I'd lecture you about filling your tank with firewater, but I do believe that getting drunk most likely worked best for you. You did freak Mary and Bo out, though. Are you okay?"

"Right now my memory needs a little recuperation time," I told him. "And no, I don't think that I'll ever be okay again after yesterday. Not the same anyway."

"What now?" he asked. "Where will this go?"

"Hell, I don't know. We wait until we know for sure it was Michael in that tree. In the meantime, one of my voice mail messages tells me to call to a federal agent immediately and to plan on a face-to-face this afternoon over at the county courthouse. I guess that I best call him back."

I called FBI agent Daniel Pohl, and tried to put him off until tomorrow when my brain would contain fewer cobwebs, but he adamantly told me that he needed me there today. We agreed to meet at the Billet County Courthouse at one o'clock. I hung up, and a picture of Snowball hanging on the office wall brought a smile to my face. He held a catfish that was as long as he was tall and was flashing a smile from ear to ear. He sure did look like Mary.

The smell of Mary's pan sausage cooking lured me out of the office. Mary said, "Man, you look like death warmed over. Then again, so do I. I believe I drank more last night that I have in years and years. How do you like your eggs? Never mind, I'm scrambling them all. Bo, get some biscuits going in the oven.

"Hope you slept well. I didn't have it too cold for you, did I? Was the bed comfortable enough? After breakfast, there's a shower you can use down the hall from the rooms. Bo took your keys. We didn't want you driving off in the middle of the night. Why don't you hang around with us today and get your land legs back under you...."

I sat and let her rattle on, which felt normal. I needed normal, and Mary Johnson provided it with her chatter, and it mattered not if I responded.

Bo handed me my keys as Mary set pork sausage patties, scrambled eggs, biscuits, homemade mustang grape jelly, and black coffee in front of us. My pains began to ease off a bit with each forkful of wonderful, fluffy, *normal*, scrambled eggs.

After a shower and a shave I might even look normal.

I shook Bo's big hand, and he reached around and slapped my back, and Mary squeezed me with one of her normal hugs, and I crawled into my truck, waved, and headed towards the county courthouse in Moorenville.

There were barely three hundred residents in the town. Most of the county courthouse employees didn't even live in town and there had been many calls over the years to move the county seat to a larger city. However, the sheer architectural beauty of the old courthouse and the numerous remodels to keep it intact overrode and vetoed every plan to relocate.

Most of the downtown businesses were antique stores, so I had tagged along with Suzie for several visits over the years. To kill time, I had read facts about the courthouse from an historical marker on the front sidewalk. The courthouse had been built in 1891 in the Romanesque Revival style, and the four story structure was on the national historical registry, so it would take an act of Congress to tear it down. Like many county seats in East Texas, the courthouse sat in the middle of the town square and confused motorists not used to having to circle the entire square to find an exit from downtown— even in tiny Moorenville.

I slid into one of the few parking spots not occupied by a county official, and I gazed up and marveled at the tall dome-topped stone towers of the red roofed structure. The center tower reached to the heavens and housed a huge clock that looked like it had not worked in years.

I was thirty minutes early, and decided to grab one more cup of coffee at Adam's café. I remembered it as a typical, small Texas town eatery—good breakfasts, great lunch, and it may or may not be open for supper. To my surprise, a Mexican restaurant had replaced Adam's. *Sign of the times, I guess.*

The waitress at Encino's directed me to a table and looked at me with raised eyebrows when asked for just a cup of coffee. They apparently had to brew a fresh pot because it took awhile to arrive. I took a couple of sips, got up, left the puzzled waitress enough to cover the tip, and walked across the street to meet the FBI.

My boots banged a rhythm on the oak floors of the old building. I headed up creaking stairs to the third floor and passed a courtroom with customers awaiting their fate on wooden benches along the wall. I finally came to a door that said *Billet County Sheriff's Department* on the frosted glass. A polite secretary behind an ancient counter pointed me to an office to the left.

Agent Pohl proved to be a long, tall drink of water, with a head that seemed small for a man his size. He dressed in a dark brown suit with an American flag pin in the lapel. I guessed him to be mid-thirties. He had short blond hair, was clean shaven, and had a weak handshake and a soft voice. He introduced Texas Ranger Jim Nelson.

"Ranger Nelson will be assisting with the investigation," he said, friendly enough, in an accent proving that he grew up a long ways from Texas.

Nelson still wore his Stetson hat on his head, but he removed it as we shook hands and he took a seat next to me and across a large desk from Agent Pohl. He seemed to be close to my five foot eleven, with a similar stocky frame.

I noticed that the name plaque on the desk read "Detective Thompson". As predicted, he'd been cut out of this part of the investigation. A couple of framed diplomas hung on the wall behind the desk, one in criminology from Sam Houston State University and a master's degree from Texas A&M. Suzie would have loved the antique desk.

Agent Pohl turned out to be all business. He started a digital recorder and asked detailed questions. I answered and noticed that both lawmen seemed extremely skeptical of Michael's theory based on Silas' story. The Ranger even rolled his eyes, as if to say, *"We've heard this kind of bullshit before"*.

"We're still waiting on positive identification of the body found in the pecan orchard." Agent Pohl said. "We could be looking at something as simple as a random burglary or drug deal gone wrong. Your story must sound far-fetched, even to you. How well did you really know Mr. Melton?"

My headache had returned with a vengeance.

"Someone silenced Silas Guyton and then silenced Michael in pretty much the same way that they took care of Silas' dad," I said. "That's too much coincidence for me. Doesn't seem like some kind of random burglary drug deal gone wrong at all."

"Who knows," the Ranger said. "Hell, the gangs in prison cut throats for no other reason than skin color. If either of these guys pissed off the Aryan Brotherhood or the Mexican Mafia and lacked reciprocal gang affiliation and protection, then they get smoked. The gang's arms reach far beyond prison walls."

"Trust me. We'll look into all the possible angles," said Agent Pohl. "Your theory has some interesting points and we'll look into it. Do us a favor. Stay in touch with us if any solid information comes your way. Answer your phone when we call. We may need more answers."

Chapter 23

I arrived at my farmhouse close to dusk and grabbed nothing but junk mail from the mailbox at the edge of the blacktop. Overwhelming fatigue set in as I headed up the drive. The last golden sunrays highlighted the yellow wildflowers that blanketed my property and invited me back home. The temperature on my dash read 103 degrees. Hottest day we'd had yet.

I stepped up on the front porch feeling lower than Brazos River mud, and my mind was as bogged down as my truck had been yesterday. *Was it yesterday?* I walked through the unlocked door, croaked back at Bud, the door frog, and headed to Suzie's Room. I twisted the thermostat lower.

Suzie's Room. Not our bedroom. Everything Suzie. I paused in the door frame. Her presence guided me in and into the overstuffed reading chair she loved so much. I lit a cinnamon candle on the lamp table—Suzie's favorite, and it always reminded me of the Neil Young song. I absorbed the scent, took my boots off, and propped my feet on the ottoman. I imagined myself floating up from my body. I could see my dazed self below as I drifted above the room and took in photos of Suzie and me, me and Suzie, us and the house and the pets. Soon our spirits mingled and floated together as one. The moment dissolved as I felt my heavy body sink lower into the chair cushions. I knew that she knew what I knew, and slumber washed me out with the low tide.

Rarely does daylight catch me sleeping, but I do believe that I could have slept until noon. However, a ferocious nightmare jolted me up and wild-eyed just after nine o'clock.

My dream sent me back to the pecan orchard. I was braver. I approached the slowly twisting body at the end of the noose and thought, *"What a nice job with the hangman's noose."* The fully clothed body hadn't been torched. The suit looked like Eddie Guyton's pinstripe and as the body kept turning, the bright red tie appeared. The face, the face, and bulging eyes had slapped me awake. Pete Bolden's dead eyes pierced my soul.

Adrenaline jackhammered in my gut as I grabbed my boots, blew out the candle and slammed out of Suzie's Room. I ran out onto the front porch in sock feet and sucked in the fresh air. There was plenty of heat and humidity already. It took a few minutes, but by golly I felt alive and refreshed, and I thanked God—and Suzie. Then the house phone rang.

"I want to hear from you just what the hell happened out there." Pete said. "I'm fifteen minutes from your house. So, Polly put the kettle on." And he hung up. *Good to hear Pete's voice.*

I punched up my iPod to shuffle on my stereo, and headed to the kitchen as Otis Rush's otherworldly voice sang "Double Trouble" and I thought, *Now ain't that the truth brother.*

Pete drove up in a mini-van. Never in my wildest dreams would I ever have said "Pete Bolden" and "mini-van" in the same sentence. Normally, I'd razz him a little, but my nightmare still clung like wet plaster which I couldn't wipe away. I met him on the porch with a large coffee mug.

"Mary gave me a rundown of what you ran into, Mitty. Man, you should see the headlines: *LYNCHING IN BILLET COUNTY*," Pete said as he took the mug from me. "Sorry that all that mess fell in your lap. Glad I didn't tag along, now. Unbelievable."

After filling in all the details for Pete, including my dream, I said, "Maybe we'd better rethink any kind of amateur detective stuff."

"Why, because you had a scary dream?" Pete asked as he removed his baseball cap to reveal a newly bald head. "Mental trauma's gonna cause lots of weird dreams. I'm here and alive. Let's just roll with it and try to stop these guys."

Pete caught me looking at his head, smiled and said, "Don't start. Beatrice gave my head a summer cut that went badly, so she shaved it all off."

"Now *that* can cause mental trauma. You don't know the half of it, Pete. Michael's spinning his tale one day, and the next time I see him he's swinging from a tree limb. They got him like they got Silas' dad. Hell, he didn't have to lure them out. They hunted him down, and they got him. These guys frighten the hell out of me because they are scary bad," I said as a cold chill swept through me.

"Silas fingered them in prison, Mitty. They took him out. They most likely targeted Michael too, but he escaped their clutches in there," Pete said. "They bided their time and attacked him at home. Michael canvassed the area for band mates, remember. He didn't exactly hide out."

"They lynched Michael, making it a federal hate crime, and some of those lawmen just may be smart enough to nab these guys," I said.

"Do these smart lawmen know about the Badou boys murdering hobby?" he asked.

"They don't put a lot of stock in that theory, but maybe they'll get there as the investigation gets going. The two guys that interrogated me seem quite competent," I said.

Pete and I talked at each other until late in the afternoon. A lot of our visiting relived the old days—at least the days prior to Pete getting strung out on drugs. Our conversation weaved back to the current crisis, but I knew neither of us had much new to say.

I always hated my tendency to repeat a problem over and over again as if the person I was talking to didn't hear me the first five times. Maybe I think repeating the details of a problem would somehow make it solve itself. My friends who are too polite to say, "Shut up, Mitty!" avoid Mitty in crisis.

Friends like Pete give me "The Look," that meant enough, already, shut up and move on to another topic or else they would walk. Today Pete was the one who kept bringing up details about the lynching. I tried giving Pete "The Look," which didn't work. Finally I said, "Shut up, Pete. We've been there already."

At five o'clock we went indoors and flipped on a Houston television news channel, and the lead story made Billet County out to be KKK country with the apparent lynching and torching of an as-yet unidentified African American man. The reporter stood on the blacktop road just before Michael's turn off and spoke in very serious tones about a very serious crime.

There was a terse interview from an FBI spokesman, whom I didn't recognize. He gave the standard "investigation is underway" sound bite.

There were interviews with half-lit clients at Snowball's Place: "I can't believe this happened around here. Nothing like this ever happens around here."

"This scares me. I didn't know no KKK rode around here anywhere. Might mean trouble. There's lots of racism, though, in these parts. Some people don't think that. There is though."

They cut to shots at the county courthouse and the county judge defending the county's residents as hard working, God fearing folks without a prejudiced bone in their bodies. There were plenty of shots of good old boys driving by in their pickup trucks and focused in on one with a Confederate flag decal on the back window.

Pete said, "They're going to play this one up like they did Jasper, which I always thought was a nice town. Played a couple of gigs over there and met nothing but friendly folks. A couple of bad seeds tainted that place forever.

The quicker they catch these guys and point out that they ain't from Texas, the better."

"I just hope the trees don't get in the way of the orchard," I said, trying a little wit and then realizing the stupidity of the comment.

"Why don't you call that county detective that you talked to first and see what he knows?"

"I'll call him tomorrow when he's on duty. I don't know if they took him completely out of the loop or not. Let's analyze things a little here, Pete."

We started by counting up harp player deaths that could possibly be contributed to one or more Badous. My theory jumped from Eddie Guyton to Joey Brooks—about a fifty-year gap.

"Then we have Bobby T about fifteen years after that. Maybe Damon Stokely, I just don't know," I said.

"What about Sonny Boy and Little Walter in Chicago? Seems like someone would have investigated the murders of such big time blues stars and found something by now," Pete said.

"Hell, Pete. Little Walter didn't even have a tombstone until fans raised the money to buy his grave one in the 1980s. Only thirty-seven and forgotten by the city he helped make famous for the blues."

"When have you had time to research all of that, Mitty?"

"Pete, I've been listening to the blues, reading about the blues, studying the blues, and playing the blues since 1968."

"I forget that you white folks took our music from us. Always surprises me when you honkies tell me more about my music than I know. Of course, I lived that stuff and didn't have to read about it," Pete said, smiling.

"Oh, bullshit. You never picked cotton in your life. You grew up as middle class as I did. The only blues you knew, you brought on yourself." I regretted the comment as it came from my mouth.

"Whoa. Now that's a low blow," he said and I immediately apologized. Pete shrugged it off and said, "Hey, I owned up to all of that a long time ago. Let's get back on topic. We can look at tons of harp players that someone just might have killed. The Lord called plenty of them home, but it doesn't mean that the Badous gave them a shove."

"You're right. Why not take out James Cotton? He's still out there gigging, or Billy Boy Arnold, who I saw perform just last year. There's got to be a method or motive to their madness."

"Okay," Pete said, "throw out some motives. All we're got so far is that Daddy Badou hated blues harp players because his wife left him for one. The Badou sons carry on the hatred because their dad was killed by the son of a blues harp player."

"Tammy's going to get back in touch with me after she researches the Badous. That'll help shed a little light on those characters. At least she can tell us whether or not such a family ever existed around that part of Louisiana."

There was another theory that had been swirling around between my ears. "OK, here's another angle. If we look at what we have, then Michael Melton's name figures prominently in most of the recent activities. Michael went to prison for nailing Joey Brooks—literally. Silas Guyton meets his maker after his visits with Michael. We can place Michael in the same city and at the last venue that Bobby T played, and now Michael meets pretty much that same fate as Eddie Guyton. Don't know much about Damon Stokely, but who knows, there might be a Michael Melton tie there, also."

Pete looked at me. "Are you saying that Michael was involved in these deaths? Maybe he wasn't the killer, but what? An accomplice? Accessory? A link?"

"I don't know exactly. But Michael was there. There's a connection."

I didn't like what I was thinking and saying. Maybe Michael had made up everything about Silas and the Badous. Maybe... I just didn't know anymore.

CHAPTER 24

B ack in the day, Pete and I would have solved all the world's problems by midnight. We'd have been skunk drunk by then, also— at least I would have been. Not sure what Pete would have been high on. As it were, we barely made it past the ten o'clock news that we didn't want to miss. There still wasn't an ID on the lynching victim. The news segment we saw regurgitated the earlier story and it became a tad more sensationalized. The newscasters began to draw parallels to the dragging death of James Byrd outside of Jasper that prompted the passing of hate crime laws.

The next morning, Pete came creeping into the kitchen to the smell of biscuits in the oven, some of those large grand ones that made enough of a meal by themselves. A jar of Suzie's dewberry jam sat on the large antique oak table. She'd always roped me into picking the succulent dewberries each spring, stirring the boiling berries, and sealing the molten delicacy into pint jars. Friends and relatives became accustomed to a jar of Suzie's Dewzie Jam, as she called it, for Christmas gifts.

I figured out how to make her jam by carefully following her recipe card. I'd watched her for years and tried to copy how she stirred and poured and sealed the jars. My jam wasn't as good as hers, but making it reminded me of her and our life together.

Disc four of Little Walter's Complete Chess Recordings blasted out an alternate take of "Everything's Gonna Be Alright" and man I felt normal again after mentally dusting my brain of the last few days of dirty filthy crap. Pete looked surprised.

"Now, that's a revelation. Where did you get that version of Little Walter's?"

"Good stuff, huh?" I said. "Just when we thought we had heard everything that the master had blown they tempt us with never before released tracks. You've got to buy the entire box set, though. Expensive. But, you know what Pete? They re-mastered these discs better than anything produced before, so just hearing a Fred Below drum roll that I missed, or a Robert Jr. Lockwood guitar lick singing and swinging with more prominence makes the purchase worth every penny."

Pete looked over at a pile of harmonica parts on my kitchen counter and said, "I see that you finally started working on your own harmonicas instead of tossing them away."

"Have you seen the prices lately?" I said. "It's kind of hard to afford for a jobless Joe like me, so it's 'Mother of Necessity'. I've gotten darn good at it too, by the way. Coffee?"

After retiring to the music room and muting "Mean Old Frisco," I dialed Detective Thompson's number.

He didn't waste time with small talk, "You didn't hear this from me, but there's a positive ID—it was Michael Ray Melton in that pecan tree.

"The feds also made an arrest during the wee hours of the morning. I expect the news will break around noon. I hear that an anonymous tipster insisted that sinister, armed and dangerous characters lived in a house set way back in the woods about a half mile from Melton's place."

There was a rustle of paper and I could tell that Detective Thompson was reading, "Deputies surprised three white male occupants at the residence. The occupants opened fire with automatic assault weapons. Deputies killed all three. The investigating officers uncovered a full blown meth lab in a shed behind the house and a pail containing bloody gloves and coveralls."

A stun gun couldn't have popped me harder than the detective's news. Pete looked my way with arched eyebrows and a quizzical look.

Deputy Thompson continued, "Preliminary identification pegged two of the three men as ex-cons sent up for—surprise—cooking and dealing meth. Tattoos indicate white supremacy gang affiliation. The third perp hasn't been identified. I'd say that kills the serial killing theories that The Wizard spun to you, unless the Badou boys dealt meth on the side and white-washed themselves."

As I sat speechless, he said, "Anyway, I thought that I owed this to you and planned to call you with the news, but you beat me to it. Again, you *did not* hear this from me, although I wanted you to hear it from me first, instead of Eyewitness News."

"Thanks, detective. I appreciate it," was all I could manage, along with, "Does Deputy Benny Williams know this? He mentioned that he knew Michael."

There was a pause. "He does."

"I guess that is that. Thank you, Detective."

Pete looked at me waiting for some sort of explanation and I told him what the detective had said. He was as speechless as I had been.

"Okay, maybe that does solve Michael's murder," he finally offered, "but now that puts us back to square one with who killed Bobby T or for that matter, framed Michael with Big Joey's murder. What now?"

"I really don't know, Pete. We need to re-evaluate all of this. I had my mind back on track and then Detective Thompson switches rails on me. Weird things are going on and I'm always leery of convenient solutions."

"How many methheads have you known, Mitty? They'll pull some crazy ass wicked evil stunts. They sure the hell ain't right in the head."

"The hell with it. Let's go jam some blues, Pete."

"We're sticking with The Wizard's plan?"

"We'll talk some more about that. I'm the scheduled jam host at Little Queenie's in a couple of nights. I thought about canceling, but I've got to get my mind off this business. Be sure you bring your butt down there," I said, attempting to jack up my own enthusiasm.

Pete and I caught the noon news before he took off, and the report repeated exactly the details given to us by Detective Thompson.

"The lynching victim has been identified as musician Michael Ray Melton, better known as 'The Wizard'."

They showed old concert clips of Michael's performances. There was another interview in front of Snowball's Place. "What a shame this happened to The Wizard. Gets out of prison and gets himself hung. Man, what a deal."

The reporters had names and mug shots of the alleged killers. Two of the three had parole violation warrants out for their arrests. They reported to their parole officers only once in North Texas, never to be seen or heard from since. The third meth cooker owned the property and was in violation of a variety of laws in Billet County, but authorities never convicted him of anything other than misdemeanor offences.

Plenty of pats on the back and kudos passed from one official to another for getting such vicious scum off the street. FBI Agent Pohl appeared on camera and lauded the cooperative team effort between his agency, the Texas Rangers, and the Billet County Sheriff's department, and I thought, *"Yeah, now we can all sleep peacefully."*

After Pete left, I pulled out my 1965 Sears Silvertone 1483 amplifier head and pulled the powers tubes and replaced them with a fresh set. The amp complained with a little noise the last time I cranked her up, and I hoped the new parts smoothed out that problem.

I plugged into my homemade cabinet with four ten inch speakers and blew a few fat, nasty tongue blocked notes through a harp in the key of "A" and my crystal element microphone. The beast was back and it thumped the floor beneath my bare feet.

"Man, that sounds good and feels good," I said out loud to myself. "Sweet therapy." And off I went blowing every note to every riff that I could think of. My psyche improved considerably, and I no longer entertained the notion to call Franklin and have him line up a substitute at Little Queenie's. I could slay a dragon now.

I laid out my Hohner Marine Band Deluxe gig harmonicas, checked the tuning on each one and adjusted the gaps as needed. There is nothing worse that hitting a note and having it balk or go blatt in mid-solo.

The thought that Pete Bolden just might share a stage with me again had me pumped, also. It had been such a long time since he cut my head with his superior technique. Woodshedding had improved my skill considerably, though—an unemployment benefit.

I booted up my ancient Dell to check the weather forecast for the rest of the week and survey the day's news.

It was storming again and I never did like getting caught in Houston traffic during a thunderstorm. There are too many impassable routes after a couple of inches of rain hit the streets. It never ceased to amaze me how many people tried to drive through the flooded underpasses and had to wade out without their vehicles.

The backlog of e-mail messages was intimidating. One from Tammy warranted opening, and she confirmed that, yes, the Badou family existed in Alexandria at one time and that, yes, they had criminal tendencies. She said that the Eddie Guyton murder investigating officer, Ray Raton, was still in Alexandria, but in a rest home. She'd get back with me. *Sweet, sweet Tammy.*

My blood ran cold as I spotted a news story out of Austin with the heading: *Austin Musician Dies From Gunshot* and a subhead naming harmonica player, Ralph Brown as the victim. My mind raced as I read the story on how the rising blues star's drummer discovered the body lying in a pool of blood in the alley in back of Cat Daddy's Club.

Authorities quoted said that the shooting appeared to be carried out execution style with one shot to the back Brown's head. They would not speculate as to whether it may have been a drug deal gone bad or some type of retribution. I dialed up The Wizard's sister, Sallie Ray, to see what she knew since Austin was her home base now.

"I just heard the news, myself," she said about Ralph Brown's murder. "First things first though. I'm burying Michael Ray tomorrow. The funeral's at 10 am in Navasota and Mary offered Snowball's for a 'Celebration of Life' party."

"That's pretty darned fast funeral plans," I said.

"Well, I told you that my cousins ran the funeral home," she said. "Are you going to make it?"

"You know it," I said.

"Okay, now," I said. "Is your take the same as mine? That Michael Ray's killers shot Ralph Brown while the Brazos River shootout took place?"

"Exactly, right," she said. "My theory is that someone set up those racist chemists next door to my brother's place. They had it coming, but I know damn well that they didn't kill Michael. I don't care if the Governor comes down and says that they did."

"Well the FBI just may pull rank over a governor on this, and they've slammed the case shut," I told her. "Did you know Ralph Brown?"

"Oh, yeah, I knew Ralph Brown." she answered quickly. "The first gig I had back in Austin had *me* open for Ralph Brown. I thought that they screwed up that booking and had to call and ask if they had it ass-backwards. They told me that this young cat just happened to be the hottest act in Austin. I couldn't even believe it, Mitty. I've got to admit it, though; he put on a hell of a show. The boy came out smoking on that harmonica, and the crowd went crazy on him. I'll tell you this; I'm glad that I didn't have to follow that kid on stage. We crossed paths several times, and he seemed like such a polite young man."

"I don't think that the authorities will tie this one in with our bad guys, with what they figure to be the dramatic ending to the case over in the Brazos River bottom," I said.

"Somebody's got to pay for framing my brother and slaughtering him, and they sure the hell haven't caught up with those heathens. Surely, they'll see it like we do, Mitty," she said.

"I don't think that Ralph Brown's execution will sway anyone in this case but us, Sallie," I said. "If they pulled the slick trick of hanging Michael's hanging on the meth heads, then no one will slip up behind these cats and surprise them, and I don't think they've sprung their last trick. Why don't you get out of town, Sallie Ray?"

"I ain't running from these assholes. I'll pop a hole in their heads if they mess with me," she said.

CHAPTER 25

The Wizard's funeral was a small and very private affair. But the wake—that was another story. Mary opened up Snowball's place for what Sallie Ray called "A Celebration of Life for Michael Ray Melton". Pete made the funeral but couldn't attend the party. He and Beatrice were going to a family reunion down on the coast.

Sallie Ray asked me to come early in the morning before the funeral. We met in her tour bus.

"I just finished cleaning out Michael's house," she said.

I shuddered, thinking of the kitchen, the blood.

Sallie Ray touched my arm, "Don't worry, the cleanup crew was there first." She pulled out a pile of sketchbooks. "Michael is... was... the real artist in the family. He'd just started drawing again," she said, flipping through the pages of a new-looking sketchbook. She stopped at drawings of an older black man.

"I think this is Silas Guyton."

I must have looked surprised. Sallie Ray said gently, "Yeah, Michael told me a little of the Silas story too. I guess I should have told you."

She flipped a little further through the book. There were rough sketches of three boys, one with a ropy scar on his neck, one with a light eye and a dark eye. "And I think these are the Badou boys from Michael's imagination."

I looked at the sketches. Michael must have drawn them from Silas' descriptions. They'd be grown men now: *what did they look like?* I looked at the sketches, tried to "age progress" them like I'd seen on crime shows. I didn't notice that Sallie Ray was holding something out to me.

It was another of Michael's plantation scenes, just a rough sketch, musicians on a porch. And the harmonica player was... me.

"A gift," said Sallie Ray, "From Michael to you."

The party started Friday and didn't end until Sunday. There was a stage set up outside. Conspicuously displayed were the permits allowing Mary to host what amounted to an outdoor music festival. Ranks of bright green Honey

Buckets were lined up across the street, along with enterprising characters selling "The Wizard Will Never Die" t-shirts, Wizard CDs and other paraphernalia out of the trunks of their cars. I had to laugh at that. I'll bet Mary chased them across the street to hang with the latrines.

Detective Thompson, Benny Williams, and other Billet County law enforcement officers were there keeping the crowd in hand.

I asked Benny how they got the permits through so fast for the event. He looked at me over the top of his sunglasses. "Are you kidding? First off, Miss Sallie Ray Melton made the request. Second, this event will probably bring big bucks into the county. Third, we gotta prove that Billet County isn't a nest of murderous racist meth heads."

It seemed like there were equal numbers of mourners and members of the media. The "modern-day-lynching" was still news and there were news people everywhere garnering interviews, snapping photos, and taping footage. I was there as a half-assed reporter too. I would be posting something in my blog, but truth be told, I was more interested in finding more connections between the deaths of blues harp musicians.

People shoved their conspiracy theories at me, that the meth heads were Aryan Nation blues music haters (I gathered that blues music was black music and therefore all blues musicians had to die); the unholy alliance between the blues and voodoo. I began to wonder if Michael's story about Silas and the Badou boys was just another theory.

Sallie Ray kicked things off with a couple of her brother's tunes and one of her own, composed for the occasion. I was sure that *"Wizard's Requiem: Get It Back"* would be her next hit and made a note to include that in the blog. After Sallie Ray's performance, everyone who had something to say or something to play for The Wizard got up on the stage. Stories were told, poems read, we cried and laughed, but mostly we jammed.

And jammed.

And jammed some more, until we couldn't play or sing another note.

"That bastard got up and blew a damned harmonica in my face," Joe Junior told his brothers. "I could have pulled my Glock and emptied that son of bitch and blew his ass off the stage."

"Why the hell didn't you?" Davey Badou asked, while Leonard flailed around flashing sign language.

"Because, stupid ass, I told you there were cops all over that place and they'd have damn sure been all over me," Joe said back.

He knew that Davey and Leonard were still angry that they had missed The Wizard's big event. He told them that they were the ones who wanted to hang around Austin long enough to sell the rest of Cousin Dwayne's dope. They were still pissed at him for not telling them about the funeral. Both of them said that they would have made a bee line back to Snowball's had they known.

"But, anyway, here I was enjoying some blues guy playing a great slide guitar. I stood inches from him while he played those licks, those same licks that I was playing the night that Silas shot Daddy," Joe said.

Right, thought Davey, *sounded like a cat being strangled to him, right before the shotgun blast that changed all their lives.*

"Then that damned Mitty guy walks up and starts wailing those notes from hell. My body trembled, he made me so mad. I told you that he was a harp blower. When I saw him walk into that Snowball place the week before we torched The Wizard and work on that little black Mexican's harmonica. He's for damn sure next."

"You already told us that, Joe Junior. Said that you figured that he knew you followed him to find out where The Wizard lived and he probably had to go next," Davey said.

"No, I told you that I followed him long enough to see where he was going. Those Snowball domino players already explained how to get to The Wizard's. Well, now that I know he blows Satan's trumpet, he's a goner for certain. Blowing a harp in my face," Joe said.

Leonard jumped up and started flapping his hands in sign language around Joe Junior.

"Get out of my face. You know I can't understand a word you say when you talk that fast," Joe said slapping at his flapping.

Davey gave both his brothers an exasperated look and said to Joe Junior, "Leonard says 'Alright Already'. Your Mitty is on our list. We'll get his ass and then get out of this damn shack of Cousin Dwayne's out in the middle of the boonies. Tell us about the party. Remember? The funeral party. The one you insisted that we miss. The one that you said that you'd circulate at and find out who knew what and believed what. Bullshit. You're just like me. You wanted to mill around and hear people talk about someone that you killed."

Joe Junior shot a fierce star into Davey's blue and brown eye and said, "I found out plenty, brother of mine."

Leonard's hand waved out an obvious, "Then, get on with it!"

"Well, to begin with, it was one hell of a party," Joe Junior said, hoping to piss Davey off. "Biggest party that I've ever been to anyway. People came from everywhere. You'd have thought that we killed the Pope. Blues stars came out of the woodwork and began jamming at noon. Some damn fine music was being played and no harmonica players in the bunch, until Mitty stepped up there. Him and the buttheads that just had to get up and say a few kind words about The Wizard ruined things for me. That wasn't until later in the evening, so I enjoyed the hell out of free beer and that Snowball lady's fine cooking. Oh, and looking at The Wizard's fine sister, Sallie Ray was a treat in itself. We've got to look up that lady real soon. She caught me staring at her. I think I put a scare in her.

"Okay, speaking of cops. I spent quite some time standing next to a couple of them and listening to them talk about those ignorant meth racists. One was a big, burly, black county cop and the other looked to be some kind of detective. The detective type wondering who the informant might have been who supplied the information about those crackers."

"He called them crackers?" Davey asked. "Good thing that Cousin Dwayne knew one of those crackers and that they lived close to The Wizard, huh?"

"Alright, shut up. You want to hear this, or not?" Joe Junior said.

"Anyway, they just thought that it was weird that all that went down the way that it did. Acted like they had suspicions," Davey said, "Hell, I knew that those idiots would shoot first and ask questions later. I don't think that they expected such an army to show up to bust a meth lab. That 'suicide by cops' cleared our ass. "

"Well, both these cops knew the owner of the property and knew that he was bad news, so it didn't hurt their feelings," Joe Junior said. "Then, the little black Mexican dude came up and started talking to the big county cop about a plan that The Wizard had to come after us. So, you were right all along, Davey. The Wizard had to be taken out."

"Well?" Davey said after Joe Junior paused his story to get up and get a beer. "What the hell was The Wizard's plan?"

"I dunno, he really didn't say other than now that The Wizard's killers were dead that he guessed that his friend Mitty wouldn't have to get himself involved," Joe Junior said. "By the way, how did the trip to Austin go brother Badous?"

Joe Junior was sure that Leonard signed, "Mission accomplished."

CHAPTER 26

The rush-hour traffic on Highway 290 thickened by the mile, but at least my path cut against the outward flow of the mass migration to the suburbs. However, in recent years development began moving back inside the 610 loop and the downtown area. The new money tore into neighborhoods like Bellaire: perfectly fine older homes were ripped out and huge three story McMansions put up in their place. Pretty soon the traffic will be awful in every direction, I thought glumly. I picked up my cell phone and called Pete, and reminded myself to look into one of those handless methods as cars flew past me doing over eighty.

He asked me, "Did you know this Austin cat that got himself shot?"

"Didn't know him, but I knew of him. Sallie Ray got to know him, and it sounds doubtful that he had enemies," I said. "I checked him out online. He played his harp at a million notes a minute, but somehow made them all count. He posted internet lessons on YouTube. I tapped into some of those, and Ralph Brown knew his shit. He also apparently ruled the Austin scene. Looks like he had generated a respectable fan base of twenty-somethings. with his brand of "blues," which had a smidgen of what you or I would call the blues in it. Not my cup of tea, but if it gets the youth of America excited about the harmonica, then I'm all for it."

"Was he the type of fellow likely to get his ass shot?"

"Sallie Ray said that she never heard of anyone calling him anything but kind and considerate," I said.

"Weird, stuff, Mitty. This business has gotten stranger by the day," Pete said. "Are we back at square one; wherever that may be?"

"Pete, we've gone way beyond weird. If Silas' tale is correct, then the Badous have stayed a step ahead of the good guys for almost forty years. Sallie Ray thinks they orchestrated the meth gang shoot-out, and then framed their racist necks. I'm inclined to believe the same." I said. "I'm in awe of their evil and they scare me."

"I don't think 'in awe' would describe my feelings towards them. Let's just go jam and blow the hell out of it and forget that the world outside of Little Queenie's exists," Pete said and hung up.

⟨◦⟩

And that's exactly what we did for the next four hours.

Franklin paid us fifty dollars per man and free drinks, so we darned sure didn't get rich from it. We just loved playing the blues. The jam host, in this case, me—opens the night with a forty-five minute set before opening the stage to musicians signed up to jam. When I host, the only constant seems to be me and the bass player, Fritz O'Donald, and sometimes he was on the road. Nonetheless, he made most of my jams and played at most of my paid gigs, too.

Pete waved at me as I wheeled my speaker cabinet through the back door. Fritz and my semi-regular drummer, Johnnie Red, asked me if they could assist with my gear, and I told them no. No one knew Johnnie's real last name, he offered no clues, and no one cared any longer. We just called him Red. Rumor had it that his last name came either from his hair or his facial color when angered, but no one dare asked about it, and no one pointed out that he had more white than red hair nowadays.

He played with Bobby T for three years, until Bobby went off to record his first album and the record company insisted on using studio musicians. Red felt shafted on the deal and took a hike. No one, including myself, ever asked him if he regretted his decision. At six-four and two-eighty-five with a trigger temper, and a tattoo on his right shoulder that indicated a motorcycle gang affiliation, we found it prudent to keep quiet. Johnnie Red could swat most of us as if we were Gulf Coast mosquitoes.

By starting time, we still had no guitar player. I recognized a youngster entering the front door from previous jams, and I liked his old school blues style, a rarity among the young pups, so I motioned him to the stage. He also never swamped us harp players with his volume. He stepped up on stage with his Telecaster and '65 Fender DeLuxe.

Pete had no amp, so I yelled over to Franklin to break out a house amp for him, but Pete said he'd rather just blow through his vocal mic and the PA. Fritz and Red kicked off a Texas shuffle, and we were off and running before the guitarist set up, but he caught us on the turnaround.

Pete and I traded fours and he totally blew me away with chops that knew no rust. Years had gone slowly by, but Pete showed no sign that any of it had caught him napping. The man blew stone cold, solid blues licks. The guitarist fell in with us and began dishing out some tasty slide guitar, indicating that he'd spent some time studying Elmore James. Franklin jumped up on stage and gave Pete a bear hug and those few early birds in the clubs had cell phones out. Some held them in the air, so their friends could hear the sounds. Some snapped pictures. I knew the messages being sent out—*"Pete Bolden's back, get your ass down to Little Queenie's"*.

Fans packed the club by the time we finished our opening set with "Key to the Highway". Pete sang his ass off and I stuck little harp fills in a call and response. We both took the song home by swapping licks back and forth, egging each on and challenging each other. Pete whipped me good before we wrapped up that old chestnut.

No harp players in the club dared followed what they had just heard, so Pete stayed up on stage and blew through my rig during the first jam set. Everyone in the club had eyes and ears glued to Pete Bolden.

Pete finally took a break and joined me at a back table, reserved for jam nights. Only a hive of bees could have generated more activity than the fans and well-wishers passing by our table to meet and greet Pete. I felt invisible, but sat and nodded to a few, "Oh, hey, Mitty" acknowledgements of my presence, glad that people still worshiped Pete's skills. Pete's faced beamed brighter with each handshake and then he said, "Uh oh, look who's coming."

Don Deal, the big boy of entertainment journalism himself, had weaseled his way past a couple of waiting fans. Our relationship revolved around a mutual hatred of each other. Since I had written my articles for a "lesser" publication than his, his opinion was that my opinion didn't count.

He had actually ripped off my ideas and complete stories with help from some sleazy mole at the *Gazette*. We only published once a week, and Devil Don would beat me to press with my own stuff. If I published my story, then it appeared as if I plagiarized the big Deal. I never threatened to sue him, but did tell him that I'd knock his fat head off his fat ass if I ever caught him out alone somewhere. He took glee in the fact that I no longer had a job.

"Damn, you boys sounded alright tonight. You too, Mitty," Deal said as he slithered up to our table. "I've never heard you play so good, Mitty. And Pete, you are as killer as ever. Nobody sings the blues like you do. You might have to take this act on the road."

Pete said nothing. He also despised the man. Pete had given me material for stories, only to see his words in a Deal "exclusive".

"Yeah, well, you know Don, I have gotten better, but how the hell would you know? You've never really heard me play," I said. And then I had an idea.

"Y'know Don, we *are* taking this act on the road," I said, as Pete's eyes widened.

"There ain't too many two harp blues bands out there like George Smith and Rod Piazza had going with Bacon Fat back in the day. We ought to be able to generate a buzz. Especially with the return of the fabulous, stupendous, tremendous Pete Bolden laying it down for them," I said.

Don asked question after question. He couldn't stand it. He had to have the details for the scoop. Pete told him that no plans had been formalized. "Move along, Donny boy and don't call us, we'll call you," Pete said. Don looked hard at him, then at me, and walked off.

"What the hell, Mitty? Since when did *we* decide to do this thing?"

"I know, I know, but Don Deal just clinched it. Look at him, Pete. He's telling everyone in the club, and by tomorrow afternoon our band will be section three front page news. Can't ask for better free publicity. Maybe Michael's plan will work," I said. "Plus, playing with you tonight has been a hell of a hoot."

"One problem," Pete said. "We don't have a band."

A racket on the stage drew our attention. Red had booted a guitarist for suggesting "Mustang Sally," which, along with "The Thrill is Gone" and "Stormy Monday" were taboo at Little Queenie's blues jams. Johnnie Red would definitely be an asset in our musical posse, and he just might go for it.

Franklin walked over and in an agitated voice wanted to know why we had kept him in the dark about forming a band.

"Are we friends or what?" he said. "The biggest blues news in the city, breaking in my own club, and I've got to hear it from Don Deal. What gives?"

No use in trying to end run Franklin on this, so after getting him to sit down, I ran down the scheme. True to form he said, "Okay, now. Let me make some phone calls. I've got lots of contacts in the business and can help get you guys booked. Just make damn sure that Little Queenie's has first dibs. I'll clear the slate any night of the week for you guys."

"Thanks, Franklin. You got it, but keep in mind that we haven't got a band yet. I'll get back with you whenever we get something firm together and make sure that we can play up to snuff. We'd hate to embarrass your good name," I said.

"Hah, like that could even be a possibility. Great playing, Pete, and great to have you back," Franklin said as he got up.

Then Pete said, "Let's go outside. My ears ain't used to this stuff and it's getting louder by the minute." A guitar wanker was cranking out some Robin Trower-type licks at maximum volume. I thought that Red would be on his case, but he'd given his drum spot up for a jammer and had sat down behind the bar with Franklin. Both were frowning at the boost in guitar volume, though.

I expected Pete to vent once we stepped into the parking lot, but he surprised me by saying, "Did you notice the skinny dude with the dark sunshades and dreadlocks sitting at the bar?"

"A black guy?

"Naw, a white dude," he answered sarcastically. "Hell yeah, a black guy. Know any white guys with dreadlocks?"

I'd seen white guys with dreads, but this wasn't the time to chit-chat about that. "Okay, okay. What about him?"

"Just a feeling. A weird feeling about him. Kind of a scary vibe about him."

This guy had shaken Pete. I said, "Are you thinking that a Badou boy might be checking us out already?"

"Just thinking, Mitty. That's all. Stupid thinking, I guess."

"Listen, Pete. Consider no thoughts stupid. We've got to follow our hunches. Hell, hunches rule with these plans. Let's go and talk to this dreadlock dude."

"Wait a minute," Pete said. "First off, you ain't getting off the hook for popping off to Don Deal. We need to get a band on the road."

"I know, Pete. I'm sorry. Mary Johnson offered Snowball's Place for a tune-up location. She's got rooms and she'll feed us while we pick and grin and put together an awesome blues band," and Pete smiled as I said it.

"You know, I've enjoyed tonight. We laid down some great grooves up there and everyone ate it up. Let's just get her done, as you honky, rednecks say. OK, now we can go see if we can corner Mr. Dreadlocks," he said.

No dreadlocks could be seen anywhere within the club when we walked back in. Someone was picking out some nice Albert King licks from the stage.

"Check the men's room, and I'll look out in the back parking lot," I said.

My Silverado occupied the slot nearest the back door. I surveyed the dozen or so other vehicles in the lot, when suddenly a loud "Whoop!" sounded from behind and I felt a body leap on my back and hands grab around my face. I reached back and grabbed a handful of hair and started to flip the intruder over onto the pavement. A familiar voice hollered, "Wait a minute, Uncle Mitty!"

I froze, the monkey on my back jumped free, and I turned to stare at the wild-eyed face of Bobby T's daughter, Tammy. Pete had walked out the back door in time to see the circus and laughed out loud.

"Good golly, I never knew you to be that jumpy, Mitty," she said.

"You're lucky that I didn't flip you over that BMW. Sorry about that, Tammy. I guess I am a little bit on edge," I said. "What brings you to Houston?"

"I just got back from Alexandria and decided to stop off at my mom's house for the night before heading back to San Antonio. Franklin called and said that you guys were holding court down here," she said. "We had been out to eat at Papadeux's, so I made a beeline over here to catch what you and Pete had going. Figured that you'd want to know what I found out."

"Yeah, I got your e-mail. I didn't plan on you going to Alexandria, though, Tammy. I figured that you could just make a few calls," I said, looking around. "Where's your mom? Be good to see her."

"Since dad died, mom just can't handle being in clubs any longer. Especially listening to blues harp players. She wanted to see you, but not hear you guys play. Speaking of which, you and Pete aren't finished for the night, are you?"

"Well, it's a jam night, but maybe we can close things out," I told her and Pete gave her the thumbs up.

"You darned well better. I might have been in diapers the last time I heard Pete Bolden play the blues," she said. "Why don't you guys drop by mom's house tomorrow? That'll give me a lot more time to discuss my investigation with you. I told my editor that sending me to Louisiana just might catch a gang of serial killers. He doubted that, but sent me anyway."

Jukebox music boomed out Howlin' Wolf singing "Killing Floor" as we reclaimed our back table. Pete and I both kept our eyes peeled for our suspect. Franklin always provided a mid-jam break, so that folks could visit a bit and buy a few more rounds of drink. Tammy ordered a round for the table over Pete's protest. She never wanted to be treated like a weaker sex, and she darned well wasn't. She calls me at all hours picking my brain on how to best tackle a story or to get a hard news assignment from an editor.

She was pretty, like her mom and had been pegged as a fashion or lifestyle reporter, but she was having none of that.

Tammy's mom had been coaxed into a beauty pageant during college, won it handily, saw the shallowness of it all, and refused the many offers to continue down that path. She became a CPA, married Bobby T, kept his ass straight, and taught her daughter well.

When the San Antonio newspaper editors attempted to pigeon-hole Tammy, they had a fight on their hands. They finally stuck her on the courthouse beat, and she hammered her way into uncovering corruption Bexar County style. She exposed a few high-powered South Texas politicians' penchant for accepting bribes and won the prestigious Texas Excellence in Journalism award for her work.

She beat the hell out of my ass when it came to writing a newsworthy, investigative piece. It worried me that she became the target of threats, but nothing fazed Tammy. She had Bobby T's guts and Jean's tenacity, plus she could shoot the eyes out of a teddy bear at thirty feet with her Walther P-38—a gift from her dad.

I really didn't want to bring up the subject of the Badou family at the moment because I was enjoying the moment. Tammy changed that mood.

Tammy said, "I'll tell you this, the Badou clan definitely fits the bill as one evil family. No one ever pinned a murder rap on any of them, but everyone suspected them of most every deadly sin around that part of Louisiana.

"Even old Ray Raton, who doubted that they killed Eddie Guyton in the beginning, eventually became a believer. The man's in a rest home, but his mind clicks pretty darned good. He's convinced that they also killed Silas' younger brother, Patrick, who went to Louisiana Tech on a band scholarship. They found Patrick dead in his car, wrapped around a pine tree. Raton's pretty sure that a Badou probably ran him off the road. He told me, 'That's how they operate. You can't pin 'em down to nothing.' Anyway, Mitty, let's enjoy tonight and I'll fill you in on details tomorrow."

"You bet, Tammy. Tell your mama to expect us," I said, as a chant began to fill Little Queenie's with "Pete, Pete, Pete, Pete".

Pete's face beamed. He truly appeared overwhelmed. "Come on, Mitty, let's take it on home."

We took the stage and rounded up those that banged out the first set with us, and away we went. We smoked Little Walter's instrumentals "Off The Wall" and "Rocker" and then segued into an original Pete Bolden shuffle, with him hitting vocal vibratos that pumped the crowd and had them bouncing as if helium filled their souls.

As Pete rocked back with the microphone stand with harp in hand, all eyes and ears tuned him in and turned him on. Pete fired off the fattest, nastiest blues licks ever played in Little Queenie's. "*Good God Almighty!*" That's all that came to mind as I watched my friend completely engulfed in his element. Then I caught a sight that snapped my head around. There was the dreadlocked stranger, standing only a few feet from Tammy's chair, with his sun-shades aimed at the stage. No feet tapping, body swaying, head bobbing—no movement.

Crowd shouts of "Pete, Pete, Pete, Pete..." brought my attention back to the stage. Pete staring at me, and me finally realizing that he expected a solo from me. Took me a minute to catch the groove again, but I whipped out some triplets and double stops and slapped a few notes, while looking for Mr. Dreadlocks, who had vanished again. The guitarist took us all home with rapid-fire tasty licks, and the crowd screamed for more, more, more, as we took our bows, said our thanks and stepped off to back slaps and high fives and hugs all around.

Tammy came up and bear-hugged me, said she wanted to head to her mom's so she wouldn't have to compete with a club full of drinkers for road rights. She said that she hadn't noticed any dreadlocked man.

"You really think that he's one of our suspects?" she asked.

"Maybe not a suspect, but suspicious," I said as the crowd began milling around, some of them cornering Pete. My eyes scanned the club. "Just a gut hunch."

"Still got the instincts, huh? Sorry that I wasn't more alert, but you and Pete had me mesmerized with the blues," she said as she gave me a tight hug. "I'll see you tomorrow."

Pete worked his way over to me with fans still grabbing at a hand to shake and said, "Where did your mind wander off to in the middle of my masterpiece?"

"Didn't you see the re-entry of our man of mystery?" I said.

Pete frowned as he looked at me and said, "No. Sorry Mitty. I got really caught up in the tunes during that last set. Should we go looking for him?'

"I don't think that we'd find him. We need to watch our backs," I said and realized that I hadn't told Pete that I had my Ruger LCP.380 strapped to my ankle. "If you're not packing Pete, then stay close, because I am. This cat might have taken the bait before we even set a trap."

"Geez, Mitty," Pete said as Red walked up and caught the tail end of the conversation, "You ever known me not to pack a piece? I'm from the old school, remember?"

Red grabbed my hand, pulled me towards him, and said, "Count me in, Mitty. Bobby T and I had our differences, but I loved him like a brother. Nabbing murdering bastards while beating drums in your band sounds like a win-win deal to me. Just let me get my paws on them."

Pete just winked at me as Red volunteered his services. He realized what an asset Johnnie Red brought to the table. We'd have a one-man wrecking crew watching our backs.

Looking at Pete again and then at Red, I said, "I'm assuming that Pete recruited you, Red. And that you know something about those dangerous gentlemen that we pursue."

"Affirmative, there, Mitty Boy," Red said, wrapping a large arm around my shoulders. "They'll never know what hit 'em if they come after us. So, as I said, count me the hell in."

CHAPTER 27

We had just finished packing up our equipment. Pete had convinced me to stay over at his house after our great jam and he took off ahead of me. Franklin and I chatted for awhile and thirty minutes later I finally got going.

Tammy's plea hit me while I was driving down Waugh Drive. "Uncle Mitty. Uncle Mitty. Can you hear me, Uncle Mitty?" Tammy's voice asked on my cell phone.

"What's up Tammy? Yeah, you are loud and clear," I said.

"A telephone pole and my jeep met up with each other on Bissonnet. Just before you get into Mission Bend," Tammy said quite calmly for someone who had just been in a wreck.

"Are you okay?" I tried to remember how much Tammy had been drinking. "Maybe I can get to you before the police. DWIs can dampen career aspirations."

"The police are here, ambulance is coming, but I'm not drunk. I'm pretty sure that one of our asshole suspects ran me off the road. Probably your dreadlocked friend. I filled the back end of his car with lead from my Walther. Don't think I hit him, though, because he hooked a left on FM 1876 and hauled ass," she reported.

"OK, I'm on my way," I said, swinging my truck up onto U.S. Highway 59 to take a freeway route over to Bissonnet.

A patrol car and an ambulance lit up that part of Southwest Houston. Flashing lights always frighten me. As far as I'm concerned, the odds that the multi-color strobes represent anything good are infinitesimal. I pulled to a stop, and saw Tammy shaking her head "NO" as a couple of EMS attendants bandaged her head and arm. They had already wrapped a swath of gauze around her forehead, and I heard one say, "That head injury just might be more extensive that you realize, miss. You should go to the emergency room."

Tammy saw me and told them, "Thanks for fixing my wounds, guys. My uncle just pulled up and he can take it from here." They shrugged, finished wrapping Tammy's arm and loaded their gear.

One of the two HPD patrolmen inquired about my involvement in the accident. The patrolman looked to be in his thirties: maybe my pro-police articles in the *Gazette* years would loosen up what seemed to be a tense situation. But he had no clue who James Phillip Andersen was. I felt irrelevant.

"Mr. Andersen, your niece discharged a firearm on a public Houston street," the man in blue said to me in an official tone. "She didn't volunteer that information. We found a recently-fired Walther P-38 beneath her back driver's side tire. She does have a concealed weapons permit, but we're still taking statements."

The officer stepped away to confer with his partner.

Tammy shrugged. "I told them that someone tried to kill me by banging me off the road. I sure as hell didn't know if they planned to U-turn for another try. I made damned sure that they kept driving."

She bobbed her head up and down for emphasis. Her crop of reddish blond hair plumed and waved wildly above the huge wad of gauze around her head. She looked like Woody Woodpecker.

I chuckled involuntarily and she glared at me. One of the officers caught the glare and smiled as he said, "Well Mr. Andersen, my boss remembers you well enough."

Before he could say more, the radio in the patrol car crackled. One officer checked it out, came back and said, "A call just came in. There's a bullet-riddled car ditched behind a Target store a couple of miles from here. Appears to be a stolen 2003 Buick LeSabre. No bodies, no blood, so I guess they live another day, but sounds as if they barely dodged your shots."

The officers swapped additional information with us and the tow truck driver who had arrived, then left.

Tammy had called her mom—several times, so Jean Tarleton knew that Tammy had dodged a bullet as well. Both insisted that at that late hour that I should stay with them. Pete lived pretty much clear across town from Jean's home, so I agreed. I called to let him know what was what.

Jean hugged Tammy as we walked through the door, and then gave her hell for not going to the hospital. "Sorry, Mitty, but mothers do have the prerogative of being mothers regardless of whether their children have gotten too big for their britches."

"I totally agree," I said, as Jean grabbed me and hugged me and held on a little too long for my comfort.

"Been way too long of a day for me," Tammy said as she headed down the hallway. "Thanks loads, Uncle Mitty. You are my savior."

"Yeah, right. If someone needs to save you, then we're all in a heap of trouble," I said. "We'll talk tomorrow."

When Jean asked if I cared for a nightcap, I told her, "Sure, I haven't had my customary second drink of the night. Whatever you're having is fine."

Which turned out to be a double shot of Chivas on the rocks.

We sipped slowly and said little. There was a comfort to the silence, though. My eyes roamed around the familiar living room. New overstuffed leather furniture replaced the mix-and-match furniture I remembered. The walls were a different color. It reminded me that it had been a while since my last visit.

Jean broke the silence, "Tammy's Louisiana trip convinces me that those Badous killed Bobby. No doubt about it. These people are evil bad. Maybe the authorities should handle things. They will kill you, Mitty."

Jean was more than slightly drunk. She slurred her words, and her eyes swam unfocused. She pulled the Chivas bottle from the lamp table next to her chair and began to top her drink off.

I got up. "Hey, Jean, why don't we call it a night?"

"You just go on off to bed, Mitty. I may need just one more," Jean said. Her head bobbed a little, as she pushed herself to her feet. "I made up Tess' old room for you."

"Okay, I'm exhausted. I'm looking forward to visiting with you tomorrow, Jean," I said.

She flung her arms around my neck, pressed herself to me and tilted her beautiful face up toward mine. The feeling of a woman clinging to me almost ripped my moral compass off its pedestal, and the warm Chivas glow invited me to lean down and meet the sensuality missing from my life for much too long.

Another Chivas and my kiss would not have landed on Jean's forehead, and I would not have said, "I love you too, Jean. I'll see you in the morning."

Tammy coaxed me into the kitchen with the smell of bacon frying, and she handed me a cup of vanilla-flavored coffee in a large pink mug. Both challenged my sense of taste. She no longer had gauze wrapped around her head, but just a large bandage held in place with paper tape in the center of her forehead. She bubbled enthusiasm, and her bright yellow blouse speckled with red flowers sent a cheerful vibe through the small room.

Jean, on the other hand, had shuffled in slowly on puppy dog slippers and a well-worn blue robe. She looked my way with sad and embarrassed eyes. When Tammy left the room, Jean said, "Mitty...." I held up a hand to stop her and my eyes told her--*enough said*. We both knew that what could have happened could easily *have* happened, but the results would have been disastrous. Her mourning for Bobby would be a long, long process. The Chivas stepped in her path last night.

Tammy returned and looked at her mom, then at me, then back at her mom, and I said, "Okay, now, tell me about your adventures in bayou country."

"Let me get some huevos rancheros cooking, and we'll eat first," she said. "Since moving to San Antonio, I can cook the hell out of Mexican food, Uncle Mitty."

Tammy and I ate the hell out of her Mexican type breakfast, as Jean sat and picked at her plate until Tammy said, "Mom, you've got to start eating better and taking care of yourself. I'm grieving here too. Good square meals will help keep you on track."

Jean took a big bite of eggs and mumbled, "You're right, sweetie. I know that. My mind just won't work right, but I'll work on it. Don't worry about me."

Tammy refused my offer to clear the table and do the dishes, and Jean told both of us to take our coffee into the living room and get our 'rap session' started.

"*Rap session?* Now does that date my mom or what?" Tammy said as she pulled out a shoulder bag filled with her reporter's notebooks. She added, "Where do you want me to begin?"

"Makes no difference to me," I said.

Tammy began with Leonard Badou's severed vocal chords.

"The story goes that Joe Badou tracked down the wife-stealing harmonica player at a gig in Vicksburg, Mississippi. He was peddling cedar fence posts and Leonard was with him.

"Joe inquired about harmonica players in every town he passed through, and he found his guy-- Glenwood Stokely --playing at a place called Pearl's on the banks of the Mississippi."

"Wait a minute," I said. "You said Stokely? Wow. Damon Stokely is one of the latest additions to our list of deceased harp players. Glenwood was

Damon's dad. Wow! It also means that Crazy Joe's wife could have been Damon's mother. Too weird to think about."

Tammy didn't look a bit surprised, but she said, "That's a lot of speculation. Anyway, witnesses said that Joe came into the club with a gun demanding to know where he could find his wife. Stokely said he had no idea because the whore dumped him in an East Texas lumber camp. Well, that made Joe Badou real mad and he fired at Stokely as he ran out the door. Leonard followed, hollering bloody murder and waving a knife. Once outside, Stokely grabbed Leonard, took the knife, and put it to Leonard's throat. Witnesses stated that Joe fired at Stokely with no regard for the safety of his son and after some struggle, Stokely cut Leonard's throat."

"Anyone get arrested?"

"No. The police took Joe in for questioning and took Leonard to the hospital. Joe's shots missed Stokely, who fled the scene before the police arrived. They charged Joe with disorderly conduct, took his load of cedar posts, and ordered him to get the hell out of Vicksburg and to never return," she said.

"I'm figuring that seeing the man who stole his wife and cut his son's throat walk away didn't sit well with Joe," I said.

"You've got it," Tammy said. "Joe went off the deep end after that and began earning that 'Crazy Joe' nickname in sincerity. He claimed that he killed every harmonica player that crossed his path. No one really took him seriously."

"What about the so-called accident that killed Patrick Guyton?" I asked.

"Okay, it's just my opinion, but that just may be the first instance that Joe Badou's sons got into the game after Crazy Joe met his maker. The Ruston Police Department investigation says that it appeared that Patrick simply ran off the road, down a steep embankment, square into a tree, and died on impact.

"Ray Raton said that he had his doubts and asked a colleague from the Lincoln Parish Sheriff's office to delve a little deeper, but found nothing could be proven. Sort of like my run in with that guy last night," Tammy said.

"So, Raton became a believer at some point?" I asked.

"Ray Raton said he became a believer after he had to arrest Silas Guyton for Joe Badou's murder," Tammy said with excitement flashing in her eyes. "He felt that Silas shouldn't have taken matters in his own hands. But the more he looked into the case, the more he felt that maybe Silas had reasons to act as he had. He believed Silas when he told him that the Badou boys gloated about murdering his dad.

"Ray tried hard to discover enough evidence to convict the Badous and uncovered nothing that put them at the scene, and they all fled the Parish, except for Davey, whom they had in custody."

Tammy rustled through her notes. "Davey ended up back in Alexandria after a stint in the juvenile criminal system. An elderly aunt from his mother's side agreed to take him in after his release, and he proved to be nothing but bad news.

"There's a statement on record from her after he allegedly attempted to burn the school down. Someone piled up books and desks in his classroom and set a fire. An alert citizen spotted the smoke and damage stayed confined to the one room. Davey's aunt provided a solid alibi, and he skated by that offence. His penchant for playing with fire became public, when he and a younger cousin doused a neighbor's cat with gasoline and set it ablaze."

"Dear God," I said.

Tammy said, "There's more. The cat ran into a hay-filled barn and torched it. The barn backed up onto one of those new—for then—housing developments and half the houses in the development burned to the ground.

"Davey disappeared, and his cousin, Dwayne Bellow, told authorities that he didn't have anything to do with the fire. He said that he just watched Davey. However, Bellow has a string of convictions for burglary, auto theft, and convenience store robberies."

Tammy said, "OK, here's where our coincidences begin tying together. Bellow ended up in East Texas and continued his bad habits until he received a sentence that would keep him in the Terrell Unit of the Texas Department of Corrections for a long time. Here's the kicker: Michael Ray Melton and Silas Guyton both served time at the Terrell prison."

Chapter 28

Our un-named band headed to Snowball's Place without a guitarist. Pete and I figured that with two harps huffing and puffing that maybe we could bounce enough rhythmic tones around to get by until we found a suitable string picker. Pete had suggested Charles Biddy, the young gun from Little Queenie's jam, but I refused to get him involved.

"No, Pete," I had said, "we need someone more grizzled and hardened, someone, like the rest of us, who wants to find out who killed Bobby T. We want someone who's willing to risk themselves to pursue that goal."

Pete agreed and said, "Yeah, we should just put good friends at risk."

I frowned my meanest scowl his way and meant it.

"Joking, Mitty. Just joking, okay? Let's just have some fun."

Pete picked up Red and his drum kit, since we couldn't fit us and all of our equipment in one vehicle. We planned to stay in Mary's boarding rooms. Our bass player, Buddy Kirkland, would drive the forty five miles from his house in Tomball each day for practice.

On the way down, I called Detective Thompson—privately—to let him in on our plans while in his jurisdiction. He didn't like it at all, but knew that we had our minds dead set on carry through with The Wizard's band plan.

"I heard about the Austin harmonica player," he said "and looked into it a little. The detective in charge of the case discounts the drug deal gone bad scenario. Everyone they interviewed said that the boy had no bad habits. No drugs, no drinking, no smoking, and loved by all. Random shooting? The execution style has them puzzled.

"I mentioned the idea of a marauding band of serial killers stalking harmonica players and as expected, he had a good laugh. But they've kept the investigation open and active.

"Mitty (that's the first time that he didn't refer to me as Mr. Andersen), if these guys killed the Austin dude, then I would say that *they* are the ones doing the baiting. My experience tells me that crazy bastards that do such things will do such things. These guys have outsmarted some smart people, and maybe it just ain't too smart to try to match wits with them. My advice? Leave it alone, Mitty."

He knew that he had not talked me out of my plans because I said, "The problem is that they've been running under the radar of the law way too long. Maybe they've gotten over-confident and we'll get 'em. Maybe they'll leave us the hell alone. In that case, we'll still get to play some blues in the bad-ass band that we're taking on the road."

Detective Thompson called me stubborn and stupid, but in the end just wished me luck and hung up.

I pulled into Snowball's Place. I didn't see my *compadres*. The sun reflecting off the caliche gravel parking lot blinded me, and intense heat rays slapped me as I stepped from the cool comfort of my pickup. Bo came out into the parking lot, grinning, and after an enthusiastic handshake, he helped me unload my amp and gear.

"You look a little better than the last time I saw you," he said, grinning widely. His chipped tooth made his mouth appear slightly goofy.

Mary hollered at us over the strains of Guitar Slim wailing on "Things I Used To Do". "Y'all can just leave all your amps and stuff plugged in on the stage. I won't book anyone 'til you're done practicing. I reckon that my customers will be mighty happy just listening to you guys play."

I heard insistent banging at the back door, behind the stage. Mary swung the doors open to reveal Pete and Red standing there with drum cases in their arms.

"My Good Gosh Almighty! I haven't seen your smiling face, for what? Ten years or more," Mary said, as she bear-hugged her stout self around Pete's skinny frame, drum cases and all.

"No, I guess it's been more like fifteen years since I last crossed your path," Pete said, flashing a smile at her. "Good to see you again, sweet lady. I hope we ain't putting you out none."

She still had him gripped firmly and said, "Oh, you hush that talk. You know that *mi casa es su casa*. When did you start wearing glasses? Makes you look like a professor or something. How's Beatrice doing? You still preaching? Why don't y'all move out of that damn big city and join us country folks? Don't you have better sense than to get mixed up with all this crazy stuff? "

Pete laughed and looked at Bo, "She hasn't changed a bit, has she Bo?"

Bo grinned widely and shook his head.

"Well, anyone crazy enough to follow Mitty down his dark road will get the royal treatment, and the place belongs to all of you," she said. "Anyone hungry?"

We declined and set up and began fooling around with Mary's stage sound system. Bo lent his experience from many nights of running sound for Mary. The Silvertone sounded mighty sweet, and Pete had set up his original '59 Fender Bassman and had it dialed in to elicit superb tones, full of fat and grit.

We took a break at five-thirty. Buddy had not shown yet. Pete checked his cell and saw that he had a missed message from our bass player.

"Don't bother returning the call from your phone, Pete. No service, remember," I said, and Pete went to use Mary's phone behind the bar.

From the look on Pete's face as he talked to Buddy, I knew that the news wasn't good. Pete hung up and said, "Buddy's out."

"I thought that Buddy had a personal stake in all of this with his Aunt Tilley's story and all," I said to Pete.

Pete nodded, but said, "That's just it. He believes in that story, and also believes that some kind of Bad Juju surrounds our plans. He thinks that we're all going to die."

"Bad juju?" I said. "What? Buddy believes in black cat bones and voodoo stuff?"

"One hundred percent," Pete said. "He thought that he could whip his superstitions and hang with us, but it seems the wicked Mojo got the best of him."

I hung my head and said, "Can't blame him. I wrestled with all this myself and still have my own doubts."

"Yeah, that's basically what I told him and that we had no hard feelings for his decision to bail, but damn, now we have no bass player to go along with no guitar player," Pete said, looking as low as I did.

"I can play bass with you guys."

We both looked Bo's way. "Hey, no sweat. I've got a Fender bass guitar back over in my room and an amp and everything. Heck, I offered to play with The Wizard, but he said no."

We both looked at Mary, who said, "Yeah, Bo can play the hell out of the bass. He's whomped it at more than a few jams here."

"You've been holding out on us? How come we're just now finding out that Bo Vega can pluck a bass?" I asked.

"Nobody asked, and you guys seemed to be squared away," he said.

We sent Bo off for his stuff, and he came back with an Ampeg bass rig and Fender P Bass guitar, and he and Red soon had the bottom end of our band anchored.

Bo was darn good, and I'd wished I had my camera to capture the wide smile on his face, and Pete's, and hell, mine too. A smattering of after-work beer drinkers hooted, whistled, and clapped after every song. For the next hour, the cares of Mitty's Gritty Blues Band melted away as we set to smoking the blues.

"Hey, guys, we've got to come up with a band name," I said during a break. "It can't be named after just me."

Behind me a deep voice said, "How about Pistol Pete and the Pistoleros?"

I turned around and saw the large man that matched the voice walking towards the stage with an amp in one big hand and a guitar case in the other.

"Or maybe The Wizard's Brew," said a smiling Benny Williams, the Billet County sheriff's deputy from Michael's murder scene. He wore an untucked, striped bowling shirt and sandals. No one looked less like a police officer.

Suzie had said that she would leave me if I ever wore a bowling shirt or a Hawaiian shirt and sandals. She claimed that every middle-aged white blues fan in America adopted them as a uniform, a replacement for the less comfortable Blues Brothers stereotypical dark suit, skinny tie, and sunshades. I had to find something to wear in between the two extremes. Benny looked fine, though.

I didn't know Benny well enough to offer a hug, I extended my hand. He hugged me, though, and said, "Heard you guys could use a guitar player and maybe an extra gunslinger."

Pete looked puzzled as Benny continued, "Mr. Andersen, The Wizard showed me how to play this thing and I think that I'm damned good. When Michael got out of prison, I volunteered to play in the band that he tried to get together. He not only said no, but said, 'Hell, no, Benny. If something happened to you on account of me, I could never, ever look your mother in the eye again,' and that was that.

"Then Detective Thompson called and told me what you guys planned on doing and he thought it might be a good idea to have an unofficial official along for the ride. An off-duty assignment, if you will. I had planned to talk my way into being a second guitarist for you guys and then Mary called and told me that you didn't have a picker at all."

Benny lifted his very heavy blackface Fender Super Reverb up to the stage as easily as if it were made of cardboard.

Pete looked at me and looked at Benny. I made hasty introductions.

Benny said, "Well, Mr. Andersen, are we gonna play some blues or what?"

"When will when you stop calling me Mr. Andersen? It's Mitty to you," I said. "Plug that Strat in and let's see what you've got."

"Wait just a damn minute," Mary yelled from the kitchen behind the bar. "Somebody's going sit their butts down right now and eat this mess of barbeque ribs, or heads will be rolling."

We grinned at each other and sat down.

Red beans and rice accompanied the ribs, along with cornbread to push the food around with and sop up bean juice. Very shortly we all had barbeque sauce covering our hands and faces regardless of how many extra napkins we asked for. Everyone washed theirs down with beer, except Pete and I. Mary's sweet tea fit the bill for us.

We lit into Rod Piazza's "Murder in the First Degree," which seemed appropriate for the occasion, after filling our bellies. Pete and I both tried to eat light because it can be uncomfortable huffing and puffing into a harmonica after a full meal. Mary's meal proved to be too tempting to pull back on, so we worked through our rumbling bellies with me singing and Pete providing excellent harp fills.

Benny nailed down just the right licks right off the bat. He bobbed when needed and weaved when we wanted. He proved that he had the knack for backing harmonica players, which eludes a lot of guitarists. After nodding at him to take a solo, he threw down some tasty, nasty blues licks. He squeezed the tones from his strings with just the right touch.

"Damn, man, that's some kind of picking," Pete said, after the song ended and he slapped his back.

"I owe all that I know to The Wizard," Benny said. "and that's why I'm here."

We had us a blues band now. The crowd had picked up considerably throughout the evening, and no one wanted to leave Snowball's Place even though most had to get to work the next morning. We gave them everything that they could possibly ask for in a blues band as we covered Muddy, the Wolf, Elmore James, Magic Sam, and every harmonica player that they could possibly know about. Bo and Benny had it going on unbelievably well. We sounded like we'd been playing together for years. We'd gotten lucky—the right musicians with the right skills and something else—a shared *desire* to play all out.

We all rode the wave that washed the blues throughout Snowball's, until Mary pulled the plug at midnight—the lawful witching hour to cease alcohol sales. She just said, "Go to bed, guys. Get up and do it again tomorrow or take it on the road. You sound darn good already."

Mary fed us the next morning with one of her huge country breakfasts, and after a break to digest it, we plugged in and spent the day working up a solid set list. Red showed Benny some tricks of the trade for providing a solid blues bottom to the rhythm section. Pete and I decided who would sing which songs, with me arguing that he take the bulk of the vocals. My voice was a squawk compared to Pete Bolden's. He refused to work out harp parts because he firmly believed in being 'in the moment' and improvising the blues, and I agreed to try and hang with him.

By the third day of woodshedding, we had a solid list of tunes that could get us through a three-set gig. We even talked Benny into singing a few, and he turned our heads with his deep-voiced soulful vocals. I volunteered to bail out of the singing department since Pete and Benny had the real goods, but they wanted my gritty ass voice on some of the gutbucket, down-in-the-alley blues songs. They might as well fire me, I told them.

"Let me just be the water boy or manager or something," I said.

"Hell no, we ain't firing you, and I know that you can't manage doodly squat," Pete said. "You can't quit either. Face it; you're just going to have to get better. Besides, this is your band.

"By the way, what's our name? And don't say, 'The Pete Bolden Blues Band' or I'll pull my piece."

"Pete and the Mitty Grittys?"

"Gritty Pete and the River Bottom Blues Band?"

I had an idea, "How about *The Re-Pete-rs*? Spell it with Pete's name in the middle."

They all looked at me and said, "Huh?"

I wrote it down for them. "See... *The Re-PETE-rs...* ?"

"Why not just 'The Repeaters'? There a good play on Pete's name in there for those in the know," Mary hollered from the bar.

Red raised his big right hand and said, "That's got my vote."

Bo and Benny both said, "Aye," and raised both hands.

"Done," I said, as Pete just sat there with a look that said that we'd just ramrodded something past him.

Chapter 29

Vast quantities of pancakes, scrambled eggs, and pork sausage greeted us for our last morning at Snowball's Place. Red pleaded for more practice time, saying that "The Repeaters" needed more polish. We saw through that ruse and knew that the fantastic food had hooked him. Mary presented the biggest obstacle to our departure.

"Now, damn it," she said, leveling fierce eyes with mine. "Why the hell ain't y'all playing your first gig here at Snowball's?"

We had been over and over the fact that Little Queenie's had dibs on our first gig and Mary seemed to understand that on the first day of our arrival. I thought that Mary feared for Bo, now that he belonged to us as much as her.

"Mary, we've been entertaining Snowball's customers for three days running. They've got to be tired of us by now. I'll bet they'll be glad to come in after a hot day to have a cool one and not have to listen to our noise," I reasoned and motioned her away from the rest of the band and out of earshot of Bo.

"We'll take damn good care of Bo. I told you to book our gig three weeks from now," I said.

She scoffed and said, "I ain't worried about no Bo. He's a grown man and can take care of himself." Then she paused, furrowed her brow, and said, "Yeah. I am worried. About all of you, and Bo especially. Mitty, you don't know if you can take damn good care of Bo or yourself or any of these guys, because you don't know what those crazy bastards will do next. None of you may be around three weeks from now."

"I'm frightened too. We just hope that we can catch these guys in the act. Then maybe we can get someone out there to investigate these murders," I said.

"I just hope you don't die trying," Mary said and walked back to the table to eat a mess of pancakes herself.

As I walked back over to finish my breakfast, Pete asked, "Did you get a hold of Franklin?"

"Yeah, we're booked to play Friday and Saturday at Little Queenie's. He called Don Deal, and I figure that he'll play up the return of Pete Bolden to the blues scene in his entertainment column today. We should have a pretty substantial crowd," I told him. "Franklin has us lined up to play PJ's in Fort Worth next Thursday and some dump in Dallas on Friday and then Booster's

Club in Shreveport the following Friday and his cousin's place in Baton Rouge on Saturday. We might can pick up something in between on our own."

Red looked at me with arched eyebrows and said, "How did Franklin round up so many bookings so quickly? I thought that we'd be lucky to get a couple of gigs this month."

"Summer months are slow for the clubs because all the big boys play the festival circuit. Besides, Franklin knows the club owners well enough to get favors granted. That reminds me. Booster's turned karaoke, but the owner remembers Pete and figures plenty of old fans will show up, so he's on board. So we've got us a road trip," I said.

⌁

"The Repeaters" rocked Little Queenie's. The blues elite showed up and things got ridiculous—we had a standing ovation at the end of every song. The woodshedding at Snowball's paid off and had tightened up our grooves, and we were hitting on all cylinders. Though we could play and do it pretty damn good, the crowd aimed most of their love towards Pete. He ate it up and pulled out all the stops.

At the end of the first set, fans and media types swamped Pete and peppered him with questions. They toted old Pete Bolden albums, with real vinyl records, up to him for a signature. I felt like a proud papa. It did my heart good to see Don Deal standing in line awaiting his turn, with a little help from a burly, big armed aficionado who insisted that he wait after he tried to muscle his way ahead of Pete's admirers.

"Good job, Mitty," Franklin said, approaching the stage.

"The band's on fire, huh, Franklin?" I said while tapping saliva out of one of my harmonicas. Damn thing balked on hole three during Little Walter's "Blues With A Feeling".

"Damn right the band's on fire," he said, "but I'm talking about getting Pete back in action. He sounds like he never left. Hell, he's sounds better than I've ever heard him. He sings with a deeper, clearer voice with no drugs getting in the way. Where the hell did you come up with the guitarist? He's got the goods."

"Yeah, Benny's our ace in the hole. And he's a cop," I said.

"Smart move, there, Mitty Boy," Franklin said as he slapped my back. "I've kept my eyes peeled and haven't seen hide nor hair of your dreaded dreadlocked dude."

"Yeah, all the band members have a cue to hit on their instruments when anyone sees something that might represent evil," I said, "and there have been no sightings yet. Thanks for the lookout."

"Hey, you know that I've always got your back," Franklin said as he walked from the stage and hollered at a waitress to quit visiting and to get her butt moving.

Pete still had a gaggle of fans surrounding his table when Red hit a drum roll, signaling second set, all hands on deck. We hit the second set harder than the first and coaxed Pete into doing most of the singing and into doing a couple of his originals, and the crowd responded with raucous whoops, whistles, and hog hollers. We barreled into the third set of the night without a pause. We had 'em and they had us. Benny backed Pete vocally and Pete backed Benny, and when they hit a dual phrase together, the crowd ignited into overdrive with their chants egging the two to greater heights. "The Repeaters" ruled the night.

CHAPTER 30

With the special addition of Sallie Ray Melton, "The Repeaters" ruled Little Queenie's again on Saturday night. She hid back in the shadows until Franklin pushed her up on stage. We scrambled to back her up. Bless her, she chose to sing old standards like "Didn't It Rain" and "Ball and Chain" that any bluesman worth his salt would know.

Franklin removed all the tables in his club to allow a standing room only crowd to squeeze in. Our fan's feet took up every inch of tile. There was no room to dance and everyone jiggled up and down in place. I glanced at the tip jars, which were overflowing.

Sallie gave us all a hug. "I had to come down and listen to y'all. Didn't plan on getting up on stage, so thanks for being gracious, boys."

Benny said it was his honor to be on the stage with blues royalty and Sallie Ray actually ducked her eyes down and thanked him politely. It meant a lot to her to hear that from him.

Sallie Ray remembered Benny from the old days, watching him sit at her brother's feet, mesmerized by Michael Ray's picking. They shared lots of old times after she graced our stage. He beamed when she told him that she recognized Michael Ray in his playing. I spotted wet eyes on them both of them before they parted ways.

She thanked us some more and wished us luck and said she had to duck out. After Tammy's experience, I wouldn't let her leave alone. Pete insisted that she stay at his house and she didn't argue.

Those two nights kicked our tour off on a hell of a good note and as we drove toward Fort Worth, we were still basking in the warmth shown us by the weekend's blues fans. Made me glad to be alive and washed away the nasty gunk that had adhered to my soul over the past few weeks.

Bo and I rode in my pickup, followed by Pete's van with Red, Benny, and our gear aboard. My pickup always pulled to the right on IH35 upon approaching the town of West, and never let me proceed until I stopped at the Czech Bakery for a few of their famous kolaches. Everything in West, at least near the freeway, had a Czech theme. The Czech Inn motel never ceased to bring a smile to my face. After loading up on poppy seed, peach, apple, fig, and sausage kolaches, we had our sustenance for the rest of the trip.

PJ's Bar and Grill on Bailey Street, just out of downtown Fort Worth, had been a popular stop for the past twenty years of every blues act touring the country. Franklin worked hard at getting us booked in on a Thursday night. The weekends would have been out of the question. Franklin called in a favor from club owner P.J. Powell and the local band booked for Thursdays had agreed to step aside for the one night.

I had been to PJ's a number of times to catch blues artists who stopped coming to Houston, which seemed to be way too much in the past five years.

Architecturally, the club had nothing special going for it. Metal building, painted cement floor, rows of long, wooden, folding tables with folding metal chairs, and a run-of-the-mill bar. A big stage took up most of one wall, and the top-of-the-line sound system showcased what was best about PJ's—the musicians. The best damn blues club in Texas booked the best damn blues artists in the country, which made them the best damn blues club in Texas.

P.J. himself met us at the door. I found out that he and Pete went back a ways. P.J. said, "Franklin filled me in on the scheme you guys have cooking and I just hope whoever killed Big Joey shows up. It'll be the last blues music they'll ever hear."

He had us sit down, explaining that his sound man hadn't shown yet and that he'd do his best to do the sound check. P.J. looked like the professional tight end that he used to be. He was tall, built sturdy as a fence post, with long, thick fingers at the end of powerful hands. He wore his long gray hair pulled back into a pony tail and his clean shaven face looked as if it had been punched upon by a prize fighter.

Our conversation ebbed and flowed here and there, and P.J. had questions, "Bobby T's death started all this stuff? I thought he overdosed? And I thought they killed those animals who lynched The Wizard. I never did believe that Michael had anything to do with Big Joey's murder."

I did my best to answer. "Bobby T never did dope and that got Pete and I looking into things. The whole mess just snowballed and all roads lead to this vicious family of cutthroats. The Wizard convinced me that the Badous framed him for Big Joey's death," I said and told a waitress that dropped by the table that I'd take a non-alcoholic brew. "Then they set up the meth heads for killing Michael. The meth heads got shot in the Brazos River bottom and, officially, that's the end of it. Pretty slick move on the Badou's part. No one's looking for them but us now."

"If they took out Bobby T and The Wizard," he said with a great deal of bravado in his voice, "then I really really hope that they show their skanky faces around here tonight. Hey, Franklin told me that 'The Repeaters' broke a club record for crowds at Little Queenie's. The word's out here, Pete. I think fans will swoop down on PJ's like the west Texas wind tonight."

They did just that. "The Repeaters" repeated as successful a gig as Little Queenie's, except with twice the crowd. Pete had them swooning—well not exactly swooning, because blues fans don't swoon—but they were with him 100% when he hit Little Walter's "Fast Boogie" and then slid seamlessly into "Key To The Highway". They were with us all the way to 2 a.m. and begged for more.

Nary a threatening look nor suspicious character showed during the evening. Pete fielded as many fans during the breaks as he had in Houston. Quite a few cornered Benny and myself also and quizzed us about our equipment and instruments. The clientele proved to be very knowledgeable blues fans. We took turns walking out into the parking lot in an attempt to lure evil out of the shadows. Someone always covered us by watching through the back door. P.J. employed the largest bouncer that I'd ever seen, and he had our backs also. Nothing. No one. Nada.

Nothing happened the next night in Dallas either, where "The Repeaters" played to a sparse crowd of twenty somethings at Swinky Dinks. The club supposedly hosted blues in the past, but now catered to bar-hopping clients who became bored easily. The few who remained with us were fans of John Mayer and Jack White and had an inkling as to what we were doing, and we did win them over. They restored my faith in America's youth and their taste in music.

We had time to kill between gigs, and we hit a couple of jams around Dallas. We played with some awesome musicians, and kept our profile high, in hopes of drawing our evil friends out. Pete and Benny kicked it up a notch once the local jam slingers challenged them and proved quickly that no one could touch them.

The guys knew that our gig money didn't cover the expense of hanging between gigs, but I had let them know up front that I would take care of that end of things. They squawked, but I insisted.

Pete complained that I kept him up all night snoring at our Best Western, and I told him that since I didn't snore that he had to be spinning a lie.

"Okay," he said adamantly, "I'll get one of those cheap tape recorders and we'll listen to you while we motor down the road."

"Tape recorders? What century are you living in? Why don't you just shoot a video of me with your cell phone?"

"Now that's a good idea," Pete said, pulling out his cell.

"I'll see if I can find some of those nose strips, and see if they work," I said as I wheeled us into an International House of Pancakes. They had an "All You Can Eat" pancake special, and Pete bet Benny that he could whip him at stuffing down pancakes.

I intervened and said, "Don't do it, Benny. Don't ever take such a challenge from someone with a hollow leg. I've seen Pete out-eat the best of them, and then eat a chicken fried steak an hour later. His skinny old butt fools people. Besides, I don't need any sick musicians on my hands."

But we all stuffed ourselves anyway before hitting IH20, heading east towards the Louisiana border. If the Badous were out there, we were driving onto their home turf.

Booster's in Shreveport turned into a real juke joint party. Its patrons, mostly middle-aged black folks, still considered it to still be a real juke joint and were set to throw down a good time. Booster's played Karaoke now, but it was Karaoke juke joint style. I think the club owner thrilled the patrons by bringing in a live blues band for a change.

Pete said that he had played the club many times back in the day, and that the lively, boisterous crowds always pumped up the atmosphere. Turned out that a large number of Booster's customers remembered Pete from those days. They put the word out and packed the place.

Pete and Benny grabbed 'em, held them down, and fed them full of what they had been waiting to hear—some damned fine blues singing. The short, stubby Bo and the tall, athletic Benny made a good Mutt and Jeff tandem when they leaned their backs against each other and plucked their strings. And when we got the dueling harp attack happening, the dancers literally shook the shack.

During our first set, a tall patron with close cropped salt and pepper hair, dressed in a tailored, embroidered cowboy type suit caught my eye. He sat, without much movement, and stared at us. No foot tapping, fingers snapping, or head bobbing that indicated that he might be enjoying our music. The red bandana around his neck drew my attention and had me thinking, *"Leonard Badou"* and had my pulse pounding. Towards the end of the set, I noticed that he had taken off his bandana. As soon as we got to a break, I walked as close to him as possible, to see if a scar stretched across his neck.

As I neared his table, he turned away from me, but suddenly reached out and grabbed my wrist with a strong grip and my pulse quickened. He said, "Say, you boys are pretty darned good. Y'all got a record out? I've got a little studio across town, and we could do something together if you guys don't have a contract signed. Those two black guys can sing their butts off. Tell 'em to come over and chat with me. Here's my card."

He had no scars, just the patter of someone filled with horse hockey.

Benny and Pete literally had my back and were standing right behind me. Benny fell sway to the BS, but Pete had been there and done that and knew better and pulled the man off Benny before any agreements were made.

"The Repeaters" could do no wrong that night in hot, steamy Shreveport. We fanned the flames during our last two sets, and the crowd just wouldn't let us leave. The club owner told us we could keep at it as long as we wanted. The hell with the law and he'd foot the tab. We blasted them with blues until three o'clock and the crowd hung with us. We worked every blues groove that we knew and turned Benny loose with a couple of Freddy King instrumentals. Sheer exhaustion finally called a halt to the evening, but we were exhilarated.

The night pumped all of us so high that I don't think we fell asleep before daylight. We barely managed to beat the eleven o'clock check-out time at our hotel.

We left the hilly, piney woods around Shreveport, and rolled across the flat, piney woods outside of Alexandria, which sat smack dab in the middle of the state and also sat along our route to Baton Rouge. Pete and I had decided to pay a visit to Ray Raton and pick his brain for a little more insight into the Badous.

Pete honked his horn and flashed his lights, and I pulled over across the street from Bringhurst Field, home to the Alexandria Aces of the Continental Baseball League, according to the information printed across the front entrance.

"Hey Mitty. The guys want to know if they can take in a ballgame while we visit that nursing home," Pete said. "Sign says they have a game in an hour."

Pete and I dropped the band off and headed over to meet up with a key figure from Silas Guyton's past.

It did not happen. The front desk lady at Pine Hollow Village informed us that Ray Raton had passed away two days ago. We tried to find out more, but since we weren't related, and had no official reason to be poking around, they shooed us away.

It seemed that Ray had no living relatives for us to question either. We dropped by Ray's former employer, the Rapides Parish Sheriffs' office, in hopes of gaining some kind of insight. The office staff exhibited plenty of friendly hospitality, but few remembered Ray Raton. A sheriff's deputy said that he knew of Ray, but he hadn't heard that he had passed away. He suggested that we check with the city police department, because some of their officers had once worked for the parish department.

We struck out with the city police and decided to join the rest of the band and watch the strikeouts that the Aces threw up against the Texarkana Gunslingers. Bo, Benny, and Red found enough shade from a second level overhang to shield them from the scorching afternoon heat. The shade and plenty of cold beer had put them in a jovial mood by the time we took a seat. I tried to enjoy the game, but my mind kept returning to Ray Raton, and whether he died naturally or not. *Were the Badous still one step ahead of us?*

Pete read my mind and said, "Pretty strange if those cats got to Raton right before we showed up. Don't you think?"

"Pretty damned strange describes every move they make," I said, looking around the stadium at the crowd. "They could be watching us right now and we'd never know it."

A chill wiggled up my spine.

We struck out in Baton Rouge, but the gig kicked it in a club frequented by LSU students. They had some appreciation for the blues, but were more interested in getting as drunk as possible as quick as possible. It didn't matter who stood on stage, as long as the beer stayed cold. Still no Badous.

Our little "gig-and-they-will-find-us" plan turned up nothing, though we had a blast and a half. We had a real blues band with real fans. We should have been thrilled. Why would we want a gang of murderous butchers show up?

Maybe because someone had to pay.

Red, Bo, and Benny begged us to stop off at a casino before we crossed back over into Texas We had time to kill, and checked into a couple of rooms at the Coushatta Casino outside of Lake Charles. Pete and I hung out and talked, while the gamblers did their thing. They did well and brought back an envelope full of money that they insisted that I take, but refused. Weeks later I found the envelope under the seat of my Silverado.

"Hell of little run there, huh, Mitty?" Pete said as we packed our bags at the hotel. "Maybe we oughta think about keeping this sweet thing going."

"Maybe, Pete. Right now we owe Mary Johnson one, so let's go light up Snowball's Place again," I said.

We crossed the Sabine River and decided to take Highway 105 out of Beaumont, instead of following IH10 through Houston. Avoiding massive traffic tangles would compensate for the additional miles on the route. With the rising sun at our backs, Pete stuck a Howlin' Wolf CD in the dashboard. The Wolf growled about getting up in the morning and hitting Highway 61 and my mind eased and cares dissolved—for the moment.

CHAPTER 31

I t looked like a hero's welcome for us at Snowball's Place. Cars over-flowed the parking lot and out along both sides of the road. The smell of barbeque filled the hot summer air, and customers had spilled out under the shade trees with their cold longnecks. Juke box blues seeped through the walls and mingled with the smoke from pits.

We pulled around back, parked in the loading zone, and walked in the back door. Everyone seemed to be off into their own party and no one seemed to notice us at all, except Mary. She came screaming around the bar and slammed Bo with a death grip style bear hug. His face beamed and bulged at the same time.

"Welcome back, guys. Oh, Bo, don't ever leave again, I really missed you," Mary said and I think Bo blushed, but I couldn't tell.

"Yeah, I see why too. This all looks like it took a ton of work to get together and you ain't used to doing that by yourself," he said to her.

"Oh, you hush now. I haven't had to lift much of a finger at all once the word got out that "The Repeaters" would be repeating themselves over here. Lots of folks just pitching in and helping out. They want a party," Mary said as she swept her arm around the room in amazement at the size of the crowd. "Did you see the chartered bus in the parking lot? Franklin got the blues soci-ety members to all chip in, and they loaded up and showed up here. Ain't this wonderful? Ain't this marvelous? And Bo's back."

Pete looked at me and said, "Hell, let's get after it, before Mary talks the ears off our heads."

We unloaded the gear, plugged in, got Bo to tweak the sound board and we were off and running though the bottom with the blues in the middle of the afternoon.

We could do no wrong in the eyes of the crowd at Snowball's. They hung on every note and every song we played. We hated sing-alongs, but the crowd sang along, so we orchestrated some gems on "Got My Mojo Working" and "Hoochie Coochie Man". We created a seismic event within the walls of Mary's place well before sundown, with a rip-roaring clientele instigating the shim-sham-shimmies. Then I thought I spotted him—our dreadlocked stranger.

It had been a fleeting glimpse of a head disappearing and reappearing within the ocean of bobbing, weaving heads in the club. I mentioned it to Pete between songs, and he hadn't seen him, but kept a wary eye out after that. During the break, we informed Red, Bo, and Benny to be on guard and tune in their radar.

Customers swamped us all with high fives, slaps on the back, and attaboys and it made looking for anyone specific impossible. My gut told me that this might be the night, and my nerves felt edgy, but alert. The mass of the crowd bothered me. The amount of alcohol being consumed bothered me more. The two together made for very unpredictable circumstances.

By ten o'clock, the mass of humanity rocked the club, and they seemed to sway in mass as one drunken wave, but had yet to get out of hand. Those who remained at midnight were the hard core party animals who normally could care less about who played on stage. We kept giving them what they wanted, until Mary flashed the 'Last Call' sign and we took it home with Benny lighting into "Hideaway" and Pete and I trading licks with him which left everyone saturated with joy by the time we stepped down to screams of "one more song".

We didn't dare push past Mary's closing. Besides, I wanted to make sure that our dreadlocked fan wasn't lurking around somewhere.

Pete and I went out the back door, Red headed out a side door, and Bo and Benny went out the front door to sweep the parking lot for any signs of our suspicious character hanging out. After partying down for hours, everyone looked a bit suspect after midnight, but most of the patrons headed to their vehicles and the parking lot quickly thinned out. Some of the customers had apparently not learned that having a designated driver on board could save them a lot of grief. There were plenty of fumbled keys stabbed at door locks. The authorities certainly could have filled the county jail.

No one spotted *our* buddy. Maybe I imagined seeing him in the club. No one else saw him. Oh well, I thought as Pete threw an arm around my shoulder and said, "Great gig tonight, wasn't it, old pal of mine?"

"Yeah, we smoked 'em on down, didn't we Pete?" I said. "Well, at least you did."

Pete turned me towards him and said, "Hey, Mitty boy. Enough of this self-effacement crap. I don't think that you realize just how good you've gotten. If you don't think that you're playing on a par with me, buddy, then you are sadly mistaken. You've got it going on, my friend. Trust me, you could hang with the best of them now."

"Thanks, Pete," I said. "That means a lot to me, especially from someone who knows the score. I'm hitting the rack, jack and I'll see all you cats and rats later."

The banging on the door and Mary's yelling blended into my dream of thousands of screaming fans cheering us on to higher musical ground. She used her key, swung the door open and said, "Damn it, Mitty! Phone call. It's one of Bobby T's daughters. You can take it in my office."

As I slung my feet to the floor, I remembered calling Tammy while in Alexandria with the news of Ray Raton's death. She had gotten to know Raton's nurses well enough that she had plans to find out the details of his death.

"Potassium chloride," she said as I picked up the receiver.

"What about it? They gave my mom potassium chloride to boost her potassium. Almost killed her when her levels dropped," I said.

"That's what killed Ray Raton," she explained. "They use high dose potassium chloride in the third stage of lethal injection executions, so you might say that someone executed him. His night nurse, Emily Jones, said that he created somewhat of a disturbance the night before he died. He said over and over, "They're here. They're here. They're going to kill me." She said that she sedated him, and the day shift nurse found him dead the next morning. An autopsy revealed the overdose of potassium chloride. Emily is in the hot seat, under suspicion of killing him with the lethal injection."

"Sounds like the Badou boys have master-minded another one of their slick frame jobs," I said. "How did they get into the nursing home? No one saw them?"

Tammy sounded genuinely upset as she said, "No one saw anyone suspicious. So, I guess the Badous strike again, Mitty. Ray was such a sweet man."

"Sounds like they want their tracks swept clean. Maybe we're making them jumpy," I said.

I could hear Tammy crying. "I caused Ray Raton's death. They could have gotten to him any time that they wanted to, but they left him alone until I went asking questions."

"You did what had to be done, Tammy. I bet Ray Raton went to his grave knowing that someone had listened to him, and that someone still wanted justice to be served. Besides that, I sent you there, remember? We can't blame ourselves. Bad things happen to good people all the time, and in our case, to really good people."

Tammy seemed to feel a little better by the time I hung up the phone. I walked back to my room. Benny sat on my bed, and he extended his hand and shook mine sincerely.

"I want you to know that I really do appreciate this opportunity that you've given me," he said, as he looked me straight in the eyes.

"Well, hell, Benny you've proved to us just how damn good you can play. I can't imagine anyone else filling those shoes," I said. He continued squeezing my hand tightly.

"Well, not only that, but being given the chance to find the scum responsible for Michael's murder," he said. "Detective Thompson would have shut the door on this case along with everybody else, if it hadn't been for you and Pete. Of course, it's not his case, but he's a believer now."

"That's good to know, Benny. I do believe that you had something to do with the convincing there, though," I said and Benny grinned at me and I ran the Ray Raton story past him. "Let your boss know what's happened. Do not let your guard down for a second."

CHAPTER 32

Thank God the second gig at Snowball's Place did not start in the early afternoon. I really didn't think that my system could absorb that much fun that early in the day again. A much more normal eight o'clock evening kick-off gave us all plenty of recuperation time. It helped all of us that we were much reformed heavy drinkers, except for Red, whose Irish roots dominated when it came to beer drinking. He'd just wished that Snowball's had stocked his Guinness Stout. Our systems had recharged, and Mary's cooking had a great deal to do to with that.

By game time, we had a respectable crowd. It didn't compare to yesterday's, yet. Even though the chartered blues society bus didn't return, many of the members had shown up again. Patrons still filtered through the door as we launched into a Texas shuffle, with Bo's bass and Red's drums driving the rhythm. Folks hit the dance floor early and kept on dancing.

We changed our first set around to make it fresh, not necessarily for those from last night: with their hangovers they wouldn't remember half of what we played anyway. We just liked to mix it up, to keep the band on its collective toes. We'd add a song, subtract a song, and shuffle the order. "The Repeaters" quickly picked up where we left off and the good time grooves bounced around the room.

During the first break, I retrieved a new preamp vacuum tube for my amp from my room. It had a slightly different tonal value, and I meant to put it into my amp earlier.

I returned to the club and stopped dead in my tracks, stunned.

Mr. Dreadlocks sat between Pete and Red at the bar—and they seemed to be having a jolly good time. I could feel the evil rolling off Mr. Dreadlocks. I wanted to scream at Pete and Red.

I took a deep breath and went about my business of replacing the tube in the amp. I waved off a waitress hawking a beer at me. I just pulled at my bottle of water and kept an eye on the bar. Maybe Pete and Red were playing it real cool, getting information, getting the goods on Mr. Dreadlocks.

Red normally returned to the bandstand first and drum rolled everyone back to stage, but he, Pete, and the mysterious stranger seemed to be having too much fun. Bo stepped up and asked if he should lay down a few bass thumps to get them moving. He asked, puzzled, "Isn't that the guy you warned us about?"

"Yeah, he is.," I said, as I watched the boys. "I'll get them up here," I said. "Hey Pete and Red, get y'all's butts to the stage." They laughed, shook hands with Mr. Dreadlocks, with smiles all around, and headed my way.

Red stepped up first, grinning and saying, "Hey, Mitty, man did we have that dude pegged wrong. He writes for *Blues Alive!* magazine and wants to do a feature on Pete."

"On all of us, Red. 'The Repeaters'," Pete said, leaping up on stage.

Red looked at me, winked, and said, "Trust me, Mitty. The guy has more interest in Pete, than the rest of us."

Pete tried to protest, but I said, "Hey, Pete. That's great and don't feel like you need to drag us into your moment of glory. Dude of mine, you deserve every stinking ounce of publicity anyone cares to shove your direction."

I still had my doubts about the guy and I let them know. "Listen, I'm still not sure about this guy. It'd be nice if our first impressions of the guy turned out to be way off base. We know the Badous are smart. He could be laying a trap."

Red glared at me. "Jeez Mitty, get over it. I'm glad that we didn't pounce on him. Hey, maybe you'll make the cover, Pete."

Pete opened his mouth, but Red shut us down with—"one, two, three, four," and Benny's slide guitar licks hit the opening notes to Elmore James' "Done Somebody Wrong".

Mr. Dreadlocks moved closer to the stage with a camera glued to his face, snapping away.

Pete played astonishingly well during the second set, and we all turned it over to him. Whenever he turned to me to swap harp licks with him, I pretended to be cussing at a defective harmonica, and he'd go another twelve bars or even twenty four. Mr. Dreadlocks had moved back to the bar, bouncing his head to the beat and apparently enjoying himself.

At the end of the set, Pete wanted us all to join him with his new found journalist friend. Red needed to work on his snare drum, Mary needed Bo's help, and I begged off, but told Benny to go let fame and fortune rub off on him.

A waitress brought both Red and I a longneck beer, courtesy of the *Blues Alive!* writer, and we turned to wave a thanks, but we saw him stepping out the front door with Pete and Benny. I gave Red a hand with his drum head and repositioned his kick drum microphone.

"Nice dude, there, Mitty," Red said. "Guess your assessment of human nature might be a little off, huh? He knows harp players, too. He said that Pete's playing had always impressed him. I've never seen anyone with one blue eye and one brown eye before, though. Have you?"

I starred at Red in disbelief and then leaped from the stage, dashed through the crowd, and headed for the parking lot with Red behind me.

"What the hell, Mitty? Was it something I said?" Red hollered after me.

"Hell, yeah! Pete and Benny just walked out the door with Davey Badou," I yelled as Red looked wide-eyed at me. "Sweep the parking lot in that direction and I'll go this way. We'll meet around back."

Frantically, my eyes jotted from car to car. Patrons milled about and shouted greetings and attempted to snatch a handshake, but I moved quickly on with my desperate mission. No Pete. No Benny. No Pete. No Benny.

I rounded Snowball's back corner. No Pete. No Pete's van. Oh, no, Benny! Benny was lying on his back between the air conditioning units and the back of my Silverado. Wide opened shock froze his face, and a bleeding chest wound looked fatal.

"Oh, Benny. Oh, Benny. Oh, Benny," I said over and over as I applied pressure to his wound, and Red showed up, staring in disbelief, "I think he's dead Mitty. I don't think that you're doing much good with the first aid."

"Damn it, then call 911 and..."

Bo had caught up with us and ran back inside to make the call.

I stood up, covered in Benny's blood, and said to Red as I ran to the club's back door, "Hold pressure on Benny's chest. I've got to find Pete."

Mary stood behind the bar, and the shocked look on her face told me that I looked a mess as I headed toward the back rooms to clean Benny's blood off of me. They followed me, shotgunning me with questions as I scrolled though my cell phone's contact list and said, "It's all my fault. It's all my fault. It's all my fault," until Mary grabbed me and shook me and said, "What the hell happened, Mitty?"

I stripped off my shirt, handed Mary my cell phone and told her, "Look up Detective Thompson's home number, and call him from your office phone. Tell him that they killed Benny, and that they have Pete. They may be in Pete's van, so have him put out an APB on it."

Mary stood looking at me with big eyes as I moved to the bathroom and began washing my arms and face. "Go Mary! I've got to find Pete. Damn, I knew it. I knew it. The man reeked of evil. I knew it. I knew it. My fault. My fault."

After grabbing a fresh shirt from my gig bag, I walked into Mary's office and she still had Detective Thompson on the office phone and she said, "He wants to talk to you, Mitty."

I grabbed my cell phone and said, "Just tell him to get his ass in gear. I'm going to find Pete."

CHAPTER 33

Bo and Red were running after me, protesting that they should go along. "The bastards are going to get exactly what they deserve. They will pay," I told them, waving them away.

"No, Red, you need to tell Detective Thompson about Davey Badou," I said. "He'll need to know what you know, since you sat and talked with the son of a bitch. Who's with Benny?"

Red looked at me ashamedly and said, "He did put on a convincing act, Mitty. He fooled us bad. Some EMS dude was here for the show and came out back and chased us away from Benny."

"It's not your fault, I should have been smarter than that evil maniac," I said. "Put this one on me."

"Bullshit," Red said. "We all went into this with eyes wide open. We're all full grown men, so quit saying that shit."

Bo piped up in agreement and then said, "Let me ride shotgun with you."

"Hell, no, Bo. Mary needs you here, big guy. Besides that, I don't know what the hell my plans are, other than to drive and look for Pete's van. I don't know where to look, but damn it, I've got to look," I said and got into my pickup.

I pulled the Ruger Security Six.357 from beneath my feet, checked to make sure that it had a full round, grabbed the half empty box of shells from the glove box, and sat it all next to me on the seat. Then I reached down to make sure that my.380 was still strapped securely to my right ankle.

Mary came running with, "Detective Thompson's on the way. He's putting all the county resources into looking for Pete's van, and he's contacting the state police. Stay here, Mitty, for God's sake."

"I'm gone, Mary," I said. "Every minute counts. I've got to try." And I backed away, looking at the concern on the faces of Red, Bo, and Mary. An ambulance came screaming into the parking lot as I left.

The only hunch I had led me back to Michael's place. It just seemed to be a likely place to haul Pete off to and do Lord knows what. On the way, my eyes scanned as far as my truck lights allow, looking for any sign of Pete's van—in a ditch, a pasture, off in the woods.

I pulled up a couple of hundred yards shy of Michael's house and grabbed my pistol, ammo, and a Maglite, and slipped into the dense undergrowth. My glasses fogged as the warm humid air descended around me in the black night. I wormed my way through the thick stands of yaupon shrubbery surrounding the post oak and cedar trees. My trip through the woods turned out to be far from silent. The thick carpet of dry dead leaves crackled and crunched beneath my feet.

The hell with it. I'll charge in with my six guns blazing if need be.

A huge spider web engulfed me and its engineer crawled up the back of my neck. I shivered, grabbed the arachnid, slung it away, and then caught a yaupon branch across the head as I darted foreword.

Sweat drenched my clothing and ran down my cheeks and nose by the time I broke out into the opening that surrounded the house, which sat in total darkness. I flicked my flashlight off, and tried to make out anything that looked like a vehicle and couldn't. I crept closer, thinking that maybe they doused the house lights to see who came tromping out of the woods. Blood pounded my brain with every heartbeat.

I held the gun ready, ready for any kind of movement. There was none. No sounds but cicadas loudly chirping their hot weather song. Yellow crime scene tape, running around the front porch, caught me at my waist. I went for broke and turned my light back on, stormed up on the porch, and swung through the front door, dropping to my knees and swinging my light and gun with both hands, sweeping the room. No sound, except my heavy breathing.

I crept from room to room and then into the kitchen, where the grisly scene had taken my breath away. Sallie Ray's crew had cleaned up much of the blood, but the scene remained in my head. I turned and ran hard from that house of Black Death.

They had Pete, they had Pete. I ran back down the road with the flashlight beam bouncing around like pinballs.

I reached the Silverado, swung it around and bright lights suddenly blinded me. I yanked off into the ditch and jumped from the passenger side door with gun in hand.

A patrol car rolled to a stop, and peeking from around the back of my truck, I heard Detective Thompson's voice say, "Just what the hell did you think you were going to do if you found those guys here? I'll tell you what. End up like the rest of their victims."

"Or try my best to put a bullet in each of their evil hearts," I said, stepping out to greet the detective as he climbed from his car. "They killed Benny and snatched Pete from under my nose. If it hadn't been for me, none of this would have happened."

"Quit whining," he said. "We can all claim some responsibility. Benny Williams is one of the best and I shouldn't have let him get involved, but he would have quit the sheriff's department and joined up with you guys no matter what I said. Trust me. This is personal for me now, and *this is* my case now. Let me and my boys take it from here. Let's just go on back to Snowball's Place and we'll take over."

I nodded, climbed back into my truck, and headed down Michael's road. Detective Thompson followed. I drove sedately right up to Snowball's Place and then gunned it and flew past. I could not simply sit and wait.

I had no plan other than trying to chase down the devil and get Pete back. I figured that these guys ditched Pete's van on the way to somewhere, but where? I pulled down every little gravel road that dead ended into the Brazos River to no avail. No van, and more wasted time.

I lost track of time, and soon had no idea exactly where I was. My dashboard compass told me that I was still pointed south, when my cell phone jangled. Pete's cell phone number flashed on the screen.

"Pete?" I said with a huge amount of hope.

"Hello, Mr. Mitty," the voice said. "How come you don't answer your phone? We've been waiting to tell you how sorry we are that another harp player has to go."

I tried a scare tactic, "If you harm a hair on Pete Bolden's head, count on me killing you and the rest of your evil family. You will reap what you sow, you slithering, slimy snake."

It sounded stupid, even to me. I meant it, though.

"Oh, really?" the voice said sarcastically, "You are scaring me, Mr. Mitty."

And then I heard it. My watch frog, Bud, croaked faintly in the background.

THEY ARE IN MY HOUSE!

I found the highway and was going 100 mph, when I flew past an intersection that I recognized. I jammed on the brakes, skidded sideways, made a U-turn.

I knew the road. Fence posts, caught in the headlights of the Silverado, flicked past me. Twenty minutes from Pete. I punched in Pete's number again, so I could talk to the bastard who called and leave the impression that I hadn't left Snowball's Place. Maybe I could sneak onto my property.

"Dammit, answer the phone, you worm!"

The house lights at the top of my hill soon glowed brightly in the distance, looking warm and inviting and reminded me that the only time that view greeted me at night was when Suzie was home awaiting my arrival. Now, the evil had invaded my home sweet home.

I eased up and pulled into a pasture a quarter of a mile from my farmhouse. I sat still for a minute to collect my thoughts and analyze the situation.

They still didn't know that I know where they are.

They called just to let me know that they had Pete.

Maybe they thought I'd be home in the morning, then they could have fun with both Pete and Mitty.

I pulled my cell phone back out, I punched up Detective Thompson's number and immediately heard, "Okay, Andersen. Just where the hell are you?" Beep, beep, beep told me that the signal had died. I threw it on the seat, grabbed my .357 and slid out of my pickup. My anxiety level rose into the red zone and beyond.

I stood next to my pickup and stared toward my house, took long deep breaths, and pulled a pair of old dark brown, long sleeved coveralls from the truck bed tool box. I reached beneath the front wheel and grabbed dirty grease from the fitting and smeared it over my face.

I imagined the dark presence within the walls of my sanctuary and suddenly developed a commando attitude. I charged across the road and up the ditch towards the house. I had a lot of open ground to cover, but it was dark enough that my move up the hill should go undetected. I decided to approach from the right side of the property and use my tool shed and pump house for cover as I closed in for the kill. *Yeah, kill. Kill those bastards. Kill every stinking one of them.*

Every light in the house beamed from the windows and gave the place a heavenly glow. Suzie was a star gazer and insisted we have none of those obnoxious security lights around the property, so I could approach the house in darkness.

As I closed in on the back of my tool shed, for the first time ever, I found myself thinking that it was a good thing that Chipper, our Australian Sheppard, had died. I would have scared her witless, and she would have barked relentlessly.

I eased from the back of the shed with gun in hand, made my way up to the kitchen window, and remained just out of the light it cast. My hand began sweating around the Ruger and beads of sweat began rolling down my face. I had soaked my long sleeved outfit.

I stood on tiptoes to peer in through the kitchen window and then through the door leading to my living room. My heart stopped when I saw Pete strapped to a chair with his back to me. His head hung low. I could see two of the Badou's, neither one the dreadlocked journalist, standing in the room. One had a syringe that he flicked with his finger, and he walked towards Pete with it.

I decided then and there that I would storm the house with guns blazing, even though I spied an assault rifle visible on the couch and one of the evil ones had a Glock stuck in his front belt. I fingered my Ruger and bent down to retrieve my.380 when...THUNK!

The last time I heard and felt that, I woke up on The Wizard's couch with a concussion. This time it glanced off the back of my head and staggered me around, and I still had my Ruger, and I spun to face my dreadlocked friend. He had on one of my shirts. My favorite Little Walter t-shirt. He screamed at me and swung an aluminum bat that might have been Michael's.

I got a shot off and it nicked Davey Badou. He screamed obscenities and hit the barrel of my gun hard enough to flip it from my grasp. I swung with my right fist and caught him on his left eye and staggered him and followed up with a hard hook to his rib cage, knocking the wind out of him. I rushed him and pinned him and planned to pound his head into *MY* dirt that he had desecrated with his evil presence. I pulled my fist back as high I could to drive his nose through his brain...Blam!

My shoulder exploded with what felt like another bat attack, and the impact wheeled me around. Four hands grabbed and dragged me across my yard. I attempted to get to my feet, and a boot caught me under my chin and flipped me to my back. I felt my legs being pulled and my body bounced up the steps and through the door. My back door alarm frog croaked at me as they drug me across the kitchen floor, and into my living room; where they propped me on my own couch.

"You goddamn asshole," said Davey Badou, mopping the blood off his arm. His left eye was beginning to swell shut. "No goddamn harmonica-playing bastard asshole TOUCHES a Badou, you got that?"

My dreadlocked nemesis stepped over to the couch and drove his knuckles into my right cheek, and it felt as if it whipped my head off.

"Welcome home, Mr. Mitty. We've been expecting you to show. Glad you made it to the party sooner than we planned, because I don't know how much more fun your friend can take," Davey said after the round house blow.

Pete's chin moved from his chest and his head wobbled around. He looked at Davey Badou and smiled faintly. His eyes glazed over and his head dropped again. Puke covered the front of his shirt and pants.

Davey put his face within inches of mine, and he stared fiercely at me with his one good eye. I chuckled. If they were going to kill me, at least I'd gotten a lick in. My vision began to double, and I felt myself fading to black, and I heard the devil's brother.

"Damn, Davey. Why'd you go and knock him out? He won't be able to watch his buddy die. You always spoil the fun," I heard as I tried to stay conscious.

Those words brought me around some, and I struggled to keep my head up and focus on Pete.

"Shut up, Junior," Davey Badou yelled back to his brother. "You think I'm going to let him get away with hitting me? Look, he's still looking around."

I tried to move and stand, but the youngest Badou jabbed his bat into my wounded shoulder, and the pain just about put me away. Leonard grabbed his arm and pulled him back, spun him around, and shot sign language at him. He manhandled the shorter Davey easily, and stuck his Glock pistol in his face for emphasis. Then he glared in my direction with dark, crazy looking eyes, and heavy black brows that met together to form a vicious frown. An ear to ear black scar stood in contrast with his brown neck. He pointed the Glock at me, and I knew my end had come.

Then Pete bounced his chair on my living room floor and looked at me wild eyed, and Leonard lowered his gun, and Davey said, "Looks like old Pete needs another dose."

"Cool it Davey," Joe Junior said. "Leonard, put the damn gun down. You are idiots. Our friends here aren't going any place. Slap the duct tape back over Pete's mouth, since he's not puking now. Let's play a little truth or dare with them."

Crushing shoulder pain shot throughout my body, and warm blood ran down my right side, so I pressed my left hand on the wound to slow the bleeding,

Davey yanked my arm down, spit in my face and hissed, "Let's kill them right now." He had the assault rifle in his hands.

Joe Junior yanked it from him and said, "We'll do this my way. You two always screw things up."

Joe Junior apparently led this merry band of pranksters. He had more of an athletic, stocky build than the shorter Davey and the tall, thinner Leonard. They both deferred to him, and his look told them that he meant business. He looked at Pete, whose head looked to be a bit steadier on his shoulders, and then over at me.

"Stay with me boys. Y'all been tracking us a long time and have been working hard for this day," Joe Junior said. He looked around proudly. "We've been tracking you guys, too, though, and look who is better at it: yep, those low-down Badou boys. Y'all have been working really hard at getting to the truth, and now we've put it all smack dab in the middle of your house, Mr. Andersen."

I looked at Pete. He still appeared dazed and confused. Attempting to lift my right arm proved useless—felt like dead heavy meat hanging. My thoughts turned to the.380 strapped to my right ankle. No way could I get to it with my dead arm. Leonard and Davey stared at Pete and me, as Joe Junior began his history lesson.

"Let me tell you how it was, how it is, and how it will always be," he began. He pulled up a chair, lit a cigarette, and got a faraway look.

"First off, Papa didn't kill those Chicago cats: Sonny Boy, Pot Strong, or Little Walter. He sure wanted people to think that he did, though, so he made stories up about going up north and killing those famous blues harp players. See, Papa wanted people scared of him, and he wanted harmonica players to keep the hell away from him. He thought that if they were scared enough of him they would quit playing the instrument of the devil.

"Now, he did take out J.P. Dillon. That fellow made the mistake of running with Glenwood Stokely when he was down in our neck of the woods. See, after Vicksburg, Papa hated anyone playing harmonica and he figured that Glenwood had gone to Chicago to hide from him. He just found J.P.

"Eddie Guyton just screwed up when he came looking for his dog, stepped onto our property, and he crossed a line with our Papa. We all felt a little satisfaction killing Eddie Guyton, especially after Davey lit him up, and he started smoking."

Pete looked up and mumbled, "Vicksburg?"

Leonard slapped Pete across the face. His nostrils flared as he turned toward me. His dark eyes glowed. I knew he intended to damage me further, but Joe Junior caught him, threw him against the wall and froze him with a stare.

"Damn it, you idiot! Let me tell Papa's story then y'all can do whatever you want with these boys. I want 'em to know why they've got to go."

Leonard sat down with a sullen look on his face. Joe Junior addressed Pete.

"Vicksburg was where we found Glenwood Stokely. That was the man who stole our mama, then called her a whore when she ran off with another man. And then he cut Leonard's throat and took his voice away."

Joe Junior paused. "We swore revenge on Glenwood and his bastard son Damon, but before we could get going on that Eddie Guyton trespassed on us and we got him.

"Then Silas Guyton came after our papa and killed him. We wanted Silas for ourselves and we wanted him dead, but didn't get the chance for a long, long time.

"We had a cousin, Dwayne Bellow, serving time with Silas Guyton. He and Davey had been running buddies. They burned down a neighborhood in Alexandria together, didn't ya Davey boy?"

Davey smiled and nodded.

"Dwayne told Davey that Silas and Michael Melton had become fast friends. We really wanted Silas for ourselves, but we let Dwayne do the deed."

I knew the rest of the story and I was sick of hearing it from Joe Junior. I looked at him with narrowed eyes and said, "OK, but what did Bobby Tarleton ever do to you?"

"Whoa now, pardner," he said. "Don't jump my story. You'll hear it all before you die, dude.

"Leonard and I had thoughts of breaking Davey out of reform school after we dealt with Guyton, but decided to lay low and search for the Stokelys. We found Glenwood blowing his evil blues harp in Baton Rouge six months after Papa's murder. We grabbed him and his boy, Damon. Glenwood begged for his life and claimed that Damon was our half-brother, and how could we possibly kill our own half-brother's daddy."

He smiled as he spoke, and it occurred to me that Joe Junior, Leonard, and Davey looked different enough to have had different mothers.

"We tied cement blocks to his legs and threw him from a bridge into the Mississippi River, and told Damon that he needed to take up with us or else. He ran from us, and ran from us most of his life. Pretty sure he became a junkie to deal with it all. We finally got him, though. He witnessed too much of our business. Word got around that we were on a mission.

"Now, we did go after some of those evil scumbag harp suckers that left Louisiana for Chicago. They knew about us, and they knew we wanted their asses. They had a pact with Lucifer and had to go. Daddy said that Walter was Satan's right hand man and started all the evil in the first place. But someone got to Little Walter before we could.

"Now, about that dude up around Dallas named Joey Brooks and your friend The Wizard. Joey's daddy played drums with Eddie Guyton the night that we followed him from the Big Club in Alexandria. Papa had planned on tracking him down to eliminate any witnesses. He had died by the time we figured out where he lived. So we took his son Big Joey out. He probably knew about us, right? Besides, he played the devil's evil harmonica.

"We had nothing against The Wizard, but it was convenient that he took the fall for killing Joey Brooks. Then we found out he was getting friendly with Silas Guyton."

I looked around at the evil in my living room and said, "So, you guys targeted Michael Melton."

Davey walked up close to the couch again, smiled, and said, "That old boy caught fire real well. I had him smoking up the forest in no time, but man did he fight. Leonard went ballistic on him with his own bat, though, and began sticking him with a hunting knife, and that took the fight out of him."

I promptly got to my feet, fighting mad and got knocked down just as promptly by Joe Junior and the butt end of the assault rifle. Thankfully, he aimed for my chest and not my face. I surprised him by leaping up and driving my head into his mid-section like a crazy linebacker. His back smashed against the wall and his finger triggered a flurry of shots that peppered my ceiling.

Leonard put an end to my assault by pinging the baseball bat off my right ear and once again I felt myself being dragged across my floor with Davey hissing some kind of black threat at me. They slammed me back onto the couch. Joe Junior just stared at me as he tried to re-gain his breath.

Davey smirked as he continued, "Yeah. We extinguished The Wizard's magic and outsmarted everyone in the process. Those cracker meth cookers never knew what hit 'em. Pretty admirable planning there, huh, Mr. Mitty?"

I ignored the question and tried to keep my head on my body. "Where does Bobby T fit into the murdering spree?"

"He hung around the wrong person at the wrong time," Joe Junior said as he grabbed both my cheeks tightly and squeezed. He put his angry face a couple of inches from mine as he spoke. "We went to Kansas City after Michael, and big assed Bobby got in our way, and as you know by now, we don't regret killing harmonica players in the least, particularly if they stick their noses into our business. Since he and Michael were pals, we figured that he had to go. Then Michael took off before we could grab him."

Leonard grabbed at Joe Junior's arm and shot some kind of sign language his way. He didn't use any signing that I knew about, but Joe Junior said, "Oh, yeah. I left out Neon Leon. We hid out in Mississippi for quite some time and caught Leon's act in a juke outside of Greenville. We started harassing the old boy a bit, old Leon got pissed, and I had to step in before Davey got us all in trouble. Then Leon spit in my face.

"We followed him over to Slidell where he shacked up with some fat woman named Tilley. We followed his butt up to Chicago and missed him. We went back to visit Tilley to find out his whereabouts, and she proudly showed us all these letters from Leon. We had scared him all the way to Europe. So hell, we had a good time with her and then took her out in the Gulf of Mexico to swim with the fishes.

"And that, my friends, brings us to you fine fellows. You two guys come along and had to stir the pot and couldn't leave well enough alone. Hey, Mitty, you can put that Austin cat on you. We had to send you and Pete a private message that we were still out there and active. Leonard wanted to fill him full of holes, but I insisted on the one shot to the back of the head. You wanted us, now you've got us.

"We tried to scare your bitch by running her off the road. She's a damn fine shot and maybe me and the boys will have some fun with her when you're gone," Joe Junior said, leering at me.

My blood boiled, but for once I sat still, not needing any more damage inflicted on my battered self. *"Over my dead body,"* I thought as I tried to hatch an escape plan.

Joe Junior peered at me closely, then shrugged. "Leonard would have stabbed and killed Pete at Snowball's Place if I hadn't stopped him. I had other plans for you two. Too bad about your guitar player. We had nothing against him, but he tried to stop us."

Joe Junior looked around proudly again, waved his arms at his brothers. "You didn't know that we were *all* in Snowball's tonight, did you? I also caught up with you guys in Baton Rouge, and you never knew it. I watched you play from right there at the bar while Leonard and Davey were back over in Alexandria, taking care of officer Raton. Hell, I even attended The Wizard's damned day of celebration and no one had a clue."

Pete began to appear more alert, so Leonard waved the drug filled syringe in front of his face. Pete bounced his chair legs off the floor and mumbled beneath the duct tape, and Davey whacked him in the head again. Not hard, just to let him know that he'd best stop it. He had passed the assault rifle off to Leonard, and Leonard passed the weapon over to Joe Junior. The notion entered my head to try to reach my ankle holster with my left hand, while everyone looked at Pete. I bent over, but thought better of it. I'd never fired a gun left handed, and Leonard stared my way again too quickly.

Pete began bopping around in his chair. Davey, smiling in my direction, stepped up behind him and held him still while Leonard set his gun down and picked up the syringe.

"Okay, Mr. Mitty, time to watch your buddy ease off into hell," Davey said.

As Leonard walked past me with the syringe, I lunged off the couch feet first and swung my leg high enough to smack the syringe. The needle stuck in the sole of my boot, and I stomped it into the floor.

Leonard smashed my head with his fists—the right, then the left, then the right, with Davey yelling, "Go Leonard, go. Kill the s.o.b."

"Stop! Stop!" Joe Junior said over and over and pulled at Leonard. He would get him off of me, and Leonard would break free and smash into me again. Finally, Joe Junior put the assault rifle to Leonard's ear and pulled the bolt back and said, "Stop it now, Leonard."

He gave me one more good blow to my chin before he relented, breathing hard like he'd run a marathon. I felt blood pouring from my nose and knew he'd broken it, and he had knocked more than one tooth out of my head.

"Sit your ass back on the couch, you stupid bastard," Joe Junior yelled.

Pete had been knocked backwards during the melee, and he looked over at me from his back with watery eyes.

Davey said, "What in the hell is wrong with you, brother? We've got to do this and clear out. The cops will be on the way."

"Fill a new syringe, Leonard," Joe Junior said. "We are sticking to the game plan. Mr. Andersen will see just how his friend Pete dies, then you guys can do whatever you want to with him. Drag him back up on the couch."

Leonard had just about beaten both my eyes shut, but I could peer through the slits and saw that they had turned Pete's chair to face me. He looked resigned to his fate, but my mind still thought that I could yank my battered body off the couch once more.

Suddenly, Buddy Guy ripping through the final refrains of "Damn Right I've Got The Blues" blasted from my stereo as the timer clicked on, and every face turned towards the music. Pure adrenaline moved my left hand to my ankle, and I yanked my.380 free and fired and fired and fired. Hoping and praying that my left handed aim wouldn't land on Pete. I hit Leonard in his throat as he dropped the new syringe and reached for the Glock. Blood shot across the room as he staggered with his hands around his neck and fell to the floor.

Three hollow points hit Joe Junior as he fired the assault rifle at full automatic, blowing my out my windows, and strafing the front door. Davey started at me with the baseball bat, but thought better of it and headed for the door. I finished emptying the pistol at his back and couldn't tell if any shots hit the mark, as he went ripping out into the night.

Muddy Waters' "Stuff You've Got To Watch" bounced around the room as I walked to Pete Bolden to free him, and the world began spinning, and the house lights dimmed and faded to black.

CHAPTER 34

I had no clue what hospital walls surrounded me when I awoke. An IV dripped something into my left arm, and my mind was fogged with pain medication. I managed to sit up, stood up, and dizzily shuffled towards the bathroom, pulling my drip bottle rack with me. I had no idea who looked back at me in the mirror. Leonard Badou had molded my face into a round purple mass that appeared twice normal size, with slits for eyes. I couldn't tell if I had a nose left.

As I left the bathroom, I saw Jean and Tammy walk past my half open door. They looked right at me and kept walking until I said, "Hey you two."

Jean backed into the door and said, "My God, Mitty. We didn't even recognize you. You look horrendously bad."

"Thanks, Jean," I said. "I resemble that remark."

My attempt at humor brought frowns from both the Tarleton women. They ordered me back to bed and began fussing with my pillow and asking should they lower or raise the bed, and then both broke down crying.

"How is Pete?" I asked.

"Pete is fine. They released him yesterday. He asked us over to his house last night, and he gave us a blow by blow—oops, sorry for the choice of words," Tammy said.

"Thanks, Mitty," Jean said. "You've given us all the closure that we needed. I just hope that you're going to be okay."

"How long have I been in here?"

"Three days," they both answered together.

"I think that I'll make it now," I said. "This ain't the first ass-whippin' I've had in my life."

"Yeah, but it was almost the last," Pete Bolden said as he walked into my room. "You took some kind of head shots, my friend. You saved my life, buddy boy, going Rambo on those guys. I'll never forget that."

I reached out my left hand, and Pete grasped it with both hands, and I asked, "What happened after I passed out?"

"Well, I sat around, tied up, and twiddled my thumbs for another thirty minutes," he said. "I had no idea if they had killed you or not. Then I heard the sirens of the cavalry off in the distance. Seemed like an army sweeping through your house, looking for the bad guys. Your Detective Thompson cut me loose. He said they'd found us by tracing the GPS signal off your cell phone."

"What about Davey Badou? Last I saw of him he was running out the front door dodging my bullets," I asked.

"The first squad car found his body stretched out in the middle of your driveway," Pete said. "You nailed him."

The room filled with the additional bodies of Franklin, Mary, and Bo. Mary brought in some red beans and rice, just in case the hospital food didn't suit me—which, of course, it didn't. Bo kept a concerned frown on his face, which starkly contrasted with his ever present wide grin. Franklin called me "Pretty Boy," which stirred nervous laughter around the room.

Mary told me that Officer Thompson sent his best wishes—and the best news I'd heard in a long time—Benny was hurt bad, but he was going to make it. I would've cried, but my eyes were too swollen.

Everyone stayed late until the evening, and things got quite cheery once they realized that I was going to be OK. We had quite a party going on, until the nurse came in and declared "Last Call".

Everyone moved out, but Pete lagged behind and gripped my left hand once more and looked deeply into my swollen eyes and didn't have to say another word. Tears began running down his cheek as he gripped my hand tighter.

"The good guys finally won one, Pete," I said.

"Nice to have less evil in the world," Pete said. "Now, get you butt out of here so we can go blow some blues."

Epilogue

With "The Repeaters" scheduled to rock the blues and shake the rafters of Little Queenie's three weeks after my hospital release, we creaked up on stage to rehearse.

My face was closer to its normal shape. My nose had shape shifted and needed more work. The shoulder bothered me and holding onto a harmonica and a microphone with both hands proved painful, but the pure joy of blowing the blues again washed that away.

The door swung open and Detective Thompson came in, followed by Benny Williams, who was walking very slowly. Benny said he had to take it easy for awhile longer, but he wanted to play a little blues.

"Mind if I sit in?" he asked as Detective Thompson nearly busted a gut getting Benny's amp on the stage.

Franklin had cordoned off a few back tables for our entourage: Mary, Bo, Sallie Ray, Tammy, Tess, and Jean. The crowd called for a song from Sallie Ray and she favored us with the "Bumble Bee Blues" and "I'd Rather Go Blind". At the break we all sat down for a visit, and Jean slipped her arm though mine and held on tight. She had tears in her eyes, and I told her that I was sorry that the blues stirred up sad memories.

"Mitty, these are tears of joy," she said. "You have touched my soul tonight. I owe you so much more than you'll ever realize."

"Nope. You will never owe me anything—ever," I said and headed for the stage as Red beat out his break ending drum rolls.

Jean blew me a kiss as we cranked up a version of one of Bobby T's originals, and I do believe that I sang better than I ever had on that one.

We immediately slid into Muddy Waters' "Standing Around Crying" with Pete singing the hell out of it, when he stopped suddenly, and I looked over and he stared wide eyed into the crowded dance floor as if he had seen Satan himself. I picked up the vocal line and looked to see just who had distracted him.

A young man stood at the edge of the stage and just looked at Pete. Pete looked at me and mouthed, "Jimbo." I almost dropped my microphone. I waved Jimbo up, and Pete grabbed him and hugged him—tightly. I handed

Jimbo my harp microphone and stepped off the stage and told Pete to take it on home.

Jimbo pulled a harmonica from his pocket and wasted no time swapping licks with Pete Bolden. Pete had been right; this kid could play the blues. Pete's eyes sparkled and his grin reached ear to ear as he listened to what his prodigy laid on the crowd at Little Queenie's.

During the break, Pete found me seated next to Jean as he walked up and introduced Jimbo Jernigan who was clearly quite alive and well. He had been off bouncing around in the military for the past several years. He had joined the service directly out of high school and been to Iraq twice and Afghanistan once, kept his harp chops up, and always wondered what the hell happened to Pete Bolden.

He told Pete, that, yeah, it disappointed him to see Pete strung out on drugs, but that he knew that it was Pete's demon to beat.

Pete looked me in the eyes and said, "Life is good Mitty. Life is good."

Jean and I both simultaneously said, "It sure is Pete."

"Hey, my shoulder really hurts," I said. "Why don't you and Jimbo kick out the last set together." They both smiled at me and hit the stage running and had the crowd jacked up in moments.

"Yeah," I said to myself, "Pete Bolden is back."

☙

-THE END-

RICKY BUSH has been reading about, writing about and playing the blues for most of his adult life. His articles have highlighted the careers of blues musicians in magazines such as *Blues Access, Hittin' the Note, Southwest Blues* and *The American Harmonica Newsmagazine*. He has also written over a hundred reviews of recorded blues music and brings his view of the blues to readers at www.bushdogblues.blogspot.com.

He spent twenty nine years teaching Texas high school students journalism, world geography, and English. After retiring from teaching, his love of the blues and writing fiction met at the crossroads, and he began fulfilling his lifelong goal to author the novel that he always said that he would. He is an active member of the Sisters in Crime organization and maintains an author website at www.richardbushbooks.com, a Facebook page under Ricky Bush, and a Twitter account @bushdog51.

Richard hangs his hat in his self-built log home in rural Texas, where he and his wife, Virginia, raised two daughters and a son. He can occasionally be coaxed into assisting with the small family oil and gas operation that they helped build. When he's not applying his fingers to the keyboard, he puts a harmonica to his lips and practices what he preaches by blowing the blues.

ABOUT BARKING RAIN PRESS

D id you know that six media conglomerates publish eighty percent of the books in the United States? As the publishing industry continues to contract, opportunities for emerging and mid-career authors are drying up. Who will write the literature of the twenty-first century if just a handful of profit-focused corporations are left to decide who—and what—is worthy of publication?

Barking Rain Press is dedicated to the creation and promotion of thoughtful and imaginative contemporary literature, which we believe is essential to a vital and diverse culture. As a nonprofit organization, Barking Rain Press is an independent publisher that seeks to cultivate relationships with new and mid-career writers over time, to be thorough in the editorial process, and to make the publishing process an experience that will add to an author's development—and ultimately enhance our literary heritage.

In selecting new titles for publication, Barking Rain Press considers authors at all points in their careers. Our goal is to support the development of emerging and mid-career authors—not just single books—as we know from experience that a writer's audience is cultivated over the course of several books.

Support for these efforts comes primarily from the sale of our publications; we also hope to attract grant funding and private donations. Whether you are a reader or a writer, we invite you to take a stand for independent publishing and become more involved with Barking Rain Press. With your support, we can make sure that talented writers thrive, and that their books reach the hands of spirited, curious readers. Find out more at our website.

WWW.BARKINGRAINPRESS.ORG

Barking Rain Press

CPSIA information can be obtained at www.ICGtesting.com
Printed in the USA
BVOW071657150312

285298BV00001B/54/P